THE SOUND OF SILENCE
(Penumbra Papers #4)

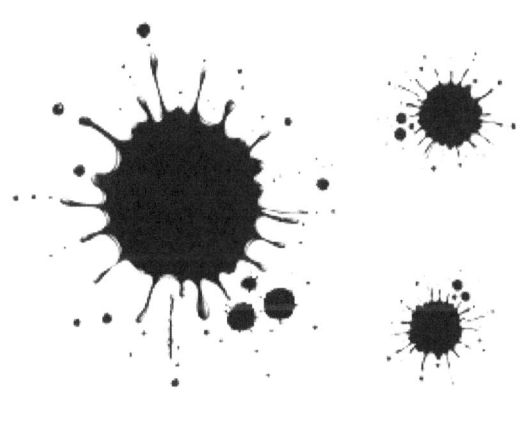

Silver James

Published in the United States of America
First Edition Print
ISBN-10: 0-9969994-4-2
ISBN-13: 978-0-9969994-4-1

DEDICATION

To lovers and dreamers and
those who love to read about both.

Acknowledgements

Writing can be a solitary business, but the lucky author has a support group of family, friends, and supporters who drag her out of the cave and into reality on a regular basis. I'd like to take this opportunity to thank those who contribute, cheer, cajole, and drag me kicking and screaming into and out of my cave.

I truly appreciate all the help I get from everyone involved in creating a book. Of course, the important ones are the readers. A big wave to all who enjoy my books. Y'all rock my world! A heartfelt "thank you" to Cate Derham for giving me the inspiration of her words and Siobhan Muir for her #ThursdayThreads flash fiction challenge. I can't count the number of scenes in this book that were written from those prompts each week.

I couldn't do this without the help and support of my wonderful husband, Greg. And last but definitely not least, I want to recognize my cover artist, Clary, for taking my blurred visions and producing wonderful covers for me.

One last caveat: Any and all mistakes are my own.

In the Beginning...

MAYBE IT STARTED with the millennium or perhaps the series of dramatic celestial events that followed in the first decade—like the stray star named The Flyer aligning with Mars in conjunction with a solar eclipse. Maybe it was a hole in the ozone. Whatever caused the Veil between the Realms to tear, all hell broke loose. Literally. It turns out there really are monsters under the bed and the things that go bump in the night are bigger and scarier than anyone ever imagined.

The world's best and brightest from every discipline—physics, theology, anthropology, chemistry, to name only a few—tried to explain the rip in the cosmic curtain. The monsters have been here all along, flying just under the radar of normal perception. They've been masquerading as mundanes—their term for humans.

Vampires. Faeries. Gargoyles. Dragons. Werewolves. Witches. Creatures of legend and nightmare. Overnight, reality took on a whole new meaning. Since the arrival of the millennium, all manner of preternatural folks intermingle with humans in ways mysterious and magical...or criminal. The FBI's answer? The Magical Activity, Grievances, and Inhuman Crimes unit is in charge of any crime involving the magicks. The FBI director handpicked Special Agent Sade Marquis to lead the unit. An agent with an X-Files mentality, it's Sade's job to deal with all the bad nasties. And she's gathered a group of dedicated agents and consultants to help.

Given the code name The Penumbra Papers, the files are buried deep within some anonymous warehouse outside of Washington, DC, inside a wooden box with a mystical marking branded into it sides...

Oh, wait. Sorry. That's the Ark of the Covenant. The

Penumbra Papers are actually buried in a bottom file drawer in the office of the Director of the FBI. Within those files resides the records of the forces of light and dark fighting in the shadows which humans had only glimpsed before the dawn of this new age.

Of course, Sade knows the truth of the matter. She was raised by a master vampire, her foster brother is a werewolf, and she has a certain immunity to magic. That's Sade's secret, and she is very, very good at keeping secrets. Which makes her very, very good at her job. In turn, that makes the magicks very, very afraid of her...*and* the MAGIC Unit. As they should be—

THE SOUND OF SILENCE
PENUMBRA PAPERS #4

And by that destiny to perform an act
Whereof what's past is prologue, what to come
In yours and my discharge. ~William Shakespeare,
The Tempest

My grief lies all within,
And these external manners of lament
Are merely shadows to the unseen grief
That swells with silence in the tortured soul. ~William
Shakespeare, Richard II

Before the Veil Ripped

DESTINY doesn't live in the stars. It doesn't give people a choice, and they have no chance of escaping it, despite what the poets, pundits, and politicians say. Destiny has a habit of showing up when least wanted, needed, or expected. It slaps people up side the head, brings them to their knees, and it is no accident when that happens. Today, Destiny landed a gut punch. My gaze raked over the chunks of shattered granite littering the courtyard. I said one word, a name. "Borac."

"Yes." Crevan, *Le Vieil* of the Gargoyle Sentinels stood beside me, stiff and deadly.

1

"What happened?"

"Someone shattered Borac and the other guards with magic and stole the Heart."

That answered why the Sentinel leader had recalled me to Paris. I am Roman Montagne, one of the oldest of my kind. I am also First Sentinel.

Crevan did not look at me as he continued. "There have been rumors and rumblings beyond the Veil. There is talk of the emergence of the Crucible of Eve."

I stiffened, becoming as still as the granite that is my true form. The last time the Crucible incarnated, the Gargoyle Realm had been left in ruins when one faction stole the Heart of Stone and used it in conjunction with the Crucible.

"We must retrieve the Heart, Roman, and secure it before the Crucible of Eve comes into power."

Crevan's order was clear but it was his unspoken command that raked against my skin, sharp as werewolf claws. If the Crucible died, crisis averted. Sentinels did not murder innocent humans, but could the Crucible truly be innocent? Or would the babe so marked have a stain on its soul so black that redemption could never be found?

A face clouded my vision and I stiffened, reading the speculation on the Old One's face. "She is many things, *Le Vieil*, but she is not the Crucible."

His sharp-eyed gaze scraped over me. "*L'Enfant de L'homme* has other destinies to fulfill, Sentinel." His disapproving tone reminded me of the schoolroom. "Perhaps you are spending too much time negotiating the affairs of vampires and fae."

Perhaps he was right. Keeping track of Sade Marquis, the human child both vampire marked and fae touched was a full-time occupation, but one I was loath to give up. When Mathias gifted the girl with a werewolf pup, I'd hoped he could take up my guard duties. The feud between Mathias and Oberon had turned into a petty playground game of tag-you're-it. I'd remained silent too long, lost in my ruminations as Crevan's hand gripping my shoulder reminded me.

"Time to hunt, Roman. This is *your* destiny."

The sound of silence swallowed my soul as I took my commander's words to heart.

CHAPTER ONE
DESTINY CALLING

———————————————————————

DESTINIES are a dime a dozen and Fate is the biggest bitch of all. The thought drummed against Roman's psyche like the rain tapping against the striped awning above his head. He toed a chunk of what appeared to be granite lying next to the curb, blocking the water running along the edge of the street. Two feet away, a stone head appeared to be crying as raindrops stained the chipped face.

Roman, First Sentinel of the Gargoyles and the Legate of New Orleans, shoved his hands deep into his pockets to keep from wrapping them around the neck of the human who stood before him, quaking in his boots and unable to meet Roman's gaze. The young man finally screwed up his courage and opened his mouth to speak but one withering look shut him up again.

The sound of wet leather slapping against humid air wasn't enough to distract Roman from his perusal of what appeared to be a shattered statue, nor did he look at the gargoyle who settled onto the sidewalk nearby.

"Roman." Crevan, leader of the Sentinels stepped up beside him.

"I don't recognize him, *Le Vieil.*" That bothered Roman on a deep, visceral level. There was a time when he'd known all of his brothers.

"He was young, barely out of L'Crèche."

"Why was he in my city?"

Crevan turned steely eyes on Roman. "*Your* city?"

"Yes, *Le Vieil.*" Roman used Crevan's title but his tone was so dry dust should have puffed from between his lips. "New Orleans is mine."

The unfortunate human chose that moment to pipe up. "Please, sir," the kid whined. "I don't know nuthin' about this. I'm innocent. It wasn't my idea."

"There is no innocence, not even in death." The words were out before Roman could stop them. He shackled his anger. Truly, it wasn't the human's fault. He stared at the broken remains of what had once been a gargoyle—one who'd had a mental age comparable to the cowering youth in front of him.

Crevan cupped the human's face in his huge hands and held the kid's gaze. Silence slithered around them, along with pewter tendrils of magic. "There," Crevan eventually said. "It is done. He'll take no memory with him and I have what he once knew." His craggy face, when he turned to face Roman, was drenched with grief.

Roman instinctively knew the verdict. "We have to hunt."

"I am calling a hajka. You have other duties, Roman. I will commission Varrick to lead it."

"You have not called a hunt in a century or more." Roman would know. He'd led the last one.

"Do we have another choice?" The Old One turned away but Roman stayed him with a hand to his arm.

"Tell me what happened here."

"It is a story of misadventure. A *nullité* on a lark, daring to seek forbidden sights. I suspect Sedge was frightened by something and turned to stone. The human boy does not remember taking up the iron bar. He does not remember damaging what he thought was a plaster statue."

"Doesn't remember?" Roman growled the words.

"He does not. There is a shadow on his mind. I believe he was compelled to commit the vandalism."

Roman stared down at the gargoyle's head. "Even a fledgling can withstand an iron bar."

"Yes."

He turned a sharp gaze on the leader of his kind before searching for the bar. There was nothing to be found. His eyes met Crevan's flinty look.

"Too bad we do not have a werewolf here. One could sniff out the spell and the caster," Crevan said.

"If a werewolf is needed, Deacon Smith will provide one." Shaking his head, Roman refused to consider the implications, should that become necessary. "New Orleans is neutral ground for all. I know the witches here. They would not perpetrate such a thing. They value their lives too much."

"Do they?" Crevan argued. "Even witches will succumb to the lure of money and power. As will wizards." A wary look crossed his face. "Or perhaps there is another to consider."

Roman stilled, contemplated, didn't like the conclusion. "A sorcerer." It wasn't a question.

"Perhaps. Varrick and his escadron will hunt. You will investigate as your duties as Legate dictate. Varrick will pursue it as a Sentinel."

Two men emerged from the empty building across the street and approached. Roman recognized them and inclined his head. Without speaking, they went about gathering up the broken pieces of granite and placing them in a wooden chest. No one spoke. At last, only the head was left. Crevan stooped and with gentle care, retrieved Sedge's head. He reverently placed it in the chest, then closed the lid. The two gargoyles disappeared back into the shadowed interior of the building. The blink of a human eye later, they were gone.

The French Quarter street was oddly quiet, as if it was holding its breath, or perhaps more fitting with the plop and drip of the rain, the hushed silence in a church before a funeral. The stillness cracked when Roman's phone chimed in his pocket. Glancing at the name flashing on the screen, he answered with a wry, "Sade."

Her voice, tinged with a slight Texas accent, held curiosity and suspicion. "Would you like to explain why the Old One is standing in the rain on a street in the French Quarter?" Silence was the better part of discretion in this instance, so he said nothing. "Roman, NOPD has a terrified kid, soaked to the skin, babbling to a desk sergeant about scary bat aliens and murder. Being the top FBI investigator that I am, I'm drawing a couple of conclusions from Crevan's presence and this kid's ramblings. Who the fuck showed up without their glamour firmly in place and who died?"

Roman returned Crevan's scowl with one of his own. "It is a matter for the Sentinels, Sade."

"Bull shit."

"Language."

"Bull shit on that too, Roman. You know the New Orleans cops are gawddamned sensitive to fuckin' Magick on Mundane crime. I thought you bein' tagged as the gawddamned Legate would take care of that shit so it didn't come rolling downhill on me."

Roman finally gave in to the urge to sigh. "It is a matter for the Sentinels, Sade. That is why *Le Vieil* has come. The young man in question will not be harmed." He recognized his mistake with the quick intake of her breath. Watching her grow up often caused him to forget that she truly was a top FBI investigator and understood the Magicks far better than any other human.

"Talk to me, Roman." There was only demand in her voice, all pretense of civility or coaxing gone. Of course, he thought ruefully, where Sade was concerned, both of those terms were relative.

"The young man currently quivering at the police station was..." He paused, knowing that no matter how he phrased events, she'd be in New Orleans by nightfall.

Roman stared directly into Crevan's eyes as he said, "Coerced to kill a fledgling."

"Holymotherfuckingswearto—"

"Do not finish that tirade, Sade." His voice was as hard and cold as sepulcher stone. "The boy is in no danger from us. In fact, he should have no memory of what occurred." And he recognized his second mistake.

"You do not leave town. Crevan does not leave town. Any fucking gargoyle involved in this does not leave town. I will be there in—"

Roman heard the soft tap on Sade's office door through the phone. Then he heard the muffled conversation.

"Your plane tickets, Sade. You will need to leave immediately to make the flight. I will text your accommodations information to your phone."

"Thanks, Alice."

Yes, the ever-efficient Alice Cooper, administrative assistant to FBI Director George Bailey, had made her predicted appearance. Roman made a mental note to look into the woman. It was a note he'd frequently made since Sade joined the FBI. He couldn't remember why he hadn't already done so.

"Bring an umbrella," he snapped into the phone and ended the call.

VERITY HUNCHED her shoulders against the steady drip drip drip of the rain. The artists who populated the walkways around Jackson Square had long since quit and gone home. Tourists and locals alike stayed inside the shops and restaurants or ducked into St. Louis Cathedral or the museums flanking it to partake of history. She tucked the plastic poncho she'd planned to wear around the arcane accoutrements of her livelihood she'd packed into her little red wagon.

Too bad her fortune telling talent never worked to predict her own life. If it did, she would have stayed home. Of course, if she had, the sun would have come out and she would have missed out on a day's earnings. Which she desperately needed. She trudged along, head down, dragging her wagon behind her. The door to Dezi's, a bar and restaurant, opened and the scents of food washed over her. Her stomach grumbled in protest. The three woman who breezed out cut their eyes her direction and scowled. She scowled back.

She wasn't deaf. She heard the disparaging remarks from the well-dressed women. From the accents, they were local but from their clothing and jewelry, they likely lived in the Garden District or one of the other ritzy neighborhoods. She also knew what she looked like because her reflection glowered at her from every plate-glass window she passed.

On her own since the age of sixteen, Verity lived by her wits and often not much more than that. She had a little gift for reading people, for seeing patterns in the cards, the crystals, and the glass ball she'd inherited from the woman who raised her. On good days, she had food in her belly with a little left over for the stray cats she fed at the back door of the room she rented. She scrounged for her clothes and pretended that she dressed so eccentrically because she was a drabani—a gypsy fortune teller.

Today she wore a broom skirt the color of corn husks in the spring. Its crinkled fabric swirled around her ankles, though she could feel its airy fingers despite the worn black leather of the combat boots encasing her feet. The blouse she wore over a dirty white tank top had been sewn together from three silky scarves, all in riotous patterns and colors. She'd belted it with the one thing she owned that had belonged to the unknown man who'd volunteered his DNA to her existence—a black leather belt with an iron buckle set with Celtic runes and a fire opal almost the size of of her fist. She'd found it under a floorboard on the night—

Verity shuddered. She put thoughts of that night and the catty women behind her. She kept her head down to avoid the puddles forming in the pitted stone slabs of the square. The materials of both blouse and skirt plastered against her body, revealing every curve. She was hungry, wet, miserable, and just wanted the solitude of her little room across the river in Algiers Point. She had enough money in her pocket to pay for the ferry ride, and if Mama Two's food truck was waiting at the Algier's Point Ferry terminal, she could get a muffaletta. Mama Two's were big enough to feed her for two days.

Verity slammed into something unyielding and hands grabbed her arms in a punishing grip. She jerked back, getting tangled in the tongue of her wagon—not that it mattered. Those hands didn't let her go.

"My apologies." The decadent voice whispered over her skin, leaving goosebumps in its wake. "I fear I was gawking at the sights rather than paying attention to where I was going."

His words carried a strange accent, one her well-trained ear couldn't place. It sounded almost French but with clipped British overtones, which probably accounted for his odd formality.

"Please, my dear, allow me to rectify my boorish inattention. May I buy you—"

A blinding light followed immediately by a deafening clap of thunder obliterated the rest of his question. Verity could smell ozone in the air and she fought the urge to cross herself—or worse, run directly to the cathedral to take refuge under its vaulted ceiling. The Church was not benevolent to her kind.

A dark shadow filtered across the periphery of her

vision and she turned her head to see what was creeping up on her. Nothing. The square was deserted. Just her and the man she'd bumped in to. Turning back, she discovered that she was alone. Then the skies opened up, drenching her to the very bone.

By the time she trudged up the ramp from the Algiers Point Ferry Terminal, her teeth were chattering, and she was so cold and exhausted that she was a block past Mama Two's when Mama's grandson ran up and tugged on her skirt.

"Mama says t'give this to you, Miss Vee. She says you need to get dry, warm, and eat it all. No savin' for a rainy day cuz it's rainin' cats and dogs t'day, yeah?" The boy shoved a plastic bag into her free hand and darted back down the street.

She yelled her thanks after him, but he didn't even raise a negligent hand to say he'd heard. She trudged on and three blocks later, she dodged down the narrow walkway between two shotgun houses. The one on her right had been bought, gutted, updated, and completely renovated by a yuppie couple who both worked and kept frou-frou dogs that barked incessantly. The shotgun she lived behind hadn't been so fortunate. The landlord divided it into two small flats and also converted the shed out back into a one-room "guest house" and rented out all three units.

Opening the door, she waited a beat before entering. Even so, the three cats—one white, one black, and one half-and-half—all but tripped her as she ducked out of the deluge that chose that moment to empty half the Gulf of Mexico on her head.

CHAPTER TWO
STICKS AND STONES

SADE BULLIED her way past the Legate's secretary and stood with only his huge antique and slightly scarred wooden desk between them. Roman remained at the window staring down into Jackson Square. "I expected you last night," he said, his voice bland. He held onto his emotions with an iron will.

"There was a fucking freak storm over Georgia and even though I was on a direct flight, we were forced to land at Hartsfield in Atlanta. I spent the gawddamned night in that motherfucking terminal. Do you have any idea how fucking uncomfortable those shitty chairs—"

He whirled, the emotion he kept off his face focused in his eyes. Flames all but shot from them as he stared her down. "Shut up, Sade."

Sade rocked back. In all the years she'd known Roman, he had never—not even once used that tone of voice with her. And she'd done some crazy-ass things as a teenager that drove her vampire godfather to drinking spiked blood, her werewolf foster brother to shift and run away from home, the fae who dogged her every step to throw up his hands and dissipate in a shower of fairy dust. Roman had simply folded his arms and braced for the storm. Easy enough to do when your natural form was made of granite. She carefully blanked her face but her mouth thinned. "The hell I—"

Roman cut her off with a slash of one hand and a voice that sent chills drag racing up and down her spine. "You will refrain from using your foul mouth in my office, Sade."

Claws slashed out of his fingers, both of them realizing what was happening at the same time. Sade didn't back away. Roman didn't attempt to control the change. In moments, all trappings of humanity fled. His clothes ripped as he grew another foot in height, his shoulders widened and leathery wings unfolded from his back.

"Jeez, that worked like a fuckin' charm," she muttered under her breath. She'd known for several months that something was wrong in Roman-ville and she'd figured a side benefit to this little excursion to New Orleans would be to cajole, harass, or irritate him out of the deep funk he'd been in. Belatedly, Sade realized what troubled Roman was far worse than a funk. This entity in front of her, with only the illusion of protection in the form of an antique wooden desk between them, should have scared her spitless. But this was Roman, the magick who fetched her from this Realm or that one when she was just a toddler and the pawn in an undeclared war between Mathias, the master vampire she considered a father figure, and Oberon, King of the Seelie Court, and once her mother's lover. He'd dried her tears. Taken her flying. Insured that she knew at least one person loved her unconditionally. And that love was returned in spades.

"You don't scare me, Roman." She jutted her chin, emerald eyes snapping with green fire hot enough to match the molten iron in his own.

"Then we will have to see what I can do about that. Because I should, Sade Marquis. You are nothing but mortal. Frail. Breakable. Unimportant. A lesser being beneath the notice of the magick races." He placed his fists on the desk and leaned forward, his gaze piercing hers. "You. Are. Nothing. I could snap your neck with one hand. There is no one here to save you if I do so. No vampire lover to turn you. No fae lover to take you to the Summerlands in hopes one of the Old Gods will revive you. The bite of a werewolf will only give you rabies." He straightened to his full height, threw back his head and laughed. The antique glass in the window rattled and papers fluttered on the desk. When he stopped, an eerie silence filled the room. His next words dropped into the void, sending ripples through the air— enough that Sade's hair lifted in their passing. "Do not make me hurt you."

He already had. His words left a bitter taste in her mouth. He knew all her secrets, knew just what to say to get to her. But he was Romo, the fairytale Prince Charming at her childhood tea parties. He was Sir Roman, the knight in granite armor who deflected the slings and arrows of a dangerous world from his Lady Sade. She loved him from the deepest well of her soul. She put every ounce of that love into her voice so that when she spoke, her voice didn't break and her conviction rang true. "You wouldn't."

Roman wasn't quite so far gone that he didn't see the flash of brittle green glass in her gaze. Yet she sounded absolutely positive, thank the One God. He wasn't damned, not yet. But if he didn't regain control, he would be. This was how it started. He'd watched it happen all those centuries ago. He'd watched the slaughter of his brothers, the near annihilation of his kind. He breathed deeply, fighting the urge to turn away from the dangerous glitter of moisture in Sade's eyes. They would both be appalled if that liquid spilled onto her cheeks. He owed her his penance so he didn't turn away, didn't flinch.

"I am sorry, Lady Sade."

"Fuck that, Roman, What in God's bloody blue- blazing hell is going on?"

His jaw hardened until the sound of his teeth grating together caused him to stop. "Will you ever grow up?"

Sade laughed, but the sound held no mirth. Her expression sobered and her eyes went soft with concern as she hitched a hip onto his desk. "Talk to me, Roman. And don't give me all the woo-woo shit about this being about magicks and therefore this stupid little mundane—" She paused to pat her own head before finishing. "Needs to just mind her own business and keep tiptoeing through the tulips. I was three the first time Tatiana tried to kill me."

Roman winced but shook his head. "No, Lady Sade. She did not try to kill. The Fae Queen never *tries* to kill someone. If she wants you dead, you are." He faced the window again. "Tell me about the storm." With the mention of Titania, Sade's initial comments were just then sinking in. There weren't many magicks who could control the weather but who else would want to keep Sade out of this situation?

"Don't know much. The pilot was too busy trying to keep us in the air and then get us on the ground safely. Seemed to me like the damn weather was following the plane. *Just* the plane. And then it camped out right over Hartsfield Airport so no one took off or landed. This morning? Blue skies and sunshine. Took a couple of hours for the airline to sort us all out and here I am."

"Where is your vampire?"

Roman's abrupt change of topic took her by surprise, but she managed to clamp her mouth shut around the words that wanted to bubble out. She flashed him a narrow-eyed look and crossed her booted legs at the ankles. "One, Sinjen is not *my* vampire, and two, he's busy. Why?"

He turned away, returning his gaze to the window. Tourists flocked Jackson Square like sea gulls and the local artists and street performers were perched around their displays like colorful birds. His eyes, as they had for months now, sought out the figure beneath the umbrella covered with gypsy scarves. Her riot of blond curls was capped with another gaudy scarf and he knew her eyes were a blue so vibrant that he could see the color from where he stood out of sight here in his office.

Sade studied him, noted where his gaze was fixed but held her own counsel. She'd find out soon enough what troubled her old friend. "I'm hungry," she announced. "And I'm buying so long as we eat at Déja Vu."

THE MORNING CROWD had been brisk then dribbled to a trickle as lunch time approached. Verity shifted her umbrella to keep up with the sun's relentless path and ignored the grumble in her stomach. She'd shared half of a half of the muffaletta sandwich Mama Two had given her with the three strays who lived under her porch. She would share the other half with them tonight. Tips had been good so far but not enough to make up for none the previous day.

Her neck prickled and she shifted on her stool to rearrange the crystals on her table so she could scan the area without being noticed. She saw two people emerge from a building across the way. She knew there were offices and apartments above the shops and restaurant that occupied the lowest floor. The man, dressed impeccably in a dark suit, was tall—probably close to seven feet but he moved like a big cat—all the sinewy grace of a hunting predator. Power brushed across her skin, leaving goosebumps in its wake. This was not a man to be ignored. She quickly changed her focus to the woman at his side. She, too, was tall, though not even close to the man. Long, dark hair fell in loose waves over her shoulders. She wore a jacket, slacks, boots, and matched the man stride for stride. There was purpose in her expression even as her gaze swept the square. She also gave off the air of a predator though there was only a whisper of power surrounding her, like a cocoon—or a protective spell.

And wasn't that an interesting thought because she'd bet money she didn't have that the woman—for all the strength and equality she showed in comparison to her companion—was human.

The two didn't look her way but Verity still felt like eyes were on her. She took another surreptitious gaze around and noticed two men standing near the entrance to St. Louis Cathedral, both obviously looking everywhere but at her. She pushed back from her table to kneel beside the old red wagon she used to transport her gear back and forth. She brushed her scarf off so that her hair curtained that side of her face and she watched the men through its veil. They both studied her now, their focus sharp as needles and her skin prickled painfully this time. One brought a phone to his ear and she watched his lips move. His eyes remained on her.

Verity continued to rummage in her wagon, head down, but eyes darting between the two men so neither of them would get the feeling of being watched. The one on the phone continued to stare but the other had turned so that he was in profile, his gaze following the path of the man and the woman she'd first noticed.

One of the guest chairs creaked and Verity jumped, whirling with such speed she lost balance and fell on her butt. Laughter punctuated her predicament and a bronze-colored hand reached for her. "Ah, cher, you do make me laugh."

She grabbed Alton's hand and he helped her up enough she could slide back into her chair. Alton, of no last name fame, was one of the living statue performers that peopled the Quarter. She'd only rarely glimpsed the real face behind the metallic paint and makeup.

Brushing back the unruly waves of her hair, she retied the scarf on her head.

"Glad to know I'm good for something," she retorted.

Alton was staring at something over her shoulder and as if a curtain closed behind his eyes, his expression blanked. Without meaning to, she turned her head to see what had caught his attention. The two men she'd noticed before were now within about twenty feet of her table. They were both glaring at Alton, as if he'd interrupted them.

"Do you know them, cher?" His voice was barely a whisper but it vibrated with repressed anger.

She shook her head and whispered back, "No, but I noticed them watching me earlier."

"Give me a reading, cher."

Verity, eyes wide, stared at him. Alton had never once asked for a reading. Full of sudden nervousness, her hands fumbled opening the wooden box holding her tarot cards. A bronze hand covered hers. "Shhh, cher. Not with the cards. Use the crystals. Focus on them. Do not worry about those men. Use the crystals."

His words all but echoed in her head. He freed one of her hands and she ran her fingers over the various crystals and stones where they rested on a scrap of soft suede leather.

"Breathe, cher. Use the crystals. Breathe."

She did. In. Out. Slow, deep breaths, her eyes narrowed in on just the tips of her fingers as they played with the baubles of her trade. Energy, like the bite of electric shocks, zapped her skin from time to time. Her vision grayed at the edges before fading to black. Her left index finger caressed a dull brown piece of granite, a piece she'd picked up along the street a few days ago. The vision ensnared her before she could prepare.

Fear. No. More than that. Terror. Absolute terror.

Can'tmovecan'tmovecan'tmove.
Run. Need to run.
Can'tmovecan'tmovecan'tmove.
It's coming. Coming closer. Closerclosercloser.
PAIN! Bright, greasy waves of pain. Shattering.
Shattered into pieces. Dust. Death. Nothing.

Verity slowly raised her head. Alton was gone. Still wrapped in the cobwebs of horror from the vision, she cast a furtive glance over her shoulder. The men were gone as well. Her left hand cramped. It took effort to unfurl her fisted fingers. A small chunk of brownish granite lay in the center of her palm. Her nails left bloody crescent moons in her skin and the rock itself had cut her, the edges as sharp as a razor. She stared at the small pool of blood gathering around it and was afraid.

CHAPTER THREE
A LITTLE HELP FROM MY FRIENDS

ENSCONCED IN her favorite booth at Deja Vu—the bar and restaurant that was Sade's unofficial home away from home in New Orleans, she watched Roman open concern. Acquiescing to him, she'd surrendered her preferred seat—the bench against the back wall in the corner—and had taken up residence on the opposite bench, but with her back against the wall, hips swiveled so she could always watch the room.

"You came alone."

She shrugged. "I've always worked alone, Roman."

"No. You've always had Caleb."

That got a rueful smile out of her. She loved her werewolf foster brother like damn and whoa but he had his own life now—one that had come precipitously close to ending in the New Mexico desert not long ago. "He's in Denver now, with his lady. Permanent transfer. The powers that be have determined the MAGIC unit should be...diversified."

An FBI agent, Sade had been perfectly poised when the Big Rip occurred, the president was unmasked as an elf, and all the big bad magicks lost their glamour. The world discovered the things that went bump in the night were bigger and badder than even their nightmares could imagine. As the goddaughter of a master vampire and of great interest to Oberon, King of the Seelie Court, Sade had been marked by both when only a toddler. As a result, glamour was lost on her and she knew an elf from a fae, a werewolf from a dragon shifter, and could call a spade a witch. She had no love for witches, since one almost killed her in Chicago just over a year ago.

At the moment, she was the head of the FBI's Magical Activities, Grievances, and Inhuman Crimes unit. To this day, Sade rolled her eyes at the federal government's love of acronyms. When the unit was first organized in response to the flood of magicks and a fear of them preying on mundane humans, only humans had been tapped. With a great deal of patience, punctuated by lots of swear words, intimidation, and events, Sade was finally weeding out the mundanes with agendas against the magicks and filling in the holes with magicks themselves—if not as actual agents, then as special consultants. Going after a rogue dragon? Yeah, took another dragon to deal with the situation. New vampire out of control? It was nice to call on a master vampire to settle things.

She'd started her FBI life in New Orleans and she kept getting called back—not that it was a big inconvenience. She loved NOLA. Always had. It was an open city with magicks and mundanes frolicking together. New Orleans was special. But murder had returned and brought Sade back.

"Diversified?" Roman's dry voice caught her attention.

"Satellite offices. Caleb's now in charge of the Denver Regional MAGIC Office. It was going to be in Chicago originally, but Caleb refused to head the unit unless the Bureau based it in Denver."

Roman allowed a touch of fondness to filter into his voice. "Caleb and Adele are doing fine?"

Jax Martine picked that moment to breeze up to the table. "Well, knock me up and slap my ass, Sade Marquis as I live and breathe. I know what you want, chere." He set four glasses of water in front of her, along with a cup of steaming-hot coffee. Then he set one glass in front of Roman. "And for you, sir?"

"Bacon cheese burger, rare, naked but for mustard. Just water." Roman hesitated a moment. "Make that two burgers. And fries."

Their waiter sailed off without a word. Sade leaned over the table and in a conspiratorial whisper said, "I swear he's got elf or fae blood. That man hasn't aged in all the years I've known him."

Roman watched the man as he bustled through the doors from the kitchen and headed behind the bar to draw a couple of beers for another table. His nostrils flared as he scented the air. "Neither. Perhaps a touch of witch." When he turned back, Sade's narrow-eyed gaze was fixed on him. "What?"

"I was paying attention that day, Roman. Witches and gargoyles are the Hatfields and McCoys of the magick realms.

He laughed at that. "That historical human feud could describe the majority of magical interactions. Fae versus vampire. Witches versus wizards..." His voice trailed off and he gazed toward the door, but his sight was somewhere far beyond the busy street just outside. "Once upon a time, true, but no longer. The last of the dark sorcerers were executed at the end of the war."

From the way he spoke, Sade mentally capitalized "The War." None of the magicks spoke of that time— only that it was bloody awful and the Veil was cemented in a magic so fierce that it took a millennium and a series of astrological events that should never have happened in alignment to bring it down. Magic spilled over when the Veil ripped. It ran wild and all the magicks were stripped bare. Only in the past few years had they been able to regain most the magic that had been theirs. To Sade's mind, most was far more than they needed because at full strength? Yeah, humans were toast.

Roman blinked and his gaze shortened to focus on

Sade as Jax glided up and slid plates onto their table. Without a word, he placed full glasses of ice water in front of her and Roman, gathered Sade's empties and disappeared.

"Elves and fae battle. Vampires and werewolves. Where there is power to be gleaned there will be conflict, Lady Sade. You know this firsthand." Before she could duck away, he fastened his fingers to her chin and jaw. Tilting her head this way and that in the ambient light of the restaurant, he gazed deeply into her eyes. He must have found what he searched for because he exhaled and freed her. "She is truly gone from you."

Sade ignored the shivers bolting up her spine, but she couldn't hide the full-body shudder that froze her muscles. She managed to swallow the saliva pooling in her mouth, but she wasn't confident enough of her voice to speak. She'd gotten up close and personal with an ancient witch in Chicago and almost died as a result. At least that's what she told herself. Deep inside the darkest, most secret part of her soul, she knew it hadn't been an *almost* thing, a close call, a near-death experience. There'd been no light at the end of the tunnel, no family and friends to greet her. No, there'd been on a vast empty darkness, and the sound of the silence deafened her.

Cool fingers caressed her cheek. She blinked her eyes open as phantom lips brushed her mouth. Sinjen, even in the sleep that is death to a vampire during daylight, had felt her distress and sought to comfort her. She didn't realize the secret smile prompted by that knowledge registered on her face. When she glanced up, Roman was studiously focused on his hamburger.

⁘ ●

A WHITE PAPER SACK, with grease staining one side

of it, landed on Verity's table. "You need to eat, cher," Alton told her. "You have somethin' to drink?"

She did, a bottle of water she'd filled from the tap the night before and left in the freezer overnight so it would be cold. "How much—"

"Don't, Vee. We're square. My tips were way over good t'day. Now eat that po'boy before the shrimp decide to swim away."

She laughed, tucking her chin and giving him a look from under raised brows and lowered lashes. "Fried shrimp are poor swimmers, Alton Smith."

"Yes, ma'am they surely are. But you need t'eat those puppies anyway." His eyes traveled over the area as people began to filter back in after the lunch hour. "An' ya need t'eat fast. I got the feelin' you'll be busy this afternoon. Lots of tourists. I'm movin' up this way. Gettin' busy down on the other side."

She knew he didn't mean more people but more street performers all vying for the same audience and tips. Verity realized he'd changed clothes. "Who you gonna be this afternoon, A?"

He did a little soft-shoe shuffle and sang a line from "Mr. Bojangles" then he tipped his hat and sauntered off. Her nerves settled a bit. Verity felt more secure knowing that Alton would be close if something happened. She smiled, thinking about how he'd shown up at her table the very first day she'd set up shop in the square. He'd been in mime white-face wearing a black-and-white striped shirt. He'd drawn her into his act, much to the amusement of the crowd. She'd been sixteen, on her own, and he'd made sure she had enough money in her tip jar to eat dinner that night.

Alton was...other, but she wasn't sure what. Maybe he was like her—part human, part witch, part something or another. She called herself a gypsy because that's how she lived. Whatever Alton was, he had a touch of

24

magic that was evident in the way he controlled his body. He'd taken her under his wing. Now he was a surrogate big brother who fussed over her and despite her proud and prickly nature, he subtly took care of her when she'd let him.

"Oh, look, George!" a woman cried. "Fortunes!"

Verity glanced up and did her best not to wince. Tourists were the lifeblood of New Orleans in general and the French Quarter in particular. Most were nice people visiting to enjoy the pleasures this place could provide. Some were like this pair—caricatures of Worst Tourists Ever—and those kind were never good tippers. George wore Bermuda shorts in an eye-searing assortment of neon brights, topped with a red tee-shirt sporting a crawfish and the words, *Laissez les bons temps rouler.* Let the good times roll. Indeed. White athletic socks clung to his skinny calves and brown Birkenstock sandals clad his feet.

"You don't need your fortune told, Margie. None of these folks are real. Remember, the nice desk clerk at the hotel told you that."

Margie wore a red straw hat with a wide brim, a tee shirt that matched her husband's only in purple, and lime green yoga pants. A lot of people probably thought a woman Margie's age should not be wearing yoga pants in public. Her crew socks matched the pants but were toned down by the white cross-trainers she wore. Verity secretly applauded Margie's *joie de vivre.*

The woman stared at Verity and huffed out a breath. "Are you a fake, little girl? How much will it cost me for you to tell me my fortune?"

Most of the other so-called psychics and fortune tellers in the Square started out by saying they'd do a free read and then fall into a patter of what they normally charged and then, after the mark was sucked in, hit them with the cost—anywhere from a hundred

25

dollars up. Verity wasn't most of them and she wasn't truly a psychic. Like Alton, she was magic touched and if she charged for her readings, the magic had a way of backlashing.

"I don't charge, ma'am," Verity said. "My gift gets jealous if I charge but nice folks, if they're pleased, will stuff a little in the tip jar so I can feed myself and put a roof over my head."

Margie settled her ample bottom in one of the small chairs and she gestured for George to join her by patting her hand on the other seat. "Can you do us two-for-one?"

Verity wasn't surprised, and as she wasn't expecting much of a tip, given George's reaction, she just smiled. "Of course. Do you prefer a palm-reading? Tarot cards? Crystals?" She spent almost ten minutes explaining how things worked and what information might be gleaned from each method of divination. The small crystal ball on its stand kept glimmering at Verity but she forced her eyes to ignore the shadows sliding through the glass and remain focused on Margie and George.

Margie wanted a crystal reading while insisting that George get the Tarot cards. The woman chattered like a magpie through the whole thing, constantly breaking Verity's concentration. She'd never been good when it came to keeping up a patter with the people who sat at her table. She needed to concentrate because she did have that elusive touch of magic and it was a harsh mistress. She gave true readings or said nothing at all.

Margie had a health problem that needed looking into, something about her chest, but she'd get to meet her first grandchild. George would get to do what he wanted with his life soon, suggesting that he was meant to retire and enjoy it. Margie was thrilled about the grandchild, especially since their daughter wasn't married but she poo-poo'd the health problem.

"Don't you people say stuff like that? To make things sound all dire so we think you're serious." She pushed up from the chair and gathered up her bag. "Give the girl a ten, George. That's about what sitting in the shade is worth." Then she was off, calling over her shoulder, "Isn't this one of those museums we're supposed to see?"

George was slower to get up, and he shook his head as he watched his wife chug across the square toward the doors of the Cabildo. "Thank you for your time," he said, his voice kind. He fumbled in his front pocket for his billfold, and without making a show of it, he pulled some bills out and stuffed them in her jar. His smile was patient as he added, "Our daughter is a lesbian. She and her partner are adopting a child next month. Margie doesn't know." His smile faded slightly. "She has several spots on her lung but has ignored the cancer for years. The doctors don't give her much longer. Once she's gone, I'm going to write a book." His expression lightened a little. "Either a romance or a spy novel." Without looking back, he headed after his wife.

It wasn't until she got home for the night that Verity discovered five hundred-dollar bills in her jar.

CHAPTER FOUR
THE STORM IS COMING

ROMAN STOOD at the window, a dark silhouette if anyone below chanced to look up. Early-morning fog swirled through Jackson Square, leaving the granite blocks and wooden benches coated with a silvery sheen as the first fingers of dawn poked through the gray miasma. Roman refused to count the number of times he'd stood here, waiting, watching for...something. He hadn't known what until—

A bright swirl of color coalesced through the murk and the constricting pressure in his chest eased, a feeling he chose to ignore. She was early this morning, lugging her wagon with the folding chairs, market umbrella, rickety wooden table, and her satchel filled with the exotic paraphernalia of her trade. Her tousled curls were tamed today, severe in a long braid snaking over one shoulder. Fog swirled around her, lightened, leaving her poised like an island tinted by riotous hues.

He couldn't remember when he'd first noticed the girl. Young woman, he corrected himself. Of course, she could be a crone of ninety and she'd still be little more than a child to him. He thought back, trying to pinpoint the moment the little gypsy had wormed her way into his psyche. Had she always been there, crouched down hiding behind all the memories of the before times? Perhaps she had.

Roman had found no peace since the first time he'd truly noticed her in front of the cathedral. Her smile tugged at his heart even as his senses warred with the knowledge of what—of *who*—she might be. Was she

28

rogue? Or perhaps unaligned, though the witches guarded their bloodlines as closely as they did their Book of Shadows. The girl was an unknown. The Witches' Council knew nothing of her that Roman could gleam from them. All magicks living or visiting in the city had to register with the Legate's office and he had no record of a gypsy girl who told fortunes on Jackson Square. That was disturbing.

He didn't know her name but this young woman with haunted shadows in her eyes and the fragile sheen of magic clinging to her skin like glitter drew him as inexorably as that proverbial moth. Would she singe his wings if he got too close? He was half tempted to find out.

The windows were open and the dank scent of the Mississippi—an odor of murky water and mud, of age and wisdom—swirled around him as the fog danced with the gypsy. She called to someone, her voice as musical as the birds who sang dawn awake. Something deep inside him stirred, something that had slumbered for hundreds of years. Desire. He'd thought himself long past the passions of the flesh. His kind was slow to feel the want or need of sex, and then only when in human guise. He'd partaken of those earthly delights once upon a time, had dallied with silky-haired sirens who tempted men. Lust was a universal thing when procreation was involved. Gargoyles only partook for fun.

The fog began to lift, and more people filtered into Jackson Square. The street folk, artists, locals on their way to their places of employment. The gypsy girl came early so she could to get the spot on the walkway right in front of the gates into the gardens surrounding the fountain and statue of General Jackson. Interesting that the so-called psychics and fortune tellers would set up their tables on the esplanade directly in front of St. Louis Cathedral as if the old gods challenged the One

God, his Son and the Holy Spirit. If that was so, the One wasn't intimidated.

Someone called out and the gypsy girl turned, her face flushing with pleasure as she waved. Roman glowered at the werewolf in his painted clothing and face. He carried a white bag with the familiar green logo of the Cafe Du Monde in one hand and a drink carrier with four coffee cups in the other. Roman ground his teeth together and was surprised by the primal growl growing in his chest. The werewolf stopped dead still and looked around, scanning every person for the threat. Interesting, he thought, until the man's eyes focused on the window where Roman stood. He didn't move, didn't look away. The werewolf eventually tilted his head to one side, quirked an eyebrow and with a deft slight of hand, transferred his goods into one hand so he could flash a two-fingered salute in Roman's direction.

What interest did the werewolf have in the gypsy? Roman continued to watch as the wolf teased her away from unpacking to join him on a nearby park bench. They ate beignets, brushing off the powdered sugar, and drank cafe au lait from the paper cups. The wolf was protective of the gypsy but not as a lover would be. Something inside him eased a bit. He stood there in the shadows and watched until the little fortune teller had her table and umbrella set up and the werewolf had gone off to perform.

Turning from the window, his eyes went straight to his desktop. A parchment envelope with its splash of blood-red wax marked by *Le Vieil's* seal sat there, a pale indictment of his dereliction of duty. He should have left the city days ago but he could not force himself to go. Not so long as the golden-haired temptress danced through his dreams. He dropped into his chair and broke the seal. He knew what would be written on the paper folded so precisely before being tucked into the envelope.

Someone was going to die.

HAIR PRICKLED on the back of Verity's neck and she wished for a moment that she'd taken the time to wash her hair instead of braiding it. When loose, she could hide behind its waves when feelings of being watched— or worse, the shivers brought on when someone walked over your grave—came over her. Her eyes were drawn to the third floor of the building on the corner of St. Peters and Chartres. A row of six tall windows fronted Jackson Square and she thought she caught movement in the third window in from the corner.

The hair on her arms joined those on her nape and she remembered the very tall, somber man and the woman she'd seen exiting from the private door leading to the second and third floors. She'd seen him a few times since but as near as she could tell, he was unaware of her existence. Why would an important man such as he take any notice of someone like her? It didn't matter that just the thought of him made her pulse flutter.

Pulling her attention away from the building, she remembered she should be paying attention to the people strolling along the esplanade. She concentrated on shifting her expression to the one Alton called her "Mona Lisa Face," a term he always enclosed in air quotes. Working to make eye contact with people, she called out to any who would meet her gaze.

"Do you want to know?" she said. "Does fate have something magical in store for you?"

Two teenage girls sauntered up. "How much?" one asked.

Verity's magic stirred again but it wasn't interested in these girls. There was something—someone—beyond them that had made her power sit up like a curious cat. He stood in the shade beneath the portico of the Cabildo, leaning against one of the square columns. Recognition stirred in the back of her mind. Did she know him? His face remained shadowed but there was something familiar about him.

"Hey!" the other girl said, snapping her fingers and popping her bubble gum at the same time. "My friend wants to know how much."

Giving the two a cool gaze, Verity let her expression turn blank. "Those who receive a reading give me what they think my words are worth. I don't want your money but I will give you this." She stared at the first girl. "Your boyfriend is not worth keeping. If you stay with him, your life will not be what you wish." She barely glanced at the second. "You should return what you took. You could afford to pay but you didn't."

Both girls sneered, and the bubble-gum chewer dug in her pocket to pull out a penny. She dropped it into Verity's tip jar. "I think your *words* are pretty worthless. C'mon, Jani."

As soon as their backs were turned, Verity dug out the penny. She cupped it in her hand and from her bag of stones and crystals, she added an agate for protection, fluorite to cleanse the negativity, and pyrite as an energy shield and for luck. Cupping both hands around stones and coin, she gently shook them, then brought her hands to her mouth so she could blow through the slit made by her thumbs. Satisfied, she put her stones back in their silk-lined bag. With the penny balanced on the curved first knuckle of her index fingers, she used her thumb to flip the coin out onto the granite blocks that made-up the walkway.

Verity checked for the man she'd seen earlier, but he was gone. She couldn't decide if she was disappointed or relieved. Smiling ruefully, she watched the people ambling past. A little girl trailed along behind her parents and she was the one who spied the penny. She squatted down on her heels and stared at the coin until her parents noticed her. Her father came back and she pointed out the money she'd found.

"A penny for luck," he said. "You can pick it up."

With Daddy's permission, that's what the child did, clenching it in her tiny hand. "Is it enough for ice cream?" she asked.

"I think it probably is," her father said, his voice full of humor and kindness.

Verity sat back, relaxed now, her heart lighter, despite a touch of melancholy. What would her father have been like? Or her mother for that matter. She had no memory of them. Only Baba Rawnie and a faint flicker of her Grandmother Zara.

"Hello again," a deep male voice said.

Startled, Verity's head jerked up and she stared at the man she'd almost knocked down in the rain.

"I think I'd like you to tell my fortune."

CHAPTER FIVE
A TIME TO HUNT

IGNORING THE STEAMING CORPSES littering the alley between two industrial buildings near the Mississippi River, Varrick felt like freaking Hansel—only the birdies obliterating this particular trail of breadcrumbs were vultures of the preternatural kind and he wasn't hunting an old witch. He smelled the rusted-iron taint of blood, tasted the copper of it around the shallow drags he pulled on his cigarette. His Gretel waited at the entrance to the alley. Sade Marquis. FBI agent. Dead sexy. She racked a new magazine in her 9mm, the metallic sound echoing. He'd already reloaded his specially modified .44 Mag. If six rounds of HE didn't take down their targets, they were dog food anyway.

"Roman, you owe me big time, brother!" Varrick snarled. He'd been called here only because Roman was stuck in a meeting with the Concilium Magicae. Hunting rogue gargoyles was a pain in the ass. Literally. A rogue was a rare creature but there'd been more of them cropping up, along with humans who'd been bespelled into destroying gargoyles frozen in their stone statue form. Varrick and his escadron had been popping in and out all over the world and he was getting freaking tired of this crap.

He rolled his head on his neck, vertebrae grinding like ancient rocks. This whole fiasco might as well be the Fed's fault. Someone was to blame. She might be stone cold—and that was a compliment coming from a gargoyle—but she was still human and if anything happened to her, more beings than Roman would be ready to grind him into dust.

A grating sound brought his head up. One idiot rogue tried to sneak up on Sade. Varrick raised the Mag, squeezed. Acrid smoke from his cigarette danced with the fog crawling across the docks as powdered granite swirled and settled, just so much dust in the wind.

The Fed glared. "I can do this. Alone. You don't have jurisdiction."

"Like hell I don't. Not to mention Roman'll take my head if you get hurt."

"I need one alive."

"Yeah, good luck with that." A bullet whistled past his ear, ricocheted. He whirled but before he could fire, the gargoyle behind him disintegrated. What the hell kind of loads was the Fed carrying?

Sade smirked and holstered her weapon. "Or maybe not." She eyed him coolly. "You do realize you almost got your ass shot off, popping in like that."

Varrick matched his tone to hers. "You do realize that you almost got your ass handed to you, and would have if I hadn't shown up."

Together, they quickly checked for survivors but found none—either gargoyle or human. Then they made sure there were no more gargoyles waiting to take them out. They cleared the area. Sade called her boss in Washington. Varrick called Roman. Roman arrived before the local police contingent. He had the advantage of teleportation.

An FBI agent for ten years, Sade had been raised by a master vampire, hunted ghouls, fought a Native American demon, and walked through blood and gore more than once. Nothing in her experience prepared her for this. The carnage was almost beyond human comprehension. Not one body was intact and it was hard to tell the human victims from the dead gargoyles.

She suspected there might be other magical victims here as well.

Having to blow up the attackers because they'd been in true gargoyle form just added to the confusion. Putting them back together in order to identify them was a job she didn't want and figured Dr. Toni Allison, the ME, would hate her for dumping all the parts into the doc's lap. Footsteps echoed behind her and she turned, expecting Varrick. She found Roman instead.

"So many." Her gaze connected with his and she didn't like what she saw in his eyes. Pain. Sorrow. Resignation. She wasn't a big student of magical history but she knew a little. Plus, there'd been rumblings of an internal fight brewing within the Gargoyle Realm. She was vaguely aware of something they called the Old War, when gargoyles fought each other. "Is this like before? Is it happening again"

"I pray not. Only a few of us survived those dark times." Roman stared out across the sluggish water of the big river, gaze fixed on some unseen speck on the far horizon, a memory only he could see. Roman shook himself and glanced around the scene. He walked away, her gaze following him as he moved through the bodies. He paused here with a look of resigned sadness and there with a look of disgust. Friend and rogue, she decided.

Roman stopped near a torso, the only one that still had a head semi-attached to it. His shoulders slumped as he dropped down beside the body. "Ah, Majid," he murmured. "Why were you here?"

Concerned, Sade followed him and glanced between his face and that of the victim. "You knew him?"

"We were brothers."

She sucked in air. Brothers? How had she not known he had a family? Her hand curled over his shoulder in a gesture of caring. "I'm sorry, Roman."

Inhaling deeply, Roman let out the breath in a slow exhale. "We were of the same fledge, his rookery next to mine."

Having not a clue what all that meant, Sade glanced up at Varrick, who'd quietly joined them, and made a wide-eyed face indicating that fact. He shook his head, his expression giving nothing away, but his eyes held chips of cold steel in them.

"I didn't recognize him until now," Varrick said, his voice choking on the emotion he struggled to hold at bay. "I've check all the others. Three of my escadron died with him." His gaze caromed over the scene like a ricocheting bullet. "Why would they come here, Roman? What lured them to this place at this time?"

"Did you recognize who attacked you?" Roman's voice grated against the stillness.

"No."

"I have checked the bodies. Neither do I."

Sade rocked back on her heels, her attention bouncing between the two gargoyles. "How can that be?" Roman and Varrick exchanged looks, shutting Sade out completely. "Now look here—"

"Shut up, Sade." Varrick barked the order and she bristled, until she caught sight of Roman.

She looked away, unable to process the utter devastation carved on Roman's face. Then she realized the face that had so captured him was staring up at her. Was there an accusation in those sightless eyes? A demand for retribution? Sade didn't know. She stood there, her gun still in her hand, watching the man who'd always known how to comfort her succumb to his grief with no idea of how to comfort him.

Roman placed his palm on Majid's forehead but there was nothing left of his brother's life force. With a gentle caress, he ran his hand down Majid's face, closing his eyes. "You are the last of us, Majid Saroyan, and perhaps the best. Together you and I stood atop that hill millenniums ago and we mourned. We lamented those we lost and we keened our sorrow to the heavens. And now I offer the same for you, my brother. My friend. My fledge mate."

He rocked and his back collided with Sade's thighs. She braced and her hands clutched his shoulders as he raised his face to the sky. "So many lost and for what purpose?" he shouted.

No answer came, save for the whispers of air as gargoyles appeared from nothing. The rest of Varrick's escadron arrived, one by one, ringing in Roman, Varrick, Sade, and the dead.

"Grief," Roman said, his voice soft once more. "Grief levels us. It is a living thing. It twines around our souls, our minds. It leaves shadows on the heart. The dark times during the Old War were terrible. Those who survived live forever with the echo of what is gone howling inside our heads. Yet there is no sound. Only silence."

Sade stared at the gargoyle—her childhood protector, now her friend. Her own heart was breaking for his. "How do you stand it?"

"What choice have we?"

Swallowing her sadness, Sade studied the broken body of Roman's oldest friend. He, and the others, had been murdered by those gargoyles she'd taken out with Varrick's assistance. Technically, this was magick on magick crime but it had been committed out in the open, in a human city. As the FBI's MAGIC liaison, she was now in charge of the investigation.

"I'm sorry, Roman. I'm sorry it came to this. He's mine now. I'll take care him. Of all of them. When I'm finished, they'll be yours again."

He pushed to his feet and Sade scrambled to give him room. Varrick steadied her and she flashed him a quick look of thanks.

"When you are finished, Lady Sade, they will be ours again. Then I shall take them home to be mourned properly as is the way of the Sentinels."

His grief grated on her heart and she touched his arm offering small solace.

"When the Silence of Sorrows ends, I will return to hunt."

"You and me both, Roman." She turned away, intent upon her task. The New Orleans police had arrived but they looked as shell-shocked as she felt. Varrick appeared at her side. "We will sort them out, Sade. And then Dr. Allison can have them for as long as she needs. The magic of the stone heart will keep them in their human guise until we release them back into the Universe.

"Okay," she said. "Okay then. I appreciate the help." She moved away, giving quiet orders to the police and then processing the scene.

Roman stood silent watch, his heart turned back into granite. What was the stain of one more death on his soul? In the face of eternity, nothing.

CHAPTER SIX
WATCHERS IN THE RYE

HE WAS BACK. The man from a few days ago. Verity didn't directly look at him as he leaned so casually against the column outside the Cabildo again. He didn't try to hide in the late-afternoon shadows. When he'd come before, demanding a fortune from her, a frisson of power had danced along her skin and her tiny spark of magic scurried into hiding. He was handsome and rich, judging by the quality of his clothes and the way he carried himself. And there was that aura of power surrounding him. Rich people carried it in the set of their shoulders, the direct way they surveyed the space around them—like they owned it, or would soon.

When what little magic she had failed, she relied upon what she knew of human nature and reading people to tell her fortunes. A true telling didn't always come to her, except lately. Lately, she'd been getting more flashes of insight, more...surety to what she foretold.

Tremaine, the man had told her. His name was Mr. Tremaine and the idea of him touching her tarot cards even to shuffle them, of his palm in her hand to read his life lines, or looking into the depths of the crystal ball made her nerves zing as tight as a bowstring. He'd settled himself on her rickety folding chair like it was a throne, offered her a knowing smile as if he saw all the way to the depths of her soul and found her infinitely lacking yet still interesting somehow, like a bug he was about to step on. Verity began her spiel but was interrupted when two artists began yelling at each other. Then one of the music combos played a loud and raucous tune. Soon, fists were thrown and the police arrived. As things settled down, she turned to apologize but the man was gone. She'd been so intent on watching the fight, she hadn't seen him slip away. Odd, that. On many levels.

But he was back now, watching her, as he had before. Verity sat very still, a field mouse under the eye of a hawk. No...not a hawk, a carrion crow. A gust of wind blew her hair into her eyes. She clawed the strands back but when she looked toward the Cabildo, He was gone. Again. Rubbing her arms to chase away the chill that had settled inside her, she scanned the Square. There was no one even faintly resembling Tremaine.

An older woman just walking past, hesitated with a little smile on her face. Smiling in return, Verity waited to see what the woman would do. Coming closer, the woman's quick gaze took in the articles of Verity's trade, the chairs, table, patched umbrella, and wagon. She read the hand-chalked sign on the small blackboard Verity propped against her tip jar. With a slightly wider smile, the woman began to settle into the nearest chair, then stopped and looked puzzled. Then she scooted over to sit on the other chair. Verity found that both odd and telling.

"Hello," the woman said. "I'm not really here for a reading, but I'll give you a tip for a bit of conversation. Fair enough?"

Verity considered. This smacked of a fae bargain but the woman held no hint of otherness about her—beyond her decision to avoid sitting where Tremaine had sat. She made a mental note to do a spirit cleansing on the chair with sage.

"I suppose it depends on what sort of conversation you are looking for," Verity answered, her voice and phrasing as noncommittal as she could make it.

The woman smiled again. "I'm Denise Long." She waited, as if she expected Verity to recognize her. When Vee didn't, Denise continued. "I'm an author. A romance author. I'm thinking about setting my new series here in New Orleans and giving it a bit of a...well, since the magicks all came out of hiding, is a book paranormal or contemporary?"

Her brows drew together as Verity attempted to make sense of the question. Denise remained smiling and placid. "Well," Vee eventually said, drawing out the word. "You do have a point."

Denise leaned on the table. "I know, right? My agent and I have been going round and round about this for weeks now because she's not sure how to position the new series to sell it to a publisher. But, I digress. What I meant by conversation is that I'm willing to pay you to let me pick your brain."

"Pick my brain?"

"Well, yes! You don't seem at all phony to me. I've talked to probably half of the so-called psychics and fortune tellers here. Between you and me, they've all pretty much been cons. They have a nice spiel and they keep talking and talking until they hit a right answer and then they mention money. By then, the poor sap has been caught hook, line, and sinker. That said, you don't appear to be that sort of person at all." Denise tapped the side of her nose. "I've been watching you."

Verity suppressed another frisson of panic. The expression—and its attendant smile—she turned on Denise was cool and professional, showing only slight interest. That's all the encouragement the writer needed. She launched into a discussion of her world-building, her characters, her plot and despite herself, Verity was drawn into the narrative. Her misgivings were allayed and she answered a few questions, made some suggestions, and ended up enjoying herself.

Denise wanted her name to use in the acknowledgments section of her book, and she stuffed a wad of twenties in the jar as she left. Verity was also the happy recipient of two new romances, autographed by the author.

Her day was definitely brighter and she'd all but forgotten the creepy sense of being watched she'd felt earlier. Verity's imagination had always been overactive and thinking she'd seen Mr. Tremaine skulking about the Cabildo was just plain silly. During the week, the crowds were always thinner. As the few who were passing by appeared to be intent on some distant destination, Verity opened one of the books and started to read.

·͘·ꞏ͘· •

ROMAN STOOD at the window behind his desk. As he often did, he stared down into Jackson Square. Long shadows stretched across the open space. Tourists were stopped in loose semi-circles around the few street performers left in the Square. A weekday meant fewer artists hanging their paintings and crafts on the wrought-iron fence, showing off their wares and hoping to entice buyers. It meant more locals and less sightseers. As the day ended, most of the traffic was local. New Orleans had two sides—day and night. Only in the early morning quiet and the evening rush did the two worlds collide, as they did now.

As it was always wont to do, his attention turned to Fortune Tellers Row. Like the artists and performers, the psychics and readers were fewer during the week. He'd long ago learned that most were charlatans but the occasional human psychic or magick appeared, which meant he had to keep his eye on their activities. His eyes sought out hair the color of sunshine capping a gamin face. She was there, tucked beneath her patched umbrella, a paperback book open in her lap and he wondered what she was reading. Her presence concerned him—far more than it should. She'd not come one day and he'd fretted all morning about it before his duties called him away. Even then, thoughts of her remained in the back of his mind, and he'd been far too relieved when she'd arrived at her usual time the day after.

He needed to return to Paris but he was still reluctant to leave New Orleans. Something kept his instincts centered here—something besides the little gypsy. There was oily darkness simmering beneath the gaudy surface of the city and the awareness of it scraped against his senses like sandpaper over sunburned skin. Evil was stalking his city and he was still guardian enough to desire battle.

An image of *Le Vieil* shimmered before his eyes and his gut roiled. Roman had a duty to his kind, as well. Crevan, the oldest of them all, had chosen him all those many years ago to fulfill the gruesome task of finding and eliminating the vessel meant to contaminate the Heart of Stone. The Crucible had been born—though none knew where or to whom. Finding her was a monumental task and all the Sentinels were looking for her. Maybe that's what was creating the sense of urgency. They'd recovered the Heart of Stone years ago and though it was hidden well, there would be no peace or safety for the Heart or the Gargoyle kindred until the Crucible was destroyed. Things were coming to a head. There'd been reports of more dead gargoyles, of others turning rogue, and the Heart was watched closely.

Movement in the sun-soaked plaza yanked him from his grim thoughts. The little gypsy had put her book away and was rearranging things on her table, filled as it was with the accoutrements of her trade— crystal ball, Tarot cards, crystals.

Four grubby men swaggered along the promenade, their voices loud and obnoxious. They approached the little gypsy's table and Roman could almost see the calculation in their eyes, and the moment gang mentality took over. Roman tore open the window and stepped out. He could taste her fear on the wind, like it was something tangible, as they surrounded the table, hemming her in their midst. He couldn't flash to her as he wished—too many prying eyes. Roman had to respond as a human would—by dashing down stairs and out the door.

One man jerked Verity to her feet and shoved her into the arms of another. He pawed her clothing as his lips sought hers. Verity clawed his face. He cursed and back-handed her. The man holding her squeezed her breast hard, his hand rough. No one came to her aid. There was no Alton today. No police.

"Help me!" she screamed but people hurried past, unwilling to get involved.

The men jeered and cussed, calling her horrible names. She caught a glimpse of her umbrella as the man who'd first grabbed her shredded it with a knife, then broke the pole over his thigh. Another kicked her table over. All of her things scattered across the granite blocks of the walk. Verity could see their mouths moving but a terrible silence took away the sounds they made. She was spun away as something ripped the pawing man from her. She blinked, fighting to stay on her feet but unable to do so. She landed on her hands and knees but scrambled to her feet, twisting this way and that looking for the next attacker. The men were gone. Now the bystanders flocked around, circling her like sharks tasting blood in the water.

Ruined. Everything was broken and ruined. Her tip jar had shattered and the bills in it danced to the silent tune played by the wind as people scrabbled for her hard-earned money. That same wind kissed her wet face and Verity dashed the back of her hand across her eyes. "No time for tears," she declared.

Dropping to her knees, she gathered the jagged pieces of the crystal ball. Her tarot cards had scattered and now decorated the bushes in Jackson Square like pagan Christmas ornaments. None of the other fortune tellers made a move to help her and everyone else just stood there, staring. A teenage boy laughed when the girl at his side made a catty remark. Others simply walked past either ignoring her or staring, as if the attack was just street theater.

Sharp pain lanced across her hand and she stared in horror as blood welled up in her palm. Her heart hurt and she couldn't process any more tribulations. Why had those men attacked her table? Why her and not one of the other fortune tellers?

Tears once again filled her eyes, blinding her despite her best efforts. Blinking to clear her vision, she realized a man stood in front of her—or at least leather boots and tailored slacks. Which was all she could see. She glanced up. And up, until she had to shade her eyes to see him clearly.

"You are hurt, little one." His voice, slightly accented and old-world, washed over her.

Roman regretted not jumping off the balcony straight to the ground. Had he done so, he would have been in time to save her. The old Legate, once a human judge who'd been turned vampire in order to accept the appointment, did not have to appear human as he was a creature of the night and the night vision of humans was easy to trick. Roman kept regular daylight hours and had to play the games demanded by the Concilium Magicae, the council that nominally ruled those of magick blood. Still, he'd arrived to deal with the four men, none of whom escaped unscathed. He had their scent and the taste of their blood and he would hunt them another time. First, though, he had to deal with the little gypsy.

Roman squatted beside her, taking her hand. Then her scent hit him and he stiffened. He stared at her face—full of innocence and pain. He couldn't turn away from her. "I am Roman Montagne. Let me help you."

Verity gulped as shivers cascaded down her spine. She realized he held one of her crystals—the rose quartz—in his other hand. Rose quartz was associated with love. Awareness, soft as a kitten paw, nudged her memory—a *knowing* beyond the awareness of seeing him from time to time. When she spoke, her question held a deeper meaning. "Do I know you?"

He inhaled deeply, and his breath caught again on the scent of her blood. Not completely human. Witch. His chest did an odd constriction then loosened. "Not yet. But you will."

Verity stared up at Roman, working very hard to mask her fear. After the first time she'd seen him with the dark-haired woman, she watched for him. She often saw him walking through Jackson Square. He was important and he was...other. Her talents didn't lean in a direction to guess. He was big—twice as tall as her, as solid as a ancient oak and his aura felt just as old. The attack from those men had scared her. This man? He scared her spitless.

He wrapped a pristine white linen handkerchief around the cut on her palm then helped her to her feet. She wanted to shove her hands into the pockets of her broom skirt to hide them. Balling them into fists didn't stop them from shaking.

"Do I make you nervous?" Roman's voice rumbled out from somewhere deep in the well of his chest.

Clenching her teeth so they didn't rattle, Verity gave a tiny shake of her head. He leaned over, bringing his face close to hers. When he spoke this time, his voice sounded like desert sand shifting in the wind. "I should."

Every muscle in her body locked and she couldn't breathe. An arm as hard as granite wrapped around her and she was lifted, her front plastered to his chest as he continued. "You are not what you seem, little one, though you are not yet what you are meant to be."

Words tumbled from her mouth. "Who are you?"

An emotion she couldn't decipher filtered over his rock-hard features. "I am the Legate of New Orleans."

Verity stared at him. She had no clue what that meant. She only knew that he scared her on some deep, visceral level. Without thinking, she asked, "What does that mean?" Surprise registered on his handsome face.

Roman studied her, watching for guile but he found none. "You are not aware of the Legation here in New Orleans? That this place is sanctuary and neutral territory for those of—" He clamped his jaw shut before he said too much. Maybe he'd been wrong about her. He caught no hint of lie or deceit from her.

Her memory snapped into place. The Legate governed the magicks in New Orleans. And he was something, something she was supposed to fear. She started shaking again and managed to squeak out, "What are you going to do to me?"

"I haven't decided." He feared the knowledge the scent of her blood confirmed. He didn't want to act, preferring to wait, to watch, before deciding. Perhaps she wasn't the one.

CHAPTER SEVEN
BROKEN DREAMS

———————————————————————————

THE LEGATE put her down...sort of. He eased the pressure of his arm around her waist and Verity slid down until her toes barely touched the granite walkway. His grip tightened and she stood there, barely balanced, afraid to breathe because touching him like this, so intimately, was wrong in so many ways. If she drew breath, her breasts would brush his abdomen because he was so very, very tall and she was...not.

Roman touched the bruise on her cheek with the tip of his index finger. Soft. Smooth. So very, very fragile. The witchling was a tiny thing, like a wild flower lost among the weeds, peeking out only when the breeze was in a teasing mood. "What am I to do with you, little gypsy?" he murmured.

He felt shivers dancing across her skin, held his breath as she leaned her forehead against his chest. She barely topped the level of his sternum. Roman needed to disengage. Walk away. If he had sense, he would run. Or at least call Varrick. He found he could do none of those things.

Breathing shallowly, Verity attempted to ignore what was suddenly pressing between her breasts. That was... He was... Her cheeks had to be flaming because her face felt so hot. Baba Rawnie's voice whispered to her.

"No, no, bebe. He is not for the likes of you. If you kiss the boys, is okay. No more though. The dark, it creeps in if you don't be careful. Gotta stay in d'light, bebe. True dis, yeah?"

49

"True dat, yeah," she whispered back. Verity turned her head but didn't have the strength to step away from the Legate. She rested her temple against him and watched the people strolling past them. No one noticed. She saw Alton coming their way, but he stopped several feet away, his metallic face smooth so as not to mess up his makeup but he still managed to convey an air of puzzlement. He lifted his head and she could see his nostrils flare. The puzzlement morphed into consternation and his eyes glittered feral red.

"Peace, werewolf." Roman's voice rumbled beneath her cheek. Werewolf? What was he talking about? *Who* was he talking about? Verity stiffened as her gaze landed back on Alton. Alton? Alton was a werewolf? Her knees went wobbly and she would have fallen into an ungainly squat had the Legate not still been holding her up.

Alton approached, but he was growling and she could almost see the shadowed overlay of a ruff standing on end. How had she missed the fact her friend wasn't human? She shrank back from him, her eyes cast down.

"Vee?" Alton's rough voice sounded hurt. She still couldn't look at him. He directed his next question to Roman. "Did you do this?"

Roman understood the wolf's anger. "No. She was attacked by four men."

A growled curse caused the little witch to press against him. His hand went to the nape of her neck and his fingers smoothed the knot of muscles bunched there.

"Why can't I smell them?"

Why indeed? Werewolves were furry lie detectors when it came to spells and magic. "You smell nothing?" Roman kept his voice very careful, then watched the werewolf quarter the area.

50

"Nothing. No magic. No scents of any kind." Now the wolf sounded confused. "I thought you'd placed a null spell, but I would have been able to detect that."

Very few magicks could create a spell a werewolf could not sniff out. "Curious. Why did you believe I'd placed a null spell?"

"Because I couldn't see anything when I first walked up. People were talking about trouble on Fortune Teller Row. I was down by Cafe Du Monde and had to finish my act before I could break away. When I walked up, I didn't see you. Didn't see Verity or her table."

Roman almost smiled. Now he at least knew the witchling's first name. The second bit of information troubled him enough the smile died before it was born. Suspicion grew and sat heavy on his mind. He needed to contact Crevan and the other Sentinels. It took far more willpower than it should have to step back from Verity. He watched her face though he spoke to the wolf. "You are?"

"Alton Smith."

He was familiar with the name. The Smith pack was large and had several sub packs throughout the south. "She is?" The werewolf bristled and clamped his mouth shut. Roman didn't want to fight. "She is not registered. That is a punishable offense."

"She doesn't have to. She's not a magick."

Roman stared at the wolf until the other man dropped his eyes and squirmed. "I have smelled her blood, Alton Smith."

Alton's shoulders hunched. "I wasn't positive. I only got occasional whiffs and never could pinpoint it around her. According to Vee, her grandmother had a little gypsy witch in the family line so I figured she might have a trace, but not enough to matter much less be registered."

Verity had unconsciously moved to Roman's side,

putting his bulk between her and Alton. Which was all kinds of wrong. Alton was her friend. Had been her friend since she'd first come to New Orleans at age sixteen. She'd been standing outside Cafe Du Monde, her mouth watering, her stomach growling and not a penny in her pocket for food. Alton had walked up with a white bag and two lidded cups of cafe au lait. He introduced himself, showed her to a bench up on the terrace surrounding a monument that overlooked both Jackson Square and the Mississippi River, and shared. He had never been anything but kind to her.

"Verity La Croix," she whispered. "My name is Verity La Croix. I didn't know I was...I didn't know."

Alton stared at her, his gaze intent. He stepped closer and she reminded herself that he was her friend, not some huge slathering beast planning on eating her for dinner. He stopped, leaned toward her and sniffed hard, drawing air deeply into his lungs. His eyes sparked again as they focused on the Legate.

"What is it?" Roman asked.

"Verity. She's the nexus of the spell." Alton tilted his head, looking very wolfish for all that he was in human form. "You said you smelled her blood?"

Roman eased her injured hand free. Red stained the white handkerchief still wrapped around her palm. "She cut it on a shard of her crystal ball," he explained.

Verity shrank back as both men stared at her—one with suspicion and the other considering.

"You didn't know," Roman said to Alton. He almost smiled. Werewolves were even less likely to suffer a witch than gargoyles. Once upon a time, witches attempted to enslave werewolves for use as familiars.

"I...no." Alton looked like he'd been hit with a Taser. He ignored Verity, keeping his gaze on Roman. "The first time we met, I saw only a scrawny kid who'd been thrown out on the street. She was hungry and sad and she needed a friend. I..." He shrugged and looked sheepish.

"Yes." Roman did smile then. "You..." and let his voice trail off just as Alton had. He glanced down at Verity. "We need to go to my office, Verity La Croix, to get you registered before there is an outcry and claims of favoritism. It will not take long." He shifted his gaze to Alton, emotion warring with duty. He wanted to keep Verity with him though that would be a very bad idea. Like, the werewolf, he was compelled to protect her. He went very still. Null spells and compulsion spells of protection weren't offensive magic. Technically speaking. Something to consider and research.

"Okay," Verity agreed in a small voice. She was looking at what was left of her livelihood and her heart sank. She didn't have the money to replace anything.

A man almost as tall as Roman walked up. His square jaw, angular face, and close-cropped dark blond hair reminded her of the actor who starred in that Viking series on cable TV. He nodded to Roman and managed to remain focused on the Legate while also taking her in, along with Alton.

"A werewolf, a witch, and gargoyle walk into a bar," the newcomer said. "Interesting developments, Roman. Why don't I clean up here then meet the three of you in your office?"

Roman nodded as he began to herd Verity toward what was nominally the west side of the square, since the park was laid on a diagonal to the compass. Alton trailed a step behind. Varrick gathered up everything he could, his preternatural eyesight finding bits and pieces others would miss. He managed to pack everything into the wagon and dragged it to the door to the Legation office. He left it parked just inside the small vestibule.

Upstairs, Roman had Verity sit in one of the plush chairs facing his desk and he handed a first aid kit to the wolf. "Make sure she won't need stitches," he ordered.

Verity steadfastly refused to look at what Alton was doing but when he showed no further signs of aggression and ignored her blood beyond a clinical observation, she relaxed and kept her attention on the imposing man who settled into the large chair on the opposite side of the massive desk. He didn't speak as he searched through some files, withdrew several forms, and picked up a pen.

"What is your full name?"

"Verity Bernadette La Croix."

"Mother's name?"

She stared at him, her mouth opening and closing a few times before she cleared her throat. She tried again, then shrank against the back of the chair as both gargoyle and werewolf stared at her. The man who she presumed was another gargoyle dropped into the chair beside her.

"Curiouser and curiouser," Varrick said. "A null spell, a compulsion spell, and now a silence spell. Someone very powerful has been messing with *la petite sorcière*, yes?"

Roman ignored the implications. "Father's name?"

This time Verity was able to shrug and shake her head. "I have no idea. No one ever told me."

"Your mother—"

"I never knew her. I was raised by my grandmother and then Baba Rawnie."

Alton, who'd still been kneeling beside her chair, rocked back and all but scampered to put a few feet between them. "Baba Rawnie? The Old Woman of Vacherie?"

Verity cocked her head, brows knitted to form deep crinkles above her nose. "Why..." She made little shakes of her head, still looking confused. "Why does it sound like a title? Baba Rawnie was very old when she died."

Her voice cracked and she gripped her hands in her lap suddenly afraid.

"Now that one *is* in the book," Alton said, his voice taut. He pushed off the floor and dashed to the wall of floor-to-ceiling bookcases. He pawed through bound volumes so old the leather was dry and cracking on the spines. "Baba Rawnie. She's in the book. Look, you'll find her."

Roman exchanged a look with Varrick, who strode over to stand just behind the frantic werewolf. "Mr. Smith, take a breath."

"No. No. She's in the book. I know she's in the book," Alton chanted. "Old. Old. So very old. Summerville Smith. She cursed him. Cursed him dead. Fine mess she made, Benton bein' not old enough to step up yet. Mama told me. Mama Two told me all about it when I was growin' up."

Verity emitted a tiny squeak filled with misery before choking off any sound by pressing both hands to her mouth. Her eyes were liquid aquamarines as she watched her only friend have an emotional melt down. It was all too much. Alton was a werewolf. And he knew Mama Two and Mama Two knew something about Baba Rawnie and there were spells and she was in trouble because *she* wasn't in the book but Baba Rawnie was. Black dots floated across her vision and her sight faded around the edges, going gray edged with black before the dots coalesced and she couldn't see a thing.

Hands. Warm hands. Gripping her arms. Lifting her. Cradling her against a hard chest. "Breathe, *mon petite bebe*."

"I'm sorry," she whispered into a shirt of very fine cloth. "I didn't mean to do it. Tell Baba Rawnie I didn't mean to do it."

"Do what, little witch?"

"Kill her."

CHAPTER EIGHT
NO SANCTUARY

ROMAN CARRIED her out of his office with no destination in mind, though his feet took him to the stairs and down one flight to the large apartment that was part of the legation's premises. The council owned the building, leasing out the first floor to a restaurant and some shops, leaving the second floor as living space for the Legate and visiting dignitaries, while the administrative offices occupied the third floor.

Acting on pure instinct, Roman shouldered open the door to his bedroom. He attempted to put her down on his bed but the girl clung to him, her body going so tense he thought her fingers would break if he attempted to loosen them from his shirt. Verity was barely breathing and her eyes were screwed tightly shut. Even so, he could see the dark circles beneath her eyes, the way delicate skin stretched tight over finely-drawn cheekbones, the white lines around her mouth.

"You need to sleep, Verity La Croix." There was power in names, though he wasn't trying to use any.

Her stomach chose that moment to growl and she grimaced. "I should go home," she whispered, still too shell-shocked to find a voice loud enough to hear. "The kittens will be hungry."

Reluctant to release her, Roman chose to sit in the massive leather chair where he often sat to read at night. He discovered it was comfortable enough to accommodate his bulk and the soft curves of the girl he held in his arms. He also discovered that she fit quite nicely into his lap. He thought she'd dozed off when her stomach made a sound similar to a bear defending her cubs. Pink crept across her cheeks in a way that charmed him, but she didn't speak so neither did he.

A few minutes later, Varrick tapped on the door and entered without invitation. He held a tray that carried the scents of seafood, sausage, and spices. He and Roman both ignored his reaction to the sight of the witchling curled into Roman's lap like a scared kitten. He set the tray on the 1930's era Art Deco side table.

"We need to talk, Roman," Varrick said, his voice all but sub-vocal.

Nodding, Roman sat forward in the chair. "You need to eat, little one. Your stomach sounds ferocious. Varrick has brought you a nice, hot gumbo and bread. Will you sit here and eat while he and I attend to some business?" Her fists clenched reflexively in his shirt. "I will be just out in the hallway and I will come back once we have talked. If you need me, simply call for me. Yes?"

Verity raised her head and looked up at him and managed a small nod. He stood, lifting her easily, then turned and settled her in the chair. Her nose twitched as the aroma of the food hit her. The other man moved silver domes off various dishes.

"Would you like rice?" His voice held little inflection. She nodded and watched him scoop rice into a shallow bowl before he ladled the steaming gumbo over the top. Shrimp and crab swam in the thick brown roux, along with a variety of vegetables. A small loaf of crusty French bread, hot from the oven, was a perfect compliment.

She waited to start eating until the two men moved away, then she fell on the bowl like a ravenous alligator.

Varrick stood patiently while Roman gave one final look at the girl before shutting the door behind them.

"What have you learned?" Away from the witchling's presence, Roman snapped back into his normal persona.

"The mother ran off shortly after her birth. Her maternal grandmother's name was Zara Cross. The old woman turned Verity over to Baba Rawnie when the child was two. Zara died three months later."

Roman leaned against the wall. "Father?"

"None listed. I'll dig deeper but I suspect we won't find one."

"What happened to Baba Rawnie?" Roman did not want to consider that Verity had truly killed the old witch.

"There's the rub. No one knows. Her house caught fire. The locals fought it and the state police investigated. They all knew a young girl had been living there for years but she pretty much stayed out of sight. Didn't attend school and no one questioned that. Even though no bodies were found, the authorities assumed both died in the fire."

Snorting, Roman gave in to the very human gesture of rolling his eyes. "And we all know that assuming anything only makes asses out of people. What about bank accounts? Anything else that could be traced?"

"Working on that too. The current bottom line is that no one—and that includes any magick source that I was able to tap on short notice—has caught even a whiff of Baba Rawnie. The girl showed up here about ten years ago. She has no ID...well, no *legal* ID. Smith met her the second or third day after she arrived. He fed her and has been unofficially looking after her ever since. Same with Mama Two. The girl lives in a shack behind a shotgun house over in Algiers Point. Has three stray cats that stick around, a few others that come and go. Smith says there's a mattress, a couple of stools, and a card table for furniture. She has a hot plate and one of those mini fridges that looks like some fraternity used it for target practice."

Full of restless energy, Roman began to pace. "No witch would live a life like that."

Varrick snorted. "No self-respecting witch would be telling fortunes in the Square."

Roman stopped and considered that. "I can see the magic on her skin," he said thoughtfully. "But I can't feel it."

That caught Varrick's attention. "Dampening spell?"

"Perhaps."

Varrick's eyes narrowed and he straightened, nothing relaxed about him now. "What are you thinking, Roman?"

"What if Verity was a changling?"

Glancing toward the closed bedroom door, Varrick didn't hide the snarl that idea put on his face. "She can't be."

"Not is. Was. A child no one ever sees growing up. A child left in a witch's care. An old witch, growing older."

"You think Baba Rawnie took the child to possess her?" Varrick sketched a few symbols in the air between him and the door. None of them flared to life.

Roman scrubbed at his forehead with the heel of one hand. "I don't know what I think. There is a terrified girl in there. She is magic touched and is convinced she killed the old witch."

⁂

THE MEN'S VOICES rumbled through the thick wooden door, but Verity couldn't understand a word they said. She finished off the gumbo by using the last piece of bread to sop up the last of it. Popping the bread into her mouth, she chewed and finally took the time to look around. Her brain was starting to clear and her curiosity came to life. The bedroom was huge—befitting the man who lived here. If she threw herself on the bed,

59

she could spread eagle across it and not come close to touching the edges. Something tingled low inside her at the thought of being in that bed.

Pushing out of the chair, Verity wandered around the room. She wasn't bold enough to open drawers despite her desire to do so. A massive armoire caught her attention. It wasn't complete latched and she couldn't resist nudging the door open and looking inside. There were robes hung there—ceremonial, she guessed from the symbols embroidered on them. A touch of fear trickled down her spine. She knew from the glimpses of his aura that he was *other* but had no clue as to what sort of magick he was. Maybe he was a wizard, because of the robes. The other man, Varrick, admitted to being a gargoyle—which scared her more than Alton being a werewolf. She quickly closed the door and bumped it gently with her hip to make sure it latched.

A writing desk caught her attention. Placed in front of a window that overlooked Chartres Street, there were books and files and papers stacked on it, much like there'd been on the massive desk in the office upstairs. With a few furtive steps, she was beside the desk and studying the papers openly displayed. The bottom of one, that looked like some sort of official proclamation, bore a flowing signature. Roman Montagne, Legate of New Orleans.

He'd mentioned that, down in the square when he'd come to her rescue. That should be familiar, she thought, and searched her memory. She bent down to read the paper. The words were hard to decipher because they were handwritten in what looked like calligraphy. Something about dragons. Dragons? She gulped and then her body was racked by a long shudder. Snatches of conversation came back to her—from people strolling past her table, from others riding the ferry with her. And she remembered Baba Rawnie's words. *New Orleans will call to you with her siren's song, Verity La Croix. You can't resist. But you must be a little mouse, child. No one must ever discover who you are. What you are. There are those who will hunt you, who will seek to destroy you. Beware the stone men for they are sworn to vengeance and retribution. Destiny will remain silent until it is time, then she will come calling with sweet sounds. Heed her warnings, witchling.*

Other voices crowded in, all those she'd caught in passing.

"The old Legate was murdered."

"Have you heard the news? A new Legate has been appointed."

"Who on the council is strong enough? Is it a witch? Another vampire?"

"A fae, probably."

"Doesn't matter. New Orleans is a sanctuary city. We may all live and play here. The Legate is here to ensure justice for all."

"I've heard he's a Sentinel."

She struggled to suck in air. She'd heard these bits and pieces about the Legate, about the magick who was in charge of New Orleans, whose word was the law all magicks were sworn to obey while within the environs of the city. She should have remembered, except she wasn't a magick. Not really. She had a touch of foresight, a smidge of intuition. She could sometimes see auras but that wasn't magic. Many humans could do the same. Except. Except Baba Rawnie was a witch and she had called Verity a witchling. And Baba Rawnie had told her over and over about the stone men, the gargoyle Sentinels who hunted witches.

"Gargoyle," she whispered, even more terrified. *Sentinel!* Gargoyle—the anathema to witch kind. Baba

Rawnie's voice was loud in her head as the old woman yelled for her to run. Verity whirled, seeking a way out. All the doors to the balcony were locked. She rattled each one to check. That left the door to the hallway. She scrambled to the door and pressed her ear against it. The voices she'd heard before were gone. Had they gone up the office? Was she alone down here?

She pressed on the brass door handle and felt it give beneath her shaking hand. Holding her breath, she eased the door open. Roman, feet spread and arms crossed over his massive chest, blocked the doorway as effectively as the Colossus of Rhodes. Not that Verity had ever seen the Colossus of Rhodes, but this huge man with his stony face, standing there as still as a statue could be one of the Seven Wonders of the World. A part of her brain noted that he looked maybe thirty-five but he seemed to carry the weight of the ages on his shoulders and in his eyes, making him seem ancient.

"And where are you going, little witch?" he rumbled.

She glanced down, well aware that she'd never win a staring contest with him. "I...I need to go. Thank you for dinner. And...stuff." She stepped to move around him only there was no place to go."

"Why did those men attack you?"

Her head jerked up. "I don't know!" Angry, she added, "Maybe *you* sent them."

His smile was positively frigid. "If I wanted to hurt you, witchling, I'm capable of doing it with my own two hands."

Verity stared at those hands. Yes, he could wring her neck in an instant, but those hands had also soothed her, made her feel safe. "Please, I need to go home."

Out in the hallway, out of sight, someone cleared their throat. "Word just came in from Deacon Smith, Roman."

"And?"

"His people found a body."

"Was it a magick?"

"No. Human."

"Then that is none of our concern."

Varrick peered around the corner of the door and studied the girl trying so very hard to appear brave and all the while her knees were knocking. "The human..." Varrick inhaled. "Maybe we should talk about this in your office."

"Say what you need to say, Varrick."

"The body was found on Verity's porch. Death magic. And he was one of the men who attacked her today."

Verity's eyes went so wide, the whites showed all the way around the blue of her irises. She began to shake and when her legs would no longer hold her, she sank to the floor, arms hugging her knees. "Why?" she mumbled.

"Who are you, Verity La Croix?" Roman demanded.

She couldn't look at him. Eyes closed, she spoke to the floor. "I'm not supposed to talk about this."

"Which means we should."

Verity jerked, her body's visceral reaction to that deep voice. Gumption. She needed to find some. She channeled her inner Baba Rawnie. The old woman had had plenty. "I'm nobody. Nothing. I'm human so this doesn't concern you and it's none of your business."

Roman grabbed her arms and hauled her to her feet. Then he leaned down—waaaay down—until they were nose-to-nose. "If it concerns you, it *is* my business."

Silver light flashed in his eyes and not for the first time, she was afraid of him. Baba Rawnie's voice whispered in her memory and Verity sketched a sign in the air. Roman didn't even blink. No one should have been impervious to that magic, taught to her by Baba

63

Rawnie to be used only as a last resort when Verity was threatened.

"Who are you?" she whispered.

"Wrong question," he grated out.

Her body was still shaking. "What are you?"

"Your worst nightmare, or your salvation. You pick."

Chapter Nine
Sound and Fury

ROMAN FELT the brush of magic as Verity's fingers moved between them but it brushed past him like a stranger on the sidewalk. He caught no sense of it on his hands where they gripped her biceps. Still, a sheen of glittering light flickered around her weakly. He glanced at Varrick, who shrugged. He'd felt nothing at all. So, her magic was weak. Perhaps she was what she appeared—a human with a touch of witch magic in her far-distant DNA.

The girl trembled beneath his hands and fire scorched his heart. Every instinct he possessed demanded that he protect the innocent and here he was terrifying a...no, not a child. Not by human measure. She was a young woman, but still naive. He could find no taint of the dark. Yet. And the Heart was safe. He'd recovered it all those years ago, avenging the deaths of Borac and his brothers.

Still, the specter of the Crucible remained as a silent reminder of what could happen. He'd been unable to fulfill that duty twenty-five years ago. The broken granite that was all that remained of Borac, the dust and rubble that was all the others lost in the Old War, in the incursions through the years, and more recently, the rain-streaked face of Sedge—those memories clapped his soul in irons. As more gargoyles died, the tug of Crevan's decree would became more insistent. He had a duty to his kindred. Protector. Guardian. First Sentinel.

"Roman!"

Varrick's voice was urgent and Roman realized the

other was squeezing his shoulder with enough force to break a human's body. He blinked, shook his head, pulled his thoughts back to present. He stared at the girl hanging limply from his hands, her head bowed, mouth slack, bruises blooming on her arms where his hands squeezed with enough force to break her bones.

His first instinct was to drop her but his body blocked Varrick's and the little gypsy would hit the floor. Hard. With infinite care, he eased the pressure of his grip, loosening fingers slightly. Roman sank to his knees, then leaned back on his heels as he gathered Verity across his thighs, his arms shifting to cradle her.

"Roman?" Varrick modulated his voice to sound calm.

"This is not who I am, Varrick. Not who I want to become. Yet I fear I no longer have a choice." Roman bent his head until his cheek rested against the top of Verity's head. "She's a child, but I sense more. Her soul is..." He shrugged, unable to put feelings into words. He felt possessive of this small human. Her fragility sparked something deep inside him but the feel of her curves pressed against him, the simple weight of her in his arms spread warmth to places that had felt no stirring for a century or more.

"Let me take her, Roman," Varrick ventured carefully. "I will put her to bed. She needs rest."

"No." The word gritted out between Roman's teeth. He would *not* relinquish her care to another. He wasn't sure what that said about him but the idea of Varrick— or any other—touching her made him edgy, unsettled. He settled Verity more firmly in his arms and rose. He strode across the room.

As soon as Roman cleared the doorway, Varrick brushed past him and was beside the bed in a flash. He pulled down the covers and rearranged the pillows, then he stepped back. He watched Roman stoop and gently place the witchling close to the center of the bed. With gentle hands, Roman removed her shoes. Then, before he could speak, Roman gestured for him to leave.

"I will sit with her," Roman explained. "She will be safe."

Varrick let out a quiet breath. "I will be in the office. Call me if you have need."

Roman didn't speak, focused as he was on Verity. Varrick slipped out the door and closed it behind him.

Roman reached for the coverlet to pull over the girl but stopped. Her breathing remained ragged, her eyes closed. He didn't believe she was feigning unconsciousness. She was too pale and when he touched her just over her heart, her spirit was a bare glimmer huddled deep inside her. He caught no sense of magic, no pulse of power and he would have. That was one of his gifts—or his curse. He pulled the covers over her and stepped away. In the bathroom, he stripped out of the tailored trappings of the Legate of New Orleans and relaxed into a worn T-shirt and a favorite pair of jeans.

Barefoot, he padded across the room and stood beside the bed. Verity slept fitfully and he wondered what dreams invaded her sleep. He knew all too well the night demons that haunted a man in slumber but she was a young woman. What—besides himself—could terrify her so? After pulling his favorite chair closer to the bed, he settled in to watch through the now silent night.

⁘ ●

VERITY LAY very still. Her heartbeat pounded in her ears, blocking any sound. She couldn't see, then she realized she'd scrunched her eyes shut. Darkness surrounded her and part of her greeted it like an old friend. Once her heart settled back into normal rhythm, she could hear voices beyond the raggedy curtain that separated her bed from the rest of the cabin.

"I doan know what'chu talkin' 'bout." Baba Rawnie used her I'm-dealing-with-yokels voice.

"Do not lie to me, old woman. Bring the child out. I want to see her." Verity had never heard the man's voice before. He didn't belong around here with his hoity-toity tone and accent.

As quiet at a little mouse, Verity crept off the bed and scooted under it. She found the hidey-hole in the wall that Baba Rawnie had shown her when she wasn't much bigger than a baby. As soon as she was inside. The spring board flipped up with a whispery *snick*. She could still hear the voices—Baba Rawnie playing the Cajun witchy woman while the man's voice rose in anger until he was yelling. The old screech owl in the cypress tree didn't like that and let the world know.

The floorboards bounced as the man stomped into the room. The legs of her bed scraped against the rough wooden floor and the man was speaking a language she didn't understand. Her skin began to prickle, like it did when she'd been in the sun too long—sort of an itching burn that she knew better than to scratch.

"See? I tole you true, magic man. Ain't no bebe here, 'specially not one can do what'chu want."

The voices faded away but Verity didn't come out. There was a rag rug lining the hidey hole and it was comfortable enough. She cradled her head on her arms and dropped back into sleep.

Verity thought her heart was going to pound out of her chest. There was yelling out in the yard. A man. Men. More than one. They were shouting and yammering like a pack of dogs after a fox. She was too big to hide in the space behind her bed. She was almost sixteen and about as tall as Baba Rawnie. There was a space behind the old Frigidaire.

"Cold iron," Baba Rawnie always told her. "It'll stop everything but the stone men and even them will have trouble findin' a little bit like you."

She squeezed into the narrow space between the fridge and the stove, also made of iron and steel. She crouched down and tried not to sneeze from the dust. She heard the front door crash open and then booted feet stomping through the house. Baba Rawnie was chanting but the men paid her no mind. Until the fire started.

"Verity." Roman kept his voice gentle, despite the panic raging in his chest. "Wake up now." He watched her, worry turning his blood to ice. Her eyes were wide open and she was staring sightlessly at something only she could see. Her mouth opened in a silent scream and her body shook. Terror rolled off her in waves.

Without thinking, Roman scooped her into his arms and he sat back down in his chair, cradling her on his lap. Her body shook so violently, he was afraid to let her go so he tightened his grip. He managed to snag a cashmere throw from the foot of the bed and he tucked it around her.

"Shhh, *petit gitan*. Shhh. You are safe." He rocked and crooned until her breathing turned less ragged and her eyes began to focus. She tucked her head under his chin and wrapped her hands in his T-shirt.

"I'm never going to be safe," she whispered. *Especially not from you.* She didn't say that out loud and as much as part of her screamed for her to get away from this man who held her so gently, a larger part was convinced he could keep her safe. She hadn't felt safe in a very, *very* long time. "I killed Baba Rawnie."

"You said that before. How did you kill her?"

"I was born."

Those three words were swallowed by a silence so

profound it echoed. No one breathed. Even the mantel clock on the ornate fireplace stopped ticking. Just when she thought her lungs might burst, time started up again and the tense arms holding her relaxed, just a little.

"What does that mean?" Roman asked despite fearing her answer.

"Everyone dies around me." The admission was difficult for her to make and her voice cracked on the word *dies*. "I don't remember my mother or my father. Just..." She paused, her eyes losing focus as she searched her memories. "There was my paridala. My grandmother, I think. I was just a baby. She gave me to Baba Rawnie and then she died. Baba Rawnie said I was the child of no one. but she told me stories of the woman—Celestine—everyone thought was my mother. Baba Rawnie said she was beautiful and that many men came to ask her to marry them, but she took none of them. Then she left one day. No one knew where'd she gone. She returned months later. With me. She lived with the old lady Baba Rawnie said was my paridala, and who was Celestine's mother, Zara. Baba Rawnie watched over me and when Zara got sick, there was just Baba Rawnie."

Roman wondered how this translated into her declaration that all those in her sphere died, but he wasn't sure how to ask. He knew how the witches worked, the tales they wove to work subtle magic on the innocent and unwary. He didn't have to when she continued.

"There was a boy. Once. Remy. He lived on the bayou and he would come to play when Baba Rawnie was away. He wasn't supposed to be there and he was my secret to keep. He climbed a tree to tease me and then he fell. Baba Rawnie came and took him away and I never saw him again. Baba Rawnie told me he had died and that I should stay away from people."

She snuggled in deeper and Roman felt such tenderness that his heart thudded beneath her cheek. Her tale was full of sorrow and he wondered at how she came to tell fortunes in Jackson Square. When she didn't speak for several minutes, he wondered if she'd fallen back asleep. Presuming so, he rose, ready to tuck her back into bed. She stirred and protested.

"May I have something to drink? And I..." Her cheeks reddened. "Uhm...the ladies room?"

Roman set her on her feet and pointed her toward the en suite bathroom. He had every intention of tucking her back into his bed but the clothes she wore looked uncomfortable to sleep in. He refused to question his motives when he stopped her, strode to his bureau and withdrew one of his T-shirts.

"You can change in the bathroom, be more comfortable when you sleep." Then he turned his back on her.

Several minutes later, she ventured out, his shirt covering her from chin to mid-calf. He ignored the male satisfaction the sight of her engendered. He'd pulled back the covers in invitation, but stepped away when she hesitated. Like a shy kitten, she skittered over and climbed into the massive bed, then jerked the covers over her body. He returned to his chair, feeling a bit disgruntled. Not that he'd enjoyed the feel of her in his lap. No, not at all.

Verity cleared her throat and he glanced at her. She was sitting up. "Would you...could you..." She cleared her throat again, not meeting his gaze. "Would you mind very much staying with me?"

He had to lean forward to hear her as she'd mostly just mouthed the words. "I'm not going anywhere, little one."

She glanced at him from behind the fall of her hair.

"Not over there." She glanced at the expanse of bed beside her. "Here. You...I...feel safe when you are near."

Taken aback, given everything that had happened that evening, he stepped closer and sank onto the bed before he could reconsider the consequences of his actions. He lay down on top of the coverlet and waited to see what she would do. It took awhile, but she eventually crept close enough to lay her cheek against his bare arm and he found his fingers tangled up with hers.

"Baba Rawnie," she murmured. "Died when men came to her cabin to take me."

He stilled, willing her to continue, willing her to stop.

"People would come, sometimes. Not coming to Baba Rawnie for magic. They came for me. There was a place under my bed where I could hide, but I was too big for it by then. I woke up to yelling and curses and I hid behind the Frigidaire because Baba Rawnie said cold iron would protect me."

Roman stopped breathing for a moment. Had the fae wanted this girl for some reason? Is that why her skin held the shimmer of magic but kept him from sensing any inside her? Perhaps she truly was a changeling in the Old sense? Or worse, a halfling.

"There was a fire and when it stopped, there was just me. Baba Rawnie and all the men were gone. There was the stove and the Frigidaire and me. Inside the stove was a wooden box. It held the crystal ball, the stones and crystals, and the Tarot cards. I took it. And I left."

She sounded so young and despite her words, innocent. She shivered and murmured something. He thought she said, "When I'm freezing, you're the flame beside me, keeping me warm." He plainly heard the next part. "But I don't understand."

"Understand what, little one?"

"How can a stone man be warm?" She squirmed past his arm and pressed against his side, her eyes closed, face serene—a sharp contrast to her earlier expression.

Stone man was a long unused term for his kind, harking back before the first cathedrals and the incantations of the holy who believed the gargoyles would protect the churches and shrines. The Christian priests named them *gargoyle*. Their realm, the dominion of the Garragyion, had often overlapped this realm, and the grand basilicas gave his kind a foothold in the world of humans.

Feared by many, revered by some, the stone men of the Garagyion had slowly transformed into the stone guardians who became gargoyles. And always, throughout their long and storied history, came the stories of the Crucible of Eve. The One who would destroy their kind with a look, a touch, a whisper of breath—or blood.

Verity La Croix might not be the slayer of the Garragyion, but she had annihilated his heart. He touched her face, all but crippled by the need to do so. The moment he'd first touched her, the chunk of rock he called a heart crumbled into dust. He wanted to fight the feeling with all the fire and fury in his soul but he could not. He needed her, here in his arms, just like this. He closed his eyes and knew. He would burn for her. And die doing it.

_____

VARRICK LEANED back in the leather wing-back chair and propped his feet on the antique desk. He was a soldier and the fine trappings of the Legate's office tended to suffocate him. He pulled a metal case from his pocket, shook out a cigar and stuck it in his mouth. Lighting it, he pursed his lips to blow smoke rings from the first, deep inhalation he took. A small *snick* of sound and the touch of cold steel pressed to the back of his head froze his lungs. A moment later, he recognized the woman who'd sneaked up behind him, though he didn't move. Sade still had her pistol pressed to the back of his head.

"Suck it up, buttercup." She waved the smoke out of her face. "And get rid of that thing."

"It's Cuban, Agent Marquis," he said, smoke now trailing from his nostrils. He probably looked like a damn dragon. "I'm not about to waste it."

"Smoking's bad for your health."

He coughed out a cloud of smoke surrounded by laughter. Thank God she'd put the pistol back in its holster. "Gargoyle, Sade. Immortal, remember?"

"Just because you're immortal doesn't mean that Roman won't kill you for smoking in his office. Or that I won't do it for him." Her arch look was spoiled when she sneezed.

In deference to her, he carefully knocked the cherry from the tip of the cigar into the Art Deco ashtray stand beside his chair and left the cigar balanced on the glass and brass receptacle. He waved his hand at the companion chair next to his and turned to face her as she sat. "I didn't expect to see you again so soon."

Sade ignored his acerbic tone. "I need information."

"About what?"

Good. She'd piqued his curiosity. When dealing with the old ones, Sade was never quite sure what would catch and hold their attention. "Roman."

"Ah." What else could he say? He watched her, waiting, hiding his wariness.

"Tell me about the Old War."

All the years of his existence suddenly weighed him down. "Not a story for my telling, child."

"I'm not a fucking child, Varrick." The anger in her tone burned him like acid. Interesting, especially since that anger wasn't necessarily directed at him. She was up and out of the chair with her words. She paced away, turned, marched back. As she reached his side, she stopped. With a move so smooth and quick the human eye couldn't truly follow, he was out of the chair, with his butt now braced on the desk so he could face her. Her lip curled up in a snarl but the words that spilled out surprised him. "Despite what Crevan calls me, despite whatever stupid prophecy, I'm not a child. And I'm not strictly human. Not any more."

Varrick considered her words. Mathias had placed vampire marks on her to combat Oberon's spells when Sade had been nothing more than a baby. While she had no magic of her own, she could, in a sense, see magic and was partially immune to it. He'd heard about the encounter with the witch in Chicago and what Sade had done. And she'd helped her werewolf foster brother face down the wendigo in New Mexico, along with help from several other magicks, including the Drakon of the most powerful dragon clan.

"You might not be a child, Sade, and not strictly human, but you are still mortal."

"Gawdammit," she spat. "Motherfucking sonava bitch."

He almost smiled. This was the Sade he'd come to know and admire. She cussed to upset those more staid members of her cadre. Him? He didn't care what language she used and as a result, her mouth wasn't typically foul. He'd pushed a button and set her off.

"Gawdammit all to hell. You just don't fucking get it, Varrick."

"Then explain it to me."

"It's...I..." She was back to pacing and she paused to swing a booted foot at the back of the upholstered chair he'd formerly been occupying. The chair and more blue words went flying. She finished with, "Ow. That was fucking stupid."

He raised a brow, which she ignored.

"This is about Roman. You assholes play your cards too fucking close to your chests. Roman was gawddamned diligent in trying to teach me Magick Races 101 but he left out a granite mountain-sized chunk of gargoyle history." She dropped her chin to her chest and rubbed the back of her neck. Her dark hair veiled her face so he couldn't see her expression.

"I don't know why I'm even bothering with you," she groused, but her voice was a whisper only supernatural ears could hear. "Stone cold. Every last one of you."

"Why is this important to you?" Varrick wanted to bite his tongue. He shouldn't be encouraging her.

Sade jerked her head up and caught a flicker of uncertainty as it crossed Varrick's features. Uncertainty was better than nothing and she could work with it far better than apathy, which is what she usually barreled into. "I'm pretty fucking sure the entire magick community knows my story. Poor little human pawn in the war between the master vampire of all vampires and the King of the Fae. Poor little girl whose father was tricked into siring her and who Oberon was almost tricked into believing she was his." She rolled her eyes. "I'm guessing you know I racked up more frequent flyer miles before I turned five than the Wicked Witch of the West."

Sade brushed past Roman's desk and stood at the window. People moved through Jackson Square even though night had fallen. New York City might claim to be the city that never slept but the French Quarter would give the Big Apple a run for its money. "Roman was the one sent to fetch me. He was the one who defied time and space to find me in whichever parallel hell I'd been stashed.

"Here was this big, scary gargoyle Sentinel, and he read me bedtime stories and tied pink ribbons in my hair." She laughed—a short bark of sound. "Only once. I hated pink, bows, and frilly dresses. Roman was...*is*...the one constant in my life, the one person who has never had an agenda where I'm concerned."

When she turned around, Varrick almost reached for her. Her bottle-glass green eyes were brilliant with tears and her voice was husky as she finally admitted the truth. "Roman is...he's family. *My* family. Something is going on with him, and whatever it might be is all tangled up in past events. There's something wrong, Varrick. Really wrong. I need to know what it is so I can help him."

Sadness and sincerity filled her voice and touched something deep inside Varrick. He wasn't sentimental. Gargoyles weren't known for having hearts. That thought dragged a dry chuckle from him. Wasn't that the whole heart of this mess? The fact that the Heart of Stone was in danger? That the Crucible of Eve had been incarnated? That gargoyles faced annihilation if the Crucible wasn't found and balance restored?

"Roman won't talk to me. Crevan might as well have his mouth glued shut for all the information he's willing to share. There are dead gargoyles."

"I'm aware of that, Sade."

She threw up her hands. "Dead *gargoyles*, Varrick! I didn't even know your kind could die."

"Everything that is alive can die, Sade. We are harder to kill than most but yes, my kind can and does die."

"What does the Old War have to do with the current situation?"

"I have no answers, Sade. I was *nullité,* barely a fledgling confined to L'Crèche when the war occurred."

Sade started to argue but snapped her jaw shut. She didn't know much about the place the gargoyles called L'Crèche. She believed it to be part nursery, part school, part training ground. It suddenly occurred to her that she didn't know much about gargoyle reproductive practices, especially since she'd never seen a female gargoyle. She tried really hard not to get squicked by the idea of Roman in a compromising position. That would be like...seeing her dad. Or her brother.

"Sade?" Varrick's voice sounded funny.

She blinked several times and concentrated on him. "Sorry. I just realized that I don't know how..." She trailed off, shook her head, and made a sour face. "Y'know what? Never mind. I don't think I want to know about gargoyle birds and bees."

Varrick threw back his head and laughed. "Good, because that's a subject I don't want to discuss with you. Roman would have my balls if he found out I had. He's rather old-fashioned that way."

Sticking her fingers in her ears, Sade chanted, "La-la-la-la."

"I thought you weren't a child." Varrick teasing her was better.

"I'm not."

"Are too."

"Am not."

They both laughed and then Sade sobered. "I need to know what happened back then because I truly believe it has a bearing on what's happening now and Roman's reaction to the situation."

"What about Roman's reaction?"

"It's...not Roman-like. I mean, he's always been reticent but he's also been open and honest. At least with me. He doesn't ignore questions. He'll tell me it's none of my business, but he's never just ignored me or worse, walked away without a word." Unaware of what she did, Sade wrapped her arms over her stomach, cupping her elbows in opposite palms.

"I hadn't noticed," Varrick admitted, while noticing far more about Sade's posture than she was aware of. She was worried about Roman, and just a little scared. That surprised him. If anything, Sade Marquis was too fearless for her own good.

"But you're one of his best friends. How could you not see how he's changed?" She knew she sounded desperate. If Varrick didn't know, Sade had no clue who to ask. Roman was on a path to self-destruction and she had no ammunition—no weapon to stop him.

"No, Sade. If Roman were to acknowledge that such a thing exists in our world, that title would fall to you. He was and is my mentor, my instructor. He is now my commander within the Sentinels. Aye, we've served centuries together, and I would name him friend but we don't...we aren't human. And those of us who live centuries seldom remember the past with pleasure. We have never discussed the Old War."

"Then tell me what the rumors were."

"Rumors—"

"Are often based on facts—facts that get twisted

with the telling but there's often a grain of truth if you dig deep enough."

Varrick settled more comfortably on the edge of the desk, deciding it was safer to stay out of Sade's way as she began pacing through the office again. "My kind calls those days the Dark Time, like other magicks refer to the killing times after the Veil ripped." He gave weight to those words and Sade nodded to indicate she'd caught the emphasis. "The gargoyles were in disarray. Holy artifacts had gone missing. There was...dissension." How much could he afford to tell her? Despite what he'd said to her, he loved Roman as well. "I have heard that a decision was made, a command given. Roman was called by Crevan, given orders."

"Orders?"

"*Le Vieil* named Roman judge, jury, and..."

Sade's heart twisted from the sudden insight and finished Varrick's sentence. "Executioner." Roman was created to be a protector, a guardian. He'd watched over her for her whole life. She almost doubled over from the pain this knowledge caused. The word she'd uttered scalded her tongue.

"Yes." A profound sadness settled around Varrick. "The guard dog was forced to hunt his flock. I believe a part of him died and—"

"Now he has to do it again." Over her dead body.

CHAPTER ELEVEN
BROKEN SILENCE

THE PHONE on Roman's desk lit up and the brash sound of its ring cut through the thick silence left in the wake of Sade's declaration. Varrick automatically answered, "Legate's office."

"Uh...this is...no, I'm nobody...uh...maybe I shouldn't have called."

"Do not hang up."

The command in Varrick's voice brought Sade to his side—not because she was compelled by the force of it but because her instincts were humming. With raised eyebrows, wide eyes, and a tilt of her head, she urged him to continue. He hit the button to put the call on speaker.

"It's just...well see..." The caller, a kid from the sound of his voice, took a sobbing breath. "My boss is a werewolf so I sort of know about stuff and when I saw those guys, they..." His voice trailed off, his fear coming through the speaker in tangible waves.

"What guys?" Varrick kept his voice neutral and calm.

"They...gargoyles, I think. I mean I don't think they're demons but maybe? Are there demons? Anyway, there was six of them. It was four on two and I didn't help because...well...four on two and they were big. I mean really big."

The kid was babbling now so Varrick cut him off. "Where?"

"Oh...yeah. Dumaine. Off of Chartres. There's like an alley...a cut through. I...think maybe some of them are dead. Maybe. I don't know. I ran."

Sade was already headed for the door. "Where's Roman?"

"He's in his room but—" She was gone before Varrick could finish. He hung up on the kid and headed after Sade.

She skipped down the stairs and headed directly to Roman's bedroom. She didn't stop to knock and was halfway into the room before her brain registered what her eyes were seeing. Roman. In bed. With a woman. *Oh fuckityfuck shit and damn*, she thought backpedaling toward the door.

Sade managed not to scream when someone grabbed her jacket and jerked her backwards out of the room. Whirling, she faced Varrick. "What in the name of fucking hell," she hissed between her teeth. "Oh my God, Varrick. I...he...she..."

Varrick continued propelling her toward the stairs. "I'll explain later. At the moment, we have something more pressing. Gargoyle attack, remember?"

Oh, yeah. She jerked her thoughts away from the woman curled half on top of Roman, of his arms around her, of the look on his sleeping face. Thank everything holy that they'd been mostly under the covers and mostly dressed. Not that she hadn't seen Roman...well, not naked, but stripped down for battle. And there'd been nothing sexy about the sight except...yeah, maybe there had been a little something sexy because...alpha male warrior totally ripped. Her sorority sisters had certainly thought so, even when they set her up with a bet they were sure would fail. Good thing Roman had played along. And yeah, her thoughts were on a hamster wheel to keep from thinking about what she'd seen up in Roman's bedroom. And what the implications might be.

They hit the back, very private and very hidden,

entrance to the Legation's building at a trot. "My car," Sade panted as she sprinted to the black SUV illegally parked down the block.

"I can fly faster."

"But I need my equipment bag."

"You aren't coming."

"The hell I'm not."

"You're human."

"I'm FBI."

Varrick didn't know why he was arguing with her. He should just take off, though it would take him a moment to shift forms and he needed to lose his shirt so his wings didn't rip it to shreds.

"Fine, but I'm—"

"I'm driving." Sade cut him off and vaulted into the driver's seat. He struggled into the passenger side even as she was hitting the electronic controls for his seat, sending it back from the dash. "Good thing I can multitask, huh!"

She hit the gas and barely tapped the brakes as she took the corner onto Chartres. Sade slowed again to navigate the posts and planters designed to keep vehicular traffic off the promenade in front of the Cabildo, St. Louis Cathedral, and the Presbytère. She had to slow on the other side of the Square for the same reason. Two blocks later, she made a sharp left turn, jammed her foot on the brakes, and skidded to a stop.

Varrick hit the pavement at the same time Sade did. A green, wooden door had been ripped from its frame in a brick wall that guarded the entrance to a narrow walkway between two buildings. Varrick peered into the thick shadows, head cocked to listen. Nothing. No screams. No moans. Not even the sound of someone breathing. He stepped into the alleyway, Sade close on his heels.

They found the first body about ten feet in. Female.

Not for the first time, Sade wished Caleb was with her. His nose for magic was the best in the business. She squatted beside the woman while Varrick kept watch. Using the green filter on a small night-vision flashlight, Sade checked the body. If she had to guess, the woman had been a witch of some sort. In New Orleans, that appellation covered a broad spectrum. From her dress, though, Sade would guess voodoo priestess and a local. The cause of death was obvious—a gaping hole in the chest. Something had ripped out her heart.

Rising to her feet, she gestured for Varrick to continue. The eerie quiet followed them, like they were enclosed in the cone of silence. Sade couldn't even hear normal street noise. A few feet further along, they found an open doorway.

Varrick swung in, called out a soft, "Clear." A moment later he stepped out. Leaning close to Sade's ear, he whispered. "The witch's abode."

Had she been ambushed on her way home? Ambushed at the door? She nodded and indicated for him to continue forward. Pistol in hand, Sade paid attention to everything—the windows above them, the walkway behind them, the area in front. The odd hush continued. There were no lights in the living spaces lining the little alley. Varrick was so broad his shoulders all but brushed against the walls on either side of them. When he stopped the next time, she got the sense of an open space beyond him.

He stepped to the side, keeping his back braced against the wall. Sade crept up beside him and swallowed hard. Faint moonlight filtered into the courtyard. Furniture lay scattered around a raised planter area, and there was a water feature. They found pieces of one gargoyle about five steps in. Another body, female again, was draped over a granite torso. She'd been a pretty girl with caramel-colored skin and black hair.

"Werewolf," Varrick muttered.

Sade gave him a startled look. "You can tell?"

He nodded absently, already dismissing the two bodies. They found another witch, face down in the fountain's pool, and two more gargoyles. Standing in the center of the courtyard, Sade slowly turned a circle. When she'd completed the action, her ears popped. That was when she realized she could hear a dog barking and traffic driving by on the street.

"There was a spell." She stared at Varrick for confirmation.

He shrugged. "Maybe. Probably. I don't get it though."

"Get what?"

"Witches don't normally hang out with werewolves and they sure don't associate with gargoyles, as a rule. At least not those who practice on the dark side."

"Seriously?"

Varrick rolled his eyes. "Magicks one-oh-one, Marquis."

"I slept through that lecture."

"That war you were asking about? It came down to witches and wizards with the help of rogue gargoyles on one side, and true gargoyles on the other."

"I thought the sorcerers caused the war and that's why there aren't any of them left."

"They did, but the magical humans came down on the wrong side."

"Varrick? Why are there so many gargoyles here in New Orleans all the sudden?"

He'd been asking himself much the same question, but had no answer. It was something he needed to discuss with Roman and Crevan. "I don't know."

"Does Roman?" Sade wanted to take that question back, because the inflection in her voice insinuated that he did. Something was going on with Roman and she had no idea of what, when, or why. And trying to be honest with herself, her feelings were hurt. Which was stupid. She held up a hand as Varrick opened his mouth and his expression shuttered. "Never mind. Just...I'm weirded out, okay? I mean, it's not okay, but fuck it. Anyway. You call your people for cleanup. I'll notify the Smith Pack alpha and the...I guess the witches' counsel? Fuck. This is stuff the Legate is supposed to handle but there is no fucking way in hell I'm calling Roman."

Varrick walked away, a cell phone to his ear. Sade used her own cell to notify Deacon Smith. The grumpy werewolf who answered—the pack's second—volunteered to inform the witch on call. Sade was almost grinning when she clicked off, thinking of the phone tree scene in the movie "Practical Magic." Still, considering how large the magick population in New Orleans was and how often mundanes and magicks rubbed up against each other, it made sense to have an "on-call desk."

Lazare Smith was the first to arrive. A tall man with shaggy auburn hair and a thick shadow beard, he shook hands with Sade. "Deacon decided I should come m'self, 'specially since the FBI was callin' an' all." He noticed the female draped over the broken granite and let out what sounded like a soft *wurfle*. "Ah, Amaline. What were you thinkin', girl?"

"You know her?"

He hit Sade with a withering glare. "Amaline Smith. So yeah. I knew her. We're all pack around here, Agent Marquis. I'd of known her besides. Any wolf who comes has t'check in with us, just like they do at the Legation office. But Ammie is—was—one of ours. A little wild, but a sweet girl. She was studyin' music at Tulane. Had a voice that'd put the First Lady of Song t'shame.

"Ella Fitzgerald?"

"Yup. Ammie could sing 'Summertime' and make a granite statue cry."

Sade flashed back to Chicago, to the coven collecting girls of unique talent. That witch was dead but could Ammie have been targeted for something similar. Gods but she hoped not. Plus, there were dead witches and gargoyles. Lots of dead gargoyles. She stepped deeper into the scene, the werewolf following her.

Near the center of the courtyard, they stopped and he studied the scene then devolved into a sneezing fit.

Sade gave him a what-the-hell look and waited. She glanced over at Varrick, who was currently talking to the two gargoyles who'd just poofed into existence. He favored her with a "no-clue" look in response.

Pinching his nose, the werewolf glowered at her. "That ain't funny, cher."

"What ain't...er...isn't funny?"

Lazare waved his hands around. "Magic spells, cher. Bad mojo. You might better take a moment an' fill this poor Cajun boy in on what the hell's goin' on."

"There was a spell here then?"

"Was and is. I did mention the bad mojo, right?"

Sade rocked back, chin tucked defensively and brow furrowed. "Wait. There *is* a spell here?"

The werewolf muttered something about mundanes under his breath. "Yeah. There was a big spell. That's what made me sneeze. And there's still a little one."

"Okay, I'm guessing here but when Varrick and I walked through the outer gate, it's like the outside was shut out, like some sort of a null spell or something."

"Can you narrow it down? What did you feel? Smell? Hear?"

"Hear. That's the weird part. I don't remember hearing anything. Not until—" She broke off, considered. "Okay. We walked through the gate. It was quiet. Too quiet considering there was supposed to be a fight going on. We found the first body. Kept walking, got here. Found the next five bodies. I remember thinking that we were in a bubble because I couldn't hear the street noise." She closed her eyes, pictured the scene. "Varrick was...standing over the body in the planter. I was...standing on the low wall around the planter, this side."

"You turned in a circle," Varrick added. He'd walked up after setting the gargoyles to work gathering up the broken stones.

Opening her eyes, Sade pursed her lips. "And my ears popped." She focused on the werewolf. "Is that significant?"

Lazare chortled. "Why you askin' me, cher? I ain't no witch or wizard. But I'd say you probably broke the spell, 'specially if you turned widdershins. That must'a been a doozy of a spell."

"Yeah, I guess." Sade glanced between the two men. "But you think there's still a spell here?"

"Yeah, but it's small magic."

"I believe one of the dead witches lived here." Varrick pointed toward the walkway. "If you don't mind confirming her scent in the open apartment?"

"Deacon tol' me t'help anyway I can. First, though, I'd like t'take care of Amaline."

Sade winced. "I'm sorry. This is a crime scene. I'll release her to you just as soon as I can. In the meantime, any information you might have or can come up with would be appreciated." She crooked an index finger at Varrick. "I need to call in a forensics team."

Gargoyle and werewolf both stared at her like she had three heads and was eating boogers. She knew what those looks meant and she resisted the urge to draw her weapon.

"There are no humans involved in this, Agent

Marquis," Lazare said very quietly but menace oozed through every word.

"This falls under the jurisdiction of the Legate, Sade," Varrick agreed.

"Dammit—"

"You are here by our leave, Sade, not the other way around."

"Fuck that, Varrick. You know Roman will—"

A bright flash of light and thundering noise cut her off. Unable to see or hear, Sade dropped to the ground, arms over her head as she tucked into a tight ball. Varrick and the wolf curled around her and they all hung on while the world rocked around them.

Fuck but she hated magic.

CHAPTER TWELVE
DARK HEARTS

VERITY WHIMPERED in her sleep and the only comfort Roman could provide was to tighten his arms around her. In many ways, lying here in the dark reminded him of nights spent watching over Sade when she'd suffered nightmares as a child. He wondered again what demons pursued Verity down the dark and silent avenues of her dreams?

He'd watched her world shatter earlier and what had he done? Duty told him to gather up the pieces and dump them in her lap. He should have walked away after turning her over to Varrick and his escadron. But after seeing her face, looking into her bruised and haunted eyes, he couldn't do his duty.

Verity La Croix was human. Mostly. She carried the taint of witch blood and his instincts writhed with a knowledge Roman repudiated with his whole being. Something dark and dangerous inside him insisted he protect her. He wanted to hold her tight, wanted to erase the hurt she'd endured, wanted to slay her demons. Wasn't he bred for that? Weren't all the gargoyles?

Magick of human stock, he reminded his heart. The gargoyles were not like other races. They had no females. They did not procreate, they were not born of male and female. They were created from rock and imbued with spirit from the Heart of Stone. Sure, in human guise, their bodies reacted like a human. They could lust and sate themselves—and often did—but they did not seek mates. Not like the werewolves and dragons. Lovers were transitory, much like they were with the fae, vampires, and the human magicks. Still, long-term couples and marriages among the other magicks were not unheard of. Those of human descent had children. Fae could have them—though a fae birth was rare.

But here he was, in bed with a human woman, holding her, touching her, soothing her. Being held in turn, touched, soothed. Roman was a being of duty. Of responsibility. He held himself aloof, never knowing when he would need to mete out justice in all its forms. Crime and punishment. Judge and executioner.

Verity stirred, emitting a soft sigh that caressed his skin with a warm wash of air, ripping his thoughts away from the precipice.

"Uhm...hi?"

Her big blue eyes looked luminescent in the low light of his bedroom. His heart actually stopped, then stuttered to a start as he fell into them. The tip of her tongue flicked out, drawing his gaze. His body stirred, blood rushing to fill his cock. While he was no stranger to the human urges created in this guise, he was surprised by the ferocity of his reaction to this...no. Verity was not a child, not a girl. She was a woman, despite her naiveté.

"Roman?" Verity didn't recognize her voice. It had grown husky, breathy, even when she spoke only his name. She also didn't understand the sensations growing deep within her. She'd read books where authors wrote of heat pooling low in the body of the heroine. She'd rolled her eyes, not understanding the sheer force of the thrilling awareness.

She gazed into his silver eyes and she wasn't sure her heart could take any more. Verity recognized so much of herself there in the mirror of his eyes. So many shadows, so much pain. He seemed caught, like she was, with no place left to run. The part of her that was barely hanging on realized there would be no second chance. She had this only moment. Was she brave enough to act?

"I just want to hold you," Roman murmured into her hair.

Was he the answer to the prayers she'd whispered in the night when dark clouds gathered around her, threatening to suffocate her with loneliness? "Don't let me go," she whispered. "Please don't let me go."

"Never." And then he was kissing her, his hands on her. *Gentle*, he chided himself, stilling the overwhelming need to claim her. Verity was young, inexperienced, soft. He was none of those things. His fingers found warm skin—the nape of her neck and her thigh. As he touched her leg, she shifted, her knee sliding across his thigh. His cock swelled even more.

Verity wanted to rub against him, a cat seeking caresses. The heat of his hands on her bare skin all but set her alight. She moved over him, breath catching until she reminded herself to exhale. Whenever she did, her breath came out as a sigh. The hand on her thigh brushed up, touched the edge of her panties, stopped. The world held its breath and then the big body beneath her rolled and she was tucked beneath him.

Gazing up at Roman, she caught a glimpse of his true form. His face was carved by savage shadows. In contrast, gentle fingertips stroked lightly over her skin. He lowered his head and his tongue grazed the soft hollow beneath her chin. Verity longed to taste him, touch him, learn the shape of him. She inhaled, filling her lungs with his scent. He smelled of sandalwood and moss, of dry leaves in autumn. She shivered as her brain attempted to sort through the emotions and sensations coiling deep within her.

She wanted him. Desperately. As a woman wants a

man. But there were whispers, here in the dark. *"No, bebe. Dis you cannot do. If you give yourself—"*

"Shut up," she hissed.

Roman froze. Verity's heart fluttered like a hummingbird's wings. Fast and furious. Her fingers clutched his shirt—the shirt he wanted fiercely to shed. Skin to skin. Hunger goaded him to rip it off, to rip off the shirt—*his* shirt—she wore as a barrier between them. He'd never experienced this urgent compulsion to take what Verity could offer. He grabbed for a fragment of sanity.

His voice sounded like gravel in his ears as he spoke her name, "Verity?"

"Kiss me," she pleaded. "Make the voices shut up!"

She moved under him, almost writhing as she pressed the center of her heat against his groin. He gritted his teeth, wrapping that thread of sanity around his mind. "What voices?"

"Baba Rawnie," she cried, tears glistening in her eyes now. "She told me to stay away from boys, to not let a man touch me. Said they'd drag me into the dark, that I had to say in the light but—" Her voice choked off as she moaned and released his shirt only to tear at her own. "I need you. I can't explain why. I...gods, Roman! Please!"

Something was wrong. Roman didn't know what it was but the fever that gripped Verity now had it's claws in him, demanding action. Demanding he take her.

Then she said his name. Said his name as his mouth ravished hers and sucked in the sound of it from the tip of her tongue. Cloth ripped and then she was bare to him. His hand slid down to cup where she was already wet. And he shot her from dreamy drift into urgent demand.

Now there was only sensation, the pounding of blood and shocks of heat, and the tangle of limbs as they rolled to find more. She ran her hands over him, thrilling herself with the angles, the smooth skin, the hard lines of muscle.

He was starved for her, needing her like he needed air to breathe. Eager, greedy, his body wanted to ravage hers. She was panting, her hands jerking at his clothing, just as hungry for him. Roman pushed off her, ignoring her cry of protest. He was back a moment later, naked now, his body sweat-sheened with desire.

Verity stared, heart thudding, breathing sheer torture as she pulled oxygen into labored lungs. She craved him with every cell of her being. Reaching for him, her hands were quick, her intentions clear as she touched the hard length of him.

"Yes," she breathed.

He was in the same desperate mood. They shared the same reckless need. She spread for him, and he sank on top of her. The tip of his erection found the soft, heated center of her and sank in. "More," he ground out. "Give me more. Give me all you have, Verity La Croix. And take all that I give you in return."

Driven half-crazy by the feel of her inner depths wrapping around him, he plunged inside her to the base of his cock. She locked her legs around him as he dragged her up, twisting so that she straddled his lap. Blue fire flickered in her eyes as she watched him, her expression unreadable. Her hips rocked against him and she clamped around him when he would withdraw from her wet heat. Her body shuddered. Was she already coming? He'd known a second after he entered her that she'd been virgin. But she was witch stock and the magic drove her now, drove them both.

Verity's breath snagged in her chest, her heart stuttering as euphoria surged through her. How could this singular act make her feeling so...enormous. Lightheaded. Fulfilled. Crazy. Jubilant. Her insides turned liquid and she could feel him swelling against her slick walls as she plunged down on him and ground her body against his.

She watched his mouth move. Was he speaking? She couldn't hear, couldn't make sense of the sounds coming from between his lips. His arms wrapped around her back and he pulled her closer, his hips arching up as she sank onto him, taking him deeper.

Just hold on, she thought. *Hold onto him. We have to do this. We're on the edge of a cliff.* And she held him while the hunger consumed them both.

Almost frantic now, Roman shifted them again, holding her beneath him. His hips jackhammered into her welcoming heat. A voice in his head told him to stop. They were strangers and there were lies between them. He didn't care. His body was burning up like a shooting star falling from the sky. There was no way out now. The darkness was already settling around his heart.

Lights flared behind his eyes as she tightened around him once more. Together. They would come together and whatever force brought them to this time and place would be appeased. Heaven or hell. He didn't know. Didn't care. His body exploded and he pumped his life force into her and she received him, taking all of him, every drop.

Shuddering, they hung onto each other until the shaking stopped, until they could see again, breathe again. Their eyes closed as the magic settled around them, cloaking them from the powers beyond the room where they lay.

When Roman's head rested between her breasts, Verity opened her eyes. He had claimed her—this gargoyle who was the anathema to all those of her kind. She was his, every atom accepting his claim. This miracle of claiming created light in the darkness that had been her world. She had no experience with the physical act they'd just completed. She knew others used sex for violence and domination, for power. When driven by passion and lust, it could consume. But what had driven this act?

Roman tasted her skin with his lips and felt her quiver beneath him. Lust flared in his belly but he quenched it. Love was needed now—for them both. With gentleness and care, he separated from her, felt her gasp brush across his shoulder, then the sob that followed.

"Shhh," he murmured. He braced on a forearm, easing his weight from her. Enough light splashed into the room that he could see her face, see her luminous blue eyes. She was both terrified and sated. His soul felt battered, his heart was bleeding and she looked as if she had experienced the same.

"It's dark," she whispered. "I feel it wrapping around me."

"Let it go, *mon coeur*. There is just you and me tonight."

Verity stared up at him. "You too. I see the darkness in you as well."

"Yes, little one. There is darkness. But there is love. Remember that. Let go of the dark thoughts and remember only me."

He saw the moment she let go, saw in her eyes that she was seeing only him, only them. He settled beside her, pulling her close. There were those of his kind who would brand him a criminal for what he'd done here in the Stygian folds of the night.

She let go—he knew the moment she did, the instant all the dark thoughts left her. And only the two of them remained in her heart, her mind. Her eyes grew hazy, then her lids drooped as she relaxed into sleep. Roman lay still, listening for sounds in the silent night.

Then he lay, still alert, to make sure the dark didn't hold Verity in it's claws while she slept. Only then did he allow himself to follow, ignoring the dark in his own heart, and still he held on to Verity. That all he could do tonight.

CHAPTER THIRTEEN
WAITING FOR THE OTHER SHOE

LEVANT TREMAINE paced from room to room in the Garden District mansion he'd claimed for his New Orleans headquarters. He wore anger like a cape, swirling it around him like a vaudeville magician. The rogue werewolf he'd hired to kidnap the witch was currently occupying a special cell. Idiots. One simply could not trust a magick who turned into an animal. He debated opening the portal so he could descend into his dungeon. Taunting the werewolf might take the edge off his need for violence. The soft clearing of a throat set his anger off again.

"What?" he barked.

The gargoyle standing in the arched doorway to his inner sanctum flinched. Levant smirked. Gargoyles were not the all-powerful beings the infernal Concilium Magicae relied upon. They were simply stone constructs, acting at his will. He glanced toward the granite bowl gracing the altar he'd set up. All he needed was a stone statue. Once he had the Crucible of Eve, he could create as many of the brutes as he needed for his army. Still, he needed the Heart of Stone to imbue them with the magic needed to win his rightful place. He could give the statues life but he had to draw upon his own magical reserves to give them human glamour—something true gargoyles did with little effort.

"I am sorry to interrupt, sire," the gargoyle said diffidently, head lowered. Though not fully the size of true gargoyles, the thing was still taller than Levant. "One of the others has reported that he is in place. He will notify us if the witch is sighted."

"Was anything learned from searching her hovel?"

"Yes and no, sire. We found a death spell. One of the humans succumbed to it. Nothing else was discovered there but some cats."

"Did you kill them?"

"They ran away. We did not chase them, knowing you wanted us to search for the source of her magic. As they were not the source, nor were they familiars, we let them go."

"And the human?"

"We left him there. A warning."

Levant nodded and waved a hand to dismiss the gargoyle, but it stayed. "Is there something else?"

"Yes, sire. We have word that an FBI agent has arrived in town."

"There is an FBI field office here. What does it matter to me if they come and go? It's the FBI, not the Concilium Magicae."

His master's disdain was evident even to the poorly formed gargoyle. "We have heard the agent is someone of note, sire. A human woman named Sade Marquis."

That name rang a bell, Levant thought. When the Veil ripped and the president of the United States had been unmasked for the cursed elf that he was, Levant vaguely recalled some movement within the government to curb the violence done by and to magicks. There's been talk of a special unit within the FBI. Then he remembered. Sade Marquis. Under the protection of the most deadly vampire in the US *and* the King of the Fae. Still, she was only human. He would deal with her as he dealt with all the others he planned to subjugate. Still, she might be an interesting ace in the hole if he had control of her.

"If the opportunity presents itself, bring this FBI agent to me."

"As you wish, sire." Bowing and scraping, the creature retreated.

Levant truly hoped the opportunity arose. Having this agent in his hands might just be the falling domino that would begin the cascade into chaos he was planning for those in the magical realms. He turned back to his altar and stared at the chunk of quartz crystal sitting in the bowl. The bloodstone embedded in the center of the quartz was barely visible. If he didn't get his hands on the Crucible soon, he would need to replenish the Heart's blood supply.

·./(\\·• ●

VERITY LAY very still in the huge bed. She was naked. And alone. The enormity of the previous night swamped her and she had to work to keep breathing. What had she done? Panic fluttered in her chest, a murmuration of starlings wheeling in mad pirouettes. With a cautious stretch, she checked out her body. She was sore between her legs but not terribly so. In a very weird way, she felt...complete. That helped the flock in her chest settle onto imaginary telephone wires.

Faint murmurs that sounded far too much like Baba Rawnie's voice echoed around her. Verity was not meant to take a lover. Ever. And now she'd crossed some invisible line that no witch worth her salt would step over. But she wasn't a witch. She'd never worked real magic, only small spells Baba Rawnie had taught her. She told fortunes. Read Tarot cards. Sometimes saw things that had been, might be, could be in a crystal ball. Used crystals to get a sense of things or to help those who came to her. She was not a witch. She was a...a what? A psychic? A seer?

Her skin itched and she could almost feel the blood in her veins pushing its way into the capillaries, feeding each cell in her body, heating it to a scorching burn. *Witch blood,* a voice whispered. *Tainted.*

Someone tapped softly on the door. She scrambled to pull the covers up to her chin and called out a tentative, "Come in?"

A woman who looked to be in her late forties opened the door and poked her head in. "Hello, little one," she said. "May I enter?"

Verity nodded even though she was unsure if she had permission to invite anyone into the room. The woman stepped through and shut the door behind her. She wore a tailored business suit that looked like it probably cost a small fortune. She carried a bundle of clothes in her hands and approached the bed. She wore a silver name tag that bore a gold fleur-de-lis and the word C-E-L-Y-N.

The woman pointed to the tag, but pronounced her name KELL-in when she said it. "I'm the Legation secretary. The Legate was called out early this morning on a situation. He asked me to look in on you. Are you hungry?" Celyn offered a brisk smile. "The Legate arranged for some clothes to be procured for you. I think you'll find everything you need. When you are presentable, come out to the sitting room and I'll have food brought to you." She set the bundle on the foot of the bed.

Staring, Verity struggled for something to say. "Are you human?" The question spurted out before she could catch it. She immediately clamped her hands over her mouth, horrified and showing it by hunching her shoulders, ducking her head, and pleading with her eyes.

Celyn laughed—a rich, boisterous sound that surprised Verity down to her toes. "Oh, child. The Legate will have his hands full with you, now won't he? No, dear. I'm not human. I'm Elvish." She brushed back her stylishly cut bob to show the top of one ear. For the barest instant, Verity could see a point. "Not get cleaned up and come out. You're looking a bit peckish this morning."

The woman turned gracefully and departed, easing the door shut behind her. Verity stared at the door, wondering if she'd dreamed the whole thing. Then the folded clothes drew her attention. She didn't recognize them. She'd assumed Alton or someone who knew her would have gone to her house to— Her cats!

Verity jumped out of bed and grabbed a wad of cloth lying on the floor. It was a man's shirt and it was huge on her but it would do. She flung open the door and raced out into the hallway. Hesitating, her head swiveled back and forth as she decided which direction to go. She heard voices and dashed in that direction. Sliding on a rug as she tried to slow down to enter the room with the voices, she pinwheeled, arms flailing. The voices stopped and Verity glimpsed the faces of a dark-haired woman and the elfin receptionist as they turned to stare at her.

An arm hard with muscles roped around her waist and lifted her off her feet. She *oofed* as air rushed out of her lungs in surprise.

"While I appreciate the sight of you in nothing but my shirt, it is not appropriate for public wear."

Roman's words in her ear sent shivers bouncing down her spine. Still holding her around the waist, he scooped her up, turned and walked back toward his bedroom. Behind her, she caught another glimpse of the dark-haired woman, who was standing now, mouth agape, looking like she'd been hit with a stun gun or something.

In the bedroom, with the door closed, he set her on her feet. "Put on clothes, Verity, then come out to talk. Yes?"

She nodded and she knew it was none of her business but the dark-haired woman was pretty and looked more like the type Roman should be with—had been with, because Verity recognized her now. Did he have a wife? Or a girlfriend? She was appalled at her actions because clearly, Roman was a man who surely would have a lover. She blurted, "The woman…is she your lover?"

Roman rocked back, confused. Lover? He didn't have one. Not until last night. "What woman?"

"In the sitting room. The pretty brunette."

Pretty brunette? He felt like he was two steps behind and running to catch up to the conversation. Sade? Was Verity talking about Sade? Celyn had pale blond hair streaked with silver. She must be talking about Sade. A burst of laughter exploded from him.

Verity didn't know whether to get mad, be more dismayed, or intimidated.

"Get dressed, little one, and I will introduce you to Sade. I think you will understand my laughter." Roman brushed his fingers across her cheek and its prominent bruise. He backed toward the door, watching her. He paused before leaving and added, "There is no one, Verity La Croix. No one but you."

And with those words, Roman sealed his fate.

CHAPTER FOURTEEN
BURNING TRUTHS

WHEN VERITY peeked shyly around the corner into the sitting room, more people had arrived. An older man with shaggy hair and a day's growth of whiskers looked out of place, despite the cut and richness of the three-piece suit he wore. He looked rumpled as he sat stiffly on the sofa, like he'd slept in his clothes. The other gargoyle who'd been in the square yesterday stood just inside the entry, one shoulder braced against the wall. The elfin woman was absent, though the dark-haired beauty remained, sitting in a high-backed chair—which Roman was currently standing behind, his forearms braced on the top of the chair. Verity fought the jealous clutch in her stomach.

As soon as Roman saw her in the doorway, Roman strode across the room and took her hands in his. "Welcome, Verity. Please..." He led her into the room. "Are you hungry?"

Of course she is, he thought. She was too thin, a sign of too many missed meals, and he'd...they'd...last night had been a vigorous one. He urged her toward the antique sideboard where various dishes were laid out buffet-style. Preparing a plate, he then settled her into the high-backed chair that was a companion to the one Sade occupied.

"Eat," he commanded softly. "I'll introduce you." He started with Varrick, since he was already somewhat familiar to her. "This is Varrick Baden. He is a Sentinel."

Verity nodded and swallowed the bite of eggs she was chewing. "Thank you for your help yesterday," she said in a quiet voice. The gargoyle nodded but said nothing.

"This is Deacon Smith. He is the Alpha of the Smith Pack. His territory runs throughout Louisiana and Mississippi."

Werewolf. The word hung in her subconscious, then she remembered what she'd learned yesterday about Alton. And Mama Two. She didn't speak but lowered her eyes and ducked her head. She'd heard about the dominant and submissive behavior necessary to navigate pack politics. Glancing up from beneath her lashes, she found the man studying her, an odd look on his face—like he was both fascinated yet slightly repulsed. She concentrated on her food as Roman continued.

"And finally, I'd like you to meet Sade Marquis."

"Hi, Verity. Roman and I are old friends."

She choked on the scrambled eggs she'd just swallowed. She knew what that meant. This woman and Roman weren't *friends*. They were...more. Her heart twisted and it was just as well she couldn't breathe. Roman gently pounded on her back as she leaned forward trying to dislodge the food in her airway. Her vision blurred until she gasped in a breath. The other woman's face immediately drew her attention.

Sade didn't need to guess at what Verity's problem was. She'd seen the furtive glances, the speculation, the worry. She waited until the younger woman sipped some water, cleared her throat, and took a real breath.

"Roman's known me since I was a toddler," Sade explained. "He practically raised me."

Verity almost choked again and her face flamed as heat and blood rushed into her cheeks, a beacon flashing out her embarrassment to everyone in the room.

Without missing a beat, Sade continued. "He still

thinks he can boss me around, like he did when I was a kid. Too bad I'm a special agent with the FBI now. I head up the MAGIC unit. I deal with all the magical crimes that happen. That's why I'm here."

Sinking back against the chair, Verity inhaled deeply and settled. Her appetite was back and she dug into the food on her plate as the others talked. She didn't pay much attention until Varrick said, "The men who attacked Verity yesterday were human, led by a werewolf."

"Are you sure?" Deacon asked. "I'm not aware of any rogues in my territory. Outsiders know they are to register here at the Legation if coming in for less that a week. Any longer period, they have to petition me. Neither has happened. Ceylin hasn't notified me of any visitors in at least a month. I admit to some surprise, what with Halloween coming up."

Sade scrunched up her nose and pressed her lips together. "No offense, Mr. Smith, but how would you know?"

"I'd know. I have people scattered everywhere. They're always on watch. It wouldn't be the first time an outside wolf slipped in but we always catch them within a day or two."

"Well, speaking of, my former partner, Caleb Jones, will be flying in next week. It's official business."

Smith nodded at her, his face a stony blank. "Duly noted."

Yeah, bad memories there, Sade thought. Caleb had once been...betrothed, for lack of a better word, to Victoria Smith. She'd been First Daughter in the Smith Pack, a familial designation that also carried rank in the whole werewolf scheme of things. After a brief affair, Victoria and Caleb went their separate ways, having no intention of ever mating. Several years later, Victoria had been murdered here in New Orleans. Sade and

Caleb caught the murderer and as a result, an uneasy truce between Deacon Smith and Caleb had come about.

"What I don't get, is why a werewolf would work with humans to go after Verity." Sade caught the flicker of the look Varrick and Roman exchanged, but before she could call them on it, Varrick spoke.

"Paid muscle," he said, his voice a low rumble. Varrick held up a hand in an attempt to smother Deacon's growl. "We all know that rogue wolves do dirty work for pay. And there have been Alphas who hired out their wolves. Back in the day." He inclined his head toward Deacon. "Present company excepted." That seemed to mollify the Alpha and he settled back on the sofa.

"Okay. I *get* the werewolf. But why *Verity*? I mean...it's not like she makes a fortune telling fortunes. Since they hired a magick, they likely don't belong to some radical group of humans wanting to harass the magical races. And why her specifically? There are what...usually ten or so psychics and fortune tellers in the Square at any one time? What made Verity stand out so much they went for her?"

"There is also the question of the null spell during the attack, and a compulsion spell." Roman pinched the bridge of his nose. With reluctance, he looked toward Deacon. "Have you done any spell hunting, Deacon?"

The werewolf leaned forward, his eyes alight with interest. "Not since I was a pup." He turned his gaze to Sade. "When is Jones due in?"

She shrugged. "Not sure. He's finishing up a case in Denver. He promised he'd be here by next week. There's not many who can follow magic scents better than Caleb."

"This is true, though I have someone I can call if time is of the essence." He eyed Verity, who ducked her head again. He tapped his index finger against his chin, lost in thought for a long moment. Then he said, "There is something about this one that draws interest. I think we need to know now."

Withdrawing a cell phone from his pocket, he scrolled through his contacts and hit the call button beneath a name. "Mama Two," he said when his call was answered. "You need to catch the next ferry and come to the Legate's office."

There wasn't much conversation for the next thirty minutes. People ate and drank coffee. Verity remained curled up in the big chair, attempting to look as unobtrusive as she could. She was still freaked out by the knowledge that Alton and Mama Two were both werewolves. A man in tailored slacks, a buttoned-up vest, and a white shirt arrived to clear away the food. He never said a word, never looked at anyone and Vee couldn't tell if he was human or something else.

Deacon fielded phone calls. Varrick held up the wall. Roman leaned on the back of Verity's chair as he'd been doing over Sade's when the young woman had arrived. Sade just watched. There was something deep—and unsettling—going on. Like Deacon, Sade sensed something *more* about Verity but she couldn't pinpoint what it was. Ever since Mathias and Oberon had both marked her as a child, she'd been able to sense magic, knew when someone was a magick, and she could usually determine their particular flavor? For anything else, Sade had to depend on the good will of any particular magick for help. Which sucked hind tit.

She suspected the gargoyles knew exactly what Verity was, but getting them to share would be a battle. How many more would have to die before she got to the bottom of things? Because, truthfully speaking? Sade didn't believe for a New York minute that *Le Vieil* would play this one close to his stone-cold chest without retribution. And that pissed her right the hell off.

The guy who'd cleared the buffet was back, this time wearing a black suit coat. Sade had a lot of experience with butlers in magical households—none of it particularly good. This guy? He was so innocuous, he was almost invisible. She might get used to this type of butler—if his silent presence wasn't so creepy.

Before the man could speak, a woman swept in, all but knocking him out of the way. Varrick straightened from his slouch against the wall. Deacon dropped his head into his hands. Roman moved from behind the chair, preparing to defend Verity. Sadie took all this in while still checking out the intruder.

The woman might be forty. She might be seventy. Her hair was confined in the wraps of a colorful scarf. Her caramel skin was smooth but for crinkles at the corners of eyes the color of dark roast coffee. She wore a flamboyant muumuu while her wrists and neck were draped with beads and chains—none of them silver. She carried a cardboard box under one arms, the bottom notched against her ample hip.

"Chile, what'chu gotten yerself messed up in now?"

Verity tucked her chin and mumbled, "I don't know, Mama Two."

"Ah, cher," the woman sighed, walking toward the object of everyone's attention. She sniffed at Roman, meeting his direct gaze with one of her own. He stepped aside. Mama dropped the box into Verity's lap. "These miscreants came t'da food truck lookin' for you."

The flaps popped open and two heads emerged. "Pen! Ink!" Verity cried delightedly. A third head appeared. "Domino!" The kittens scrambled out of the box and clawed their way into her arms. One was snow white but for its tail—which was a tiger-stripe orange topped with a black tip. The second was pure black and the third was black with white markings on its face, chest, and paws.

Mama Two fisted her hands on her hips and inhaled as her head swiveled from one side of the room to the other. She curled her nose at Roman and Varrick, furrowed her brow at Sade, then she focused on Verity.

"Spells," the old woman muttered. "Deep and dark. Spells that mark. Spells to hide. Spells that have not yet died." She pointed a finger at Sade. "Move away. You have dark inside you that hides the rest. And you carry vampire marks."

Sade rolled her eyes. "I've been touched by the fae as well."

"*Pffft*," Mama Two responded, brushing that off with a flip of her hand. "You have death magic in you, child. It interferes with my hunt."

"Yeah, yeah, whatever," Sade groused, but she pushed out of the chair and joined Varrick in leaning on the wall by the door. With her out of the way, Mama focused on Verity.

"Magic...yes. Hidden away. Dampened down. Ooh, cher, some ol' witch did not want you found. Tangled webs she did weave to keep the silence."

The kittens had frozen, their eyes wide and unblinking as they stared at Mama Two. Verity's face resembled theirs. Mama leaned in close, sniffing, holding her breath, sniffing again. Then she straightened and turned to Deacon.

"Dampening spell. Compulsion spell. Null spell. And a binding to keep this chile' from usin' her magic. The binding spell is oldest, the caster one I knew. Baba Rawnie. She's dead. Burned to death years ago."

Verity flinched, unable to stop the visceral reaction. Everyone noticed.

"The null spell was weak, meant only to hide the holder's action for a short time. I know this caster too. She sells her charms and such in the Quarter. Claims to be a voodoo priestess but unless she draws on death magic, she has no real power. I suspect a werewolf bought it, likely for far more money than it was worth."

Deacon growled. "You smell wolf?"

Mama favored him with a look insinuating he was an imbecile. "I smell at least one wolf in the spell. If the girl wasn't covered in gargoyle, you would smell him around her too." She held up a hand as he growled again. "Not one of ours. I don't recognize the scent." The narrow-eyed look she sent Verity was speculative. "Nor do I recognize the scent of the compulsion spellcaster. Male, I think, but he took pains to hide his magic. As a result, the spell was weak. I think he meant for Verity to go to him. When she didn't, he sent his thugs to take her."

She stopped speaking and her expression turned troubled before she shook herself. Roman regarded her solemnly and realized with a flash of intuition that he would not like the words she spoke next.

"There is something else, another spell. One of binding but so ancient as to be lost in time. Old, old magic. Earth magic. Soul magic. A truth burned into stone." Her gaze settled on Roman and she frowned. "Only one with a heart of stone can undo it."

BY THE TIME darkness came, Verity was exhausted. The debates, plans, and downright arguments lasted all day. Words swirled around and over her as she sat trapped in the chair, her legs curled under her, Pen and Ink in her lap, Domino curled around her shoulder. Roman insisted she eat something when food arrived but for her life, she couldn't remember what she'd put in her mouth. More food arrived as shadows lengthened outside the windows. The man who Verity finally decided was a butler of some sort, came and went like a dark-suited ghost with disapproving eyes. She thought she might have heard him sniff once or twice and mutter something about the proper place for meals was the dining room.

Roman and Varrick stood near one of the tall windows, nose to nose, their hands slashing in angry gestures as they spoke in low tones. The werewolf Alpha and Mama Two sat on the sofa looking for all the world like predators lying in wait for their prey. The FBI agent had a phone glued to her ear and ignored everyone else. Even the cats had deserted Verity. She had no idea where they'd disappeared to and she was almost afraid to speculate. With its expensive antique furniture, rich carpets and draperies, and far too many breakables, this was not a pet friendly home.

Verity jerked awake for the third time. No one had moved and she wondered if they would miss her if she slipped away. She wanted a shower. She wanted sleep. She wanted away from the pressure of anger and ramped-up emotions. With great caution, she stood up. Her eyes darted around the room. No one noticed. A moment later, she was out of the room and all but running down the hall to Roman's bedroom.

WELL AFTER MIDNIGHT, Roman ended the cold war going on in the sitting room by simply walking out. He heard Sade say, "Well...alrighty then. I'm going to Déja Vu for a cold beer. Anyone want to come?" He paid no attention, far too intent on his destination. Slipping into his bedroom, his eyes adjusted immediately to the dim light lit softly by a lamp she'd left on to chase away the dark. Verity lay on her side, one hand tucked under her cheek, the coverlet falling away from her bare shoulder. He stood beside the bed, taking her in.

He'd awakened that morning wanting her, but he'd slipped away. Duty was carved into him and the harsh demand of its call drove him to get up. Now, after a frustrating day of arguments and recrimination, he just wanted the warm comfort of Verity's body. Roman had never craved a woman. Enjoyed them yes, but desiring one to the point that every cell in his body burned? Never. Until Verity. He had only to look at her, touch her, to need her in the very depths of his soul. The whole notion was alien to him but some instinct urged him to accept the gift of her.

Fingertips as gentle and light as a summer breeze stroked over her skin, heating flesh and feelings both. The slide of a tongue followed by lips brushing over her mouth roused and aroused her. Verity floated on the cusp of wakefulness, a sweet drowsiness dragging on her eyelids.

Roman kissed her closed eyelids, then found her ear. His erotic whisper put a sweet smile on her face. She reached for him, her movements languid. He was hyper-aware of her, as if she'd been imprinted on his body. She sighed, her breath teasing the skin on his neck as he held her.

"Clothes," she murmured, as desire bloomed despite her sleep-blurred mind.

He smiled and pushed off the bed. Roman kicked off his boots and stripped, his clothes dropping on the floor without a thought. When he rejoined Verity on the bed, he was determined to go slow. To ease her into this...thing...these feelings he had no name for because he had no experience with them. All he was certain of was that he wanted to savor this time with Verity. To go slow. He buried his nose against her throat. She smelled of... His brain fought to decipher emotions and his overloaded senses. Mate. His. Yes. Compelled to claim her, he tasted her, shaped her body with his hands, learning her. Committing everything about her to his memory.

"Forever," he whispered as she moved beneath him.

The staggering fatigue drained away, replaced by quixotic awe as she rose to meet him, to accept him. He would give her everything he had to give, knowing what he bequeathed to her would be returned tenfold. She was his solace, his peace. She offered comfort with her touch, her kisses, the simple fact of her being.

Verity stroked him, fully awake now. His skin was chilled and when she looked deep into his eyes, she saw a coldness buried so deep she feared touching it. But she would. She was patient. Her hands on his skin were already warming it. She smiled and her eyes misted. She might not be able to say the words, but she could tell him this way that he was loved, that he was desired.

Words came then, though she didn't understand them. She thought they might be French but they weren't. They came from a place far older, more remote. Roman murmured them against her skin, in her ear, in between the kisses he bestowed upon her. Something in her stilled, listened, understood, and the horrible ache, the excruciating loneliness eased. His words were a caress, and a promise.

Roman was a warrior, a guardian, a man taught not to seek comfort. Verity knew this instinctively, just as she knew she was the one chosen to care for him, to tend the gentle heart he hid beneath his stone facade. He filled her slowly and she rode the sensation—a long sweet wave. She threaded her fingers through his thick, silky hair and pulled him down to her. "Yes," she murmured in his ear.

He spoke more words, from his heart, his soul. She gave them back to him, words from her own heart. He just wanted to touch her, to hold her close, cherish her. She was a miracle. *His* miracle.

They made love. Long. Slow. Sweet. They touched. They kissed. They each gave in turn. Together they rode the rising waves of passion, cresting on one and crashing down on another until it felt like a hurricane was breaking around them. The waves eventually gentled as their desire was spent.

Roman cradled Verity to his heart. She wrapped around him, holding on to him. "Sleep, little witchling," he whispered into her hair.

She looked up at him and he was staggered by what he saw. The trust in her eyes was a living thing—fragile, a gossamer thread of spider web easily broken by a careless word. He stopped breathing for a moment, struck by the wonder of it. He would die before he erased that look.

He felt her slip away as dreams took her. Roman was exhausted and should follow her into sleep but he couldn't. He lay awake for a long time, to ensure no nightmares chased her but that was only half truth. He wanted to cherish this time with her. She was his touchstone, had become his truth. She was his constant. And that terrified him down to the very center of his heart of stone.

CHAPTER FIFTEEN
WHATEVER IT TAKES

EVERY MORNING since she'd been here, Verity woke up to some part of her old life installed in Roman's bedroom. Or was it her bedroom now? A part of her protested that the gargoyle was taking over her life and that she should fight it. But she was still adrift, a leaf caught up in the current of events. And she was frightened. When Roman was with her, she felt safe— safer than she'd felt in her entire life. Still, there was something inside her, a pressure building, a need coiled and waiting. She didn't understand what was happening to her.

For what seemed like the first time in her life, she had plenty of food. A soft bed. A man who held her through the tears and nightmares. A man who made love to her. Someone had found all of her Tarot cards and returned the deck to her. Most of her crystals and stones had been retrieved as well. Verity wasn't sure if she missed the crystal ball or not. It had belonged to Baba Rawnie and its power, while useful, always felt...*off* to Verity. It radiated a dissonance that never truly resonated with her.

Roman, as was his custom, was up and gone with the rising sun. She wondered if that was a gargoyle thing or just Roman's habit. He was a busy man, spending long hours in his office dealing with the magicks coming and going in New Orleans and he was also hunting for the man she knew as Mr. Tremaine. Everyone involved was convinced he was a sorcerer, and that was very bad.

Bored, she wandered through the apartment, Pen and Ink winding between her ankles as they played hide and seek. She'd left Domino curled up on her pillow, fast asleep. She found a door slightly ajar and realized she'd never been in this room. As curious as the cats, she peeked inside. Heavy velvet curtains draped the tall windows, casting a gloomy pall over the room. One slender ray of sunlight slashed through a slit in the material and arrowed toward a curio cabinet set against the far wall. Something glittered and winked in the sunbeam and it drew Verity like a siren's song.

She approached the cabinet as if mesmerized. There on the middle shelf, toward the back was something made of glass. Not just glass, something finer, like the stuff cut crystal glasses were formed from. Her fingers literally ached to touch the crystal ball. A little voice in the back of mind demanded that she do whatever it took to claim this treasure. She reached out and touched the latch. The cabinet wasn't locked. Opening the door, she reached in. A tingle jolted through her as her fingers touched it.

Verity let out a little squeak and almost dropped the ball, but her fingers instinctively clutched it tighter. She glanced over her shoulder, afraid someone would catch her. Only then did she notice that Pen and Ink paced just beyond the room's open door, meowing in distress. Odd, she thought, but she had the crystal ball now and that's all that mattered.

With great care, she closed and latched the cabinet then darted back to the hallway. She left the door partially ajar as she'd found it but as she walked away, the door closed with a snick. Concerned, she returned. Raising her hand hesitantly, she grasped the door handle. She pressed down but it didn't move. The door was locked. Verity checked the hallway, and with furtive glances over her shoulder, she all but ran to Roman's bedroom.

Climbing up onto the bed, she sat cross-legged in the middle, elbows on her knees, the crystal ball resting in her cupped palms. While Baba Rawnie's ball allowed her blurry visions, peering into the heart of this one was like turning on a high-definition TV and holding the change-channel button on the remote so that the channels flashed by in a kaleidoscope of images. In moments, she was lost.

Pen and Ink, the fur on their stiff tails bristled, huddled together in the large chair that Roman normally sat in, anxious eyes watching Verity. Domino sat beside her, eyes unblinking.

⁘ ⚫

SADE LEANED back in the worn chair, her booted feet propped on the desk in her purloined office. The two FBI agents occupying chairs across from her looked a little anxious. She didn't plan on alleviating their concern any time soon.

"So," she began, her gaze catching and holding both of theirs. "You two are assigned to the local MAGIC unit."

The woman glared and jutted her chin in Sade's direction. It didn't take a mind-reader to know the agent did not like Sade. The male agent leaned back in his chair, crossed his legs, ankle to knee, and smiled—or at least the corners of his mouth quirked up. His eyes remained cold and flat. "We *are* the Magic unit," he said.

Sade didn't need to check the files on the desk to know these two would be trouble. She made a mental note to have another sit-down with her boss, FBI Director George Bailey. The personnel office was totally fucking up assignments again.

"When was the last time you two worked a magical crime?" Sade thought she'd kept her voice neutral, but evidently not because the woman leaned forward, eyes narrowed and hands fisted on the arms of the chair she occupied.

"You know damn good and well that we responded to that fiasco on the docks the other night. You were already on scene and you sandbagged us."

"Ease down, Campos," the man said, his tone patronizing. "I'm sure Agent Marquis had things under control."

Sade flashed him her patented cold-eyed smirk. "That's Senior Special Agent Marquis to you, Reed." She shouldn't have been so happy when his throat worked in a convulsive gulp, but it was the little things that counted. "And I would be the Senior Special Agent in charge of the MAGIC unit. That makes me your boss." Her gaze flicked to Campos. "And yes, my reputation for being a bitch precedes me. In this case, all the rumors are true. Suck it up, buttercup."

Uncrossing her ankles, Sade pushed one of the files across the desk using her heel. "What have you found on Levant Tremaine?"

Campos lowered her eyes and muttered, "Nothing." She followed that with a quick, "Yet."

Some of Reed's bravado had seeped back in because his own smirk was back in place. Sade ate agents like him for breakfast. She crossed her arms over her chest and waited.

"We only have the word of a street entertainer to go on. Personally, I don't think the man exists. Plus, from my research, there hasn't been a confirmed sorcerer in what? A century or more? We have better things to do than run down vague leads."

Sade watched Campos, beginning to understand the dynamics here. Reed would be the problem. She had hopes for Campos. "Check for long-term rentals and leases. Something large and private. He's not local but he's been here awhile and plans to stay longer. I don't think he'd buy but tug that thread if the rentals don't turn out. We need to do whatever it takes to run him to ground." She cut her eyes to Reed, dismissing Campos. He was smiling at her like he was sitting in the catbird seat. She smiled back, knowing he wasn't.

Campos hadn't moved. "You have an assignment, Campos," Sade reminded her.

The woman glared at Sade then at Reed before she stood, grabbed the file and marched to the door, her spine stiff. Sade watched her very carefully open then close the door after she passed through. She'd lay odds Campos remained just on the other side, ear pressed to the door in hopes of overhearing what Sade and Reed talked about. She'd make sure Campos got an earful.

⁕

TWO DAYS Sade had been looking for her suspect. The werewolves and the gargoyles had no more luck finding a trace of Levant Tremaine than the FBI. Campos had removed the chip on her shoulder and was working hard. Reed, was...still a misogynistic asshole. Sade would deal with him later, when she had the time to enjoy taking him down a few pegs. Sade would be so fucking happy when Caleb arrived. She missed having him cover her back.

She glanced at her watch. It was after sundown in Washington. She pulled out her cell phone, but it rang before she could dial. The name on the phone's screen put a smile on her face.

"Great minds," Sade said in lieu of a greeting. "I was just pulling out my phone to call you."

"You are unsettled, Lady Sade."

"Naw. It's just this case. I keep running into dead ends."

"Then I can presume you won't be coming home any time soon?"

"Probably not. Caleb is flying in Monday. That'll help. The fucking—"

"Language, Sade."

"Bloody gargoyles are a pain in my ass. Why are all the fucking—"

"Sade..."

"Bleeding magicks are such tight asses."

"Magicks are used to dealing with our own affairs, Sade. You are well aware of this by now."

"Yeah, yeah. I know. But this is Roman, Sinjen."

"Yes, it is. And he is special to you."

"He won't talk to me. It's all...gargoyle shit. Like what's going on is a big gawddamned secret that only the cool kids get to know and I'm not one of the cool kids. It sucks."

Sinjen's laughter rolled from the phone's speaker and it heated Sade's blood. Damn but she missed him. "You don't exactly play nice with others, Sade. Perhaps it is good for you to see how that feels from the flip side of the coin."

She muttered a lot of curse words under her breath. "There's something else, Sinjen." He waited in silence for her to continue. "About Roman. He...ah...you see...there's a girl. Well, a woman. A young one. Younger than me. He's..."

"He's taken her as a lover?" Sinjen asked softly.

"Well...yeah. And its fucking weird!"

"Why is it weird?"

"He's...so much older than her for one thing!"

Sinjen chuckled softly. "Pot, kettle, my love."

"That's different. *We're* different."

"And how is it different? I am over a thousand years

old."

"True, but you're human. Were human. Roman is…"

"A gargoyle."

"Well, yeah. And this girl…I don't care that she's in her twenties, she a girl compared to him."

"Sade, while some magicks may not be human, they all have the basic urge to…"

"To what? Mate? Procreate? Get down and have wild monkey sex? I get that. But the gargoyles? I mean…" She shuddered, and found herself at a loss. "They…according to Varrick, they aren't…you know…born." She whispered the last word.

"I am aware of that fact," Sinjen said dryly.

"See? It's all weird."

"Have you asked him about it?"

"Ewww. No! That would be like…asking Mathias. Or my dad. Caleb." She shuddered again. "Just…no. I don't want to think about any of them having sex."

"Up to you. I suggest that you think about us having sex instead." That startled a laugh out of her. "I must go, but consider discussing the situation, at least in general terms, with Roman. I love you, Lady Sade."

"I…uhm…yeah. Me too you." Sinjen's laughter in her ear carried her toward the Legation. She always suffered a bout of awkwardness when it came to telling the man she loved how she felt about him.

As she approached the door, Varrick appeared. "Is Roman upstairs?" she asked.

Varrick, looking more like a homeless person than a gargoyle warrior, shook his head. "No. I haven't seen him all day."

"Where are you off to all dressed up?"

Rolling his eyes, he side-stepped her. "Hot date."

"Dude! Seriously? If you're going out with the hot doc, you better change." He offered her a one-fingered salute as he sauntered off. "You'll be sorry," she called to his retreating back, laughing as she did so.

Her laughter faded as she stood on the walkway, deciding what to do next. She was frustrated from the lack of progress in the investigation. She should grab something to eat and head to her hotel to get some sleep, but she was too restless to settle. Turning on her heel, she headed toward the Mississippi River, just across Decatur Street. There was a promenade lined with benches along the river. When she'd been assigned to the New Orleans office as a young agent, Sade often sought the peace sitting beside the river brought.

The humid air hadn't cooled much from the heat of day and it had been a hot one for October. Sade swiped at the sweat on her forehead as she approached a bench where a familiar figure sat. She stood staring out across the water but watched Roman in her peripheral vision. She shoved her hands into her pockets, debating what to say. She eventually moved to the bench and dropped down beside the gargoyle.

"I remember a time when I sat here just like this. You had some very wise words for me then, Roman."

He said nothing so they sat in silence. No sounds echoed around them, not from the barges sliding by on the dark river, not from the traffic or people crowding the French Quarter scant blocks away. They could be sitting in a bubble.

"Who is she?" They both knew Sade was asking about Verity, and not just her name and pedigree.

Roman didn't move, didn't blink, his human facade as stony as his real form. He knew what he had to say. Honor. Duty. Both demanded his reply. His heart had no place here.

"No one. She is nothing." *She is everything*, his psyche screamed. She was his heart, his soul, and very likely his end.

"Uh huh." Sade continued to watch from the corner

of her eye. Very little got past her and she knew Roman as well as he knew her. She didn't miss the slight hesitation, the gravelly sound of dismay in that first word. "I call fucking bullshit."

He didn't chide her for her language. Feeling hollow inside, the on-going contest about her use of curse words seemed more effort than it was worth. Sade was her own woman now, responsible for her life and actions.

"Now I know something is wrong. Talk to me, Roman. You know I'll do whatever it takes to fix it." She'd noticed the lack of reprimand too.

"No." He pushed to his feet. "This does not concern you or the FBI." He walked away.

Sade jumped up, made to follow him. He shed all pretense of humanity, shifting in the blink of an eye into his natural form—a winged gargoyle with a visage meant to haunt demons. He spread his wings, launched into the air. With great sweeping beats, he surged into the sky. He glanced back, recognized both anger and determination on Sade's face as she shook her fist at him.

"This isn't over, Roman!"

He almost smiled.

CHAPTER SIXTEEN
THIS WILL NEVER END

ROMAN IGNORED the summons in his head. He was taking a chance, but he had things to do, provisions to make before he answered Crevan's demand for his presence. There was too much at stake. Too much he didn't know. Too much emotion. He gazed down at the sleeping Verity. She was his—in ways he couldn't comprehend but felt to the very core of him. He still had no proof as to her identity and until he did, he would not acquiesce to the order handed down by *Le Viele*.

The soft brush of awareness in his mind pulled his attention away from Verity. Leaving her sleeping in his bed each morning was becoming harder and harder. Maybe she truly was the black witch Crevan named her and even now her magic was wending its way through him, wrapping webs of deceit around him. If that was true, he was helpless because she filled with with light, with love. She filled the silence in his soul with a tender song.

Again, awareness touched him. He'd gotten lost in his thoughts—lost in Verity once again. He bent to kiss her—a firm touch of lips to her forehead, a gentle stroke of his lips across hers. She smiled in her sleep and he smiled in response.

Duty, he remembered. Straightening, he turned his back on her. He had much to set in motion before this day was done.

Varrick waited outside his door, a shoulder leaned against the wall that was his usual stance when he wasn't fighting. Roman closed the door and gestured for the other man to follow him. They climbed the stairs to the third floor. Darkness clung to the world outside the windows of his office. They were alone—two battle-hardened creatures unfit for anything but war. Except there was a woman asleep downstairs in his bed, a woman who had taught him how to be tender, how to make love, how to love.

"You have it bad, Roman."

He glanced at Varrick, acknowledgment of that statement plain on his face. "And I will face the consequences. Crevan has summoned me."

Varrick nodded. "I'm aware. I've been tasked with assuring you appear."

With a rueful shake of his head, Roman stared out the window into the pre-dawn silence. He was a gargoyle. First Sentinel. Defender. Guardian. Bringer of justice. He was not born. He was created. He was not supposed to have a heart. Yet still, the organ in his chest beat out a steady rhythm when he was in human guise. The office door *snicked*. Soft steps swept across the thick Persian rug covering the aged wooden floor.

"I haven't been to bed yet so this better be good, Roman. And there better be a fuck-ton of coffee." Sade dropped into one of the side chairs and plopped her booted feet on the antique desk. "How was your date, Varrick?"

"Better than yours," the gargoyle smirked, but he did hand her a mug of black coffee.

Sade inhaled deeply, drawing the coffee's aroma into her lungs. Dark roast with a touch of chicory. Oh yeah. She might just survive whatever the hell this meeting was about after all. "Am I to presume this is a strategy session?" She raised the mug to her mouth and took a big drink.

Roman continued staring out the window, measuring time by the minute increments of the earth's rotation. Throughout his life, time had been a constant. Others spoke of it slowing down or rushing past, but to him? And to all of the gargoyle race, he suspected, time was constant. Until the first time he saw Verity. Now, time was in constant flux. Sometimes, he wished for the safety from whence he once viewed the world. Before Verity, life was steady as he watched the world go by, one year passing to the next in the same rhythm that dawn turned to dusk, noon to midnight, each day, week, month, year holding a sameness that he knew and understood.

Then came Verity. Human with a touch of magick in her blood but a lifetime as short as a day in his existence. No, he amended, as he glanced over his shoulder. The first touch of mortality had come from Sade, when the bright-eyed toddler had wrapped her arms around his neck and whispered, *"I love you, Romo."*

In the years since, he had learned, watching the child grow into an awkward teen, the teen into an accomplished woman. If not for Sade, there would be no Verity. The passing years had taught him that, though he'd refused to acknowledge the lesson until that moment.

Now the clock was barreling forward and he had to race to catch up before time ran out. Until the sorcerer was found, until the Heart was safe, until the Crucible was...no. Verity was not the Crucible. Verity would not die. Not at his hands. Not at the hands of his brothers.

He turned away from the dark and faced the only two people he could trust in that moment. "I must be away for a while," he announced.

Sade dropped her feet to the floor and leaned forward in a motion so smooth the coffee in the mug didn't even ripple. She caught the glance Varrick gave Roman. "Where are you going?"

"The where doesn't matter." Roman raised his hand, palm out as Sade opened her mouth. "Nor does the why. Suffice it to say that I must go away. I leave you—each of you—with a charge." He waited until Sade's jaw snapped shut. "Verity will need to be watched over. She has a part to play in this."

"This *what*, Roman?" Sade persisted. "I'm fucking tired of all the innuendo, secrets, and half-truths you're feeding me. I can't do my job under these constraints. Hell, I can't even help because I don't gawdamn know what the fuck is going on."

"You have to trust me."

Sade's face contorted, her lips pressing together before her mouth formed a frown, forehead wrinkled, and then eyes scrunched closed before her expression cleared. She'd come to a decision. "No, Roman. I don't *have* to trust you." Her shoulders lifted in the barest of shrugs. "I just do."

Roman dropped his chin in acknowledgment then turned his gaze on Varrick. Everything that needed to be communicated was done in that one look. Varrick looked resigned but he, too, dropped his chin in agreement.

"Promise me," Roman said, his voice grating from the emotion welling in his chest. "Promise to keep her safe."

And then he was gone.

Sade snarled. "I fucking hate it when he does that." She glowered at Varrick. "Where did he go?"

Varrick didn't reply. He, too, teleported out, leaving Sade alone in the office. She let loose a string of curses, dug her cell out of her pocket, and stabbed out a phone number. The sleepy answer didn't improve her mood.

"I need you here yesterday."

A muffled voice said, "It's for you, Caleb."

ROMAN STOOD alone on the walkway outside the basilica built in the center of Le Creche. Flying buttresses soared above him, and stone gargoyles stared down from between the pinnacles, heights, and bell tower. None of them moved to acknowledge him. He approached the massive wood and iron doors. Archivolts, like steepled fingers, closed overhead. Jamb figures lined the walls, pointing the way to the entrance. Four steps from the portal, the double doors opened soundlessly.

He strode into the hushed expanse of the basilica. Sunlight streamed in from the high clerestory windows lining the upper reaches of the nave. His booted feet echoed on the stone floor.

Crevan, flanked by four other gargoyles, waited in the transept near the front of the church. Roman stopped before *Le Vieil*. Wordlessly, the gargoyle leader turned on his heel and led the way up the six steps to the apse. Two additional gargoyles waited on the opposite side of the altar. Crevan joined them. Roman's back was exposed to the empty cathedral. His four guards took up their positions—two at his sides, the others slightly to his rear.

"Do you know why you have been summoned to the Conclave, Roman Montagne?" Crevan's voice echoed through the soaring spaces.

Roman remained stoically silent. It was up to the one or more members of the Conclave to prove him renegade.

"I'll say it out loud." Jago Laron, Second Counselor, glowered at Roman. "I proclaim you traitor, Roman Montagne, and by the Codex of Garregyion, I call upon the Conclave to find you guilty and sentence you to the maximum punishment."

"Do you confess?" Crevan's voice came straight from the icy sepulcher hidden below their feet. Roman knew of the secret room. Knew what occurred there. He was First Sentinel. He had taken miscreants to that room, held them there, witnessed the punishment meted out, had doled it out when called upon.

"I confess to doing my duty as First Sentinel." Roman's voice rang with conviction. "I confess to loving the brotherhood. I con—"

"Do you confess to fornicating with the witch?" Jago interrupted. "To breaking the sacred commandment recorded within the Codex? To conspiring with she who is the Crucible of Eve to subjugate the realm of Garregyion to the will of a sorcerer?"

Roman ignored Jago, keeping his gaze focused on Crevan. While the Conclave had a vote in this matter, it was *Le Vieil* who held the ultimate authority. "From the first," he said in a voice as soft as rain pattering on stones. "You charged me with protecting the Heart. If I and my brothers were sung a lullaby as fledglings, it was your voice reciting the Prophecy.

Raising his eyes to the stone guardians perched along the upper reaches of the apse, Roman began to recite. "From the heart of darkness came the First, she who made no cry upon her birth to break the silence of the beyond. This Crucible of Eve carried within her the Heart of Stone and when she touched us with its magic, she bequeathed power to those of the Garregyion. Silent sentinels, were we. The seekers of truth, the bringers of justice, the guardians of the weak. As a daughter of Eve, the Crucible lived and died, only to live again, throughout the ages.

"Then came the first dark times, when magic and men fought. The Crucible was taken and sacrificed by the forces of evil, for they knew that to control the Heart was to control the Garregyion. We mourned as our brothers lay shattered upon the field of battle but we reclaimed the Heart and with it, a new brotherhood was created. Once more, we, the sentinels, stand against the dark.

"Time and again, the Crucible has returned to claim the Heart. Witchborn, the Crucible has been, and each time the Sentinels have sent her back into darkness for it is written: The one, true Crucible of Eve is lost to the shadows until the Heart of Stone echoes within the sound of silence. Suffer not to live the witch who is born marked as the Crucible of Eve for she brings only death and destruction.

"This we have vowed. Thus shall we honor our promise."

As Roman finished, the echoes of the last line of the prophecy whispered through every corner. Murmurs arose, a susurrus of sound like wings beating against the wind.

"We know the words of the tale," Jago snarled. "Why think you to remind us?"

"Because I believe there is truth to be found in Verity La Croix. I believe that she is the echo in the silence, the answer to the riddle, the Crucible of Eve destined to reclaim the Heart of Stone."

"Take him," Jago ordered. None of the guards moved, all of them looking to *Le Vieil* for his verdict.

"What riddle?" the Old One asked.

"Why does the Heart of Stone give us life but does not give us love?"

A veil of silence descended. Roman and Crevan might have been the only two beings present. Dust motes danced in rays of sunlight to music no one heard. The hush became almost deafening.

"We are incapable of love," Crevan said.

Roman countered, "Are we?"

"I would never have suspected you to be the one to

betray us, Roman. As you have pointed out, I have no heart for you to break yet I feel profound sadness at your unfaithfulness. You have challenged the very foundations of the Garregyion. My hands are tied." Crevan's human facade might as well have been carved from stone for all the emotion he displayed. He dipped his chin. The guards on either side of Roman closed in, securing him with steely grips.

Roman didn't resist. "This will never end," Roman said. "Until you answer the riddle. Until we become what we are truly meant to be. Until the prophecy is fulfilled."

"SILENCE!" Crevan turned away. His back to Roman, he threw back his head and roared. Then he walked away.

Bowing his head, Roman awaited his fate. He could only hope that when it came for him, Death would be kind.

CHAPTER SEVENTEEN
TURNING THE KNIFE

_____

AS HE HAD ONCE BEFORE, Tremaine sank onto the chair across from Verity and stretched his arm over a second chair. "I'm still waiting for my fortune," he purred.

Why had she escaped the Legate's offices? Fresh air, she'd said. Cabin fever. She missed the life swirling through the crowds inhabiting the French Quarter. She'd wanted to walk among the people, to sit in the open air. To feel...what? Human? She didn't know what was going on in the grand scheme of things, especially given the...*things* going on with Roman. She'd been foolish to leave the sanctuary of his home, but she hadn't seen him in several days. He'd abandoned the bed they shared, and no one would tell her his whereabouts—not Varrick, not Sade, and especially not the elfin woman, Ceylin.

"Well?" he snapped, wrenching her thoughts back to him.

The power emanating from the man occupying the chair across the table raised every hair on her body. What did he want with her? Deciding to bluff her way out of this until she could escape, she raised her chin. "I'm no longer in that business."

"Liar."

She blinked and jerked back, almost as if he'd hit her. The satisfied smile blooming on his coldly handsome face terrified her. There were lots of people here in the restaurant. Surely Tremaine would do nothing in front of witnesses. She was just across

Jackson Square from the Legation. The restaurant wall was lined with tall folding doors, most of them open to the cool breeze blowing in from the Mississippi. If she took off running, he might not be able to catch her.

Tremaine leaned in closer. "I have been searching my whole life for you, Verity Bernadette La Croix."

Somehow, her brain was still working despite the panic welling up in her chest. How did he know her full name? She shivered as his magic coiled around her, oily and noxious.

"What are you?"

A hard glint appeared in his eyes and she realized they were the color of polished black obsidian. Reflexively, she slid her hand into her pocket and wrapped it around the purple amethyst she'd secreted there before leaving.

"I am the man you were made to serve."

His imperial tone got her dander up. Verity pushed up out of her chair, tossing her napkin on the table. "Yeah, right. That's not gonna happen."

As quick as a snake, his hand darted out and fastened onto her arm. Fingers bit into her skin with icy ferocity. "Let. Me. Go." She bit out each word.

All conversation stopped and Verity felt every eye watching them. Good. She wanted an audience. "I said, let me go."

Tremaine's smile turned more calculating and he ignored the waiter approaching them. Verity vowed to come back and leave a big tip, then she shoved the table into the man holding her. Startled, he let her go and she ran for the nearest opening, only to bounce off a very hard, very tall, very irate man. She froze as Tremaine stopped a few feet away.

Her stare ping-ponged between the two men and she fought the urge to run. *No, don't run*, she reminded herself. Running attracted the attention of predators.

She really wished her magic would let her shapeshift into a little mouse so she could find a hole to creep into and hide until the power choking the room dissipated and things were safe.

Tremaine, elegant in his hand-tailored suit, Egyptian cotton shirt, and silk tie, appeared aloof but she saw the red flames of anger banked in his eyes. She eased away from him, one minute move at a time while he kept his gaze fixed on the interloper.

The other man—all six and a half feet and linebacker shoulders of him—blocked the door. His clothing was as rough as his demeanor. Ratty jeans, worn leather jacket, scuffed biker boots. There was no refinement in his bearing—just lethal intent. *This* was the man who had been in Roman's office the night of her attack, the one who'd who had gathered her scattered belongings and packed her wagon afterward. The other times she'd seen him at Roman's he'd been more suitably attired for business in the Legation offices. Why was Varrick here? And why was he protecting her? He hadn't seemed friendly to her at all, not in all the times she'd been around him.

"She's comin' with me." Tremaine's manicured hand shot out, wrapped around her arm. A desperate yelp escaped as strong fingers squeezed hard. She would have bruises later.

"No," the tall man decreed.

The hand on her arm burned her skin. She cried out, jerked away, but Tremaine's grip remained implacable. Magic surged, choking her, and then Alton was there, too. He snarled and people screamed. *Werewolf*, she suddenly remembered. Was he crazy enough to change right here? There were laws...weren't there?

Her brain felt fuzzy and she was having trouble making her muscles work. She stumbled as Tremaine jerked her through a different opening and they stepped onto the covered walk just outside. She blinked and now she and Tremaine were standing closer to the square as people scattered, leaving them positioned in an open space.

"Let me go," she protested weakly. Had the words even left her mouth? She focused on the arm Tremaine held and pulled. Nothing happened. Her legs were wobbly so she decided sitting would be a very good idea. Verity stopped fighting the lethargy in her muscles and went limp. She watched Alton clap hands over his ears, his mouth open in a howl she couldn't hear. They were only feet away from each other. She should be able to hear him. The gargoyle rushed forward. Her butt hit granite seconds before thunder and lightning left her deaf and blind. Then darkness swallowed her.

⁙ •

PEOPLE SCREAMED and ran. Alton, his ears bleeding, knelt beside the prone body of the gargoyle. He howled again, asking for help from those of his kind. He didn't expect aid to appear in the form of a leggy brunette and another werewolf wearing a suit. He needed to shift to heal himself. He didn't know what that fucker had done but it had to have been mega magic to take down a gargoyle and a werewolf.

"Caleb, look after Metallic Man there. I've got Varrick."

Either his hearing was coming back or Alton had learned to read lips. His nose twitched. There was something about the woman. He tilted his head and whined a little. She wasn't a magick. Not exactly. A strong hand clapped his shoulder.

"Yeah, Sade has that effect on a lot of people," the strange werewolf said. "You must be a Smith?" Alton managed a nod. "I'm Caleb Jones. I'm also an FBI agent. I'll call Deacon."

He managed another nod. Deacon coming would be a good thing. His brain felt like bread pudding while his insides felt much more like gumbo. Something white fluttered in his peripheral vision. A waiter from the restaurant was holding out a towel. The man gestured toward his own ears then stared at Alton's.

"You're bleeding," the waiter said.

"Uh huh."

The man knelt and used a second, damp towel to wipe away the blood before pressing the dry towel to Alton's ear. "Turn your head, cher, so I can see the other side."

Alton found himself leaning against the waiter's chest and the sense of safety, of rightness almost brought tears to his eyes. What the freak was wrong with him?

"I see you every day," the waiter said, his voice low and husky. "Entertaining the people. And knowing what you are, I tried to stay away."

Alton furrowed his brow as he processed the man's words. "You know?"

"I'm Rene," the waiter said. "And yes. I know." He dropped his glamour and Alton caught a glimpse of pointed ears.

"Elf?"

Rene nodded. "The FBI wolf called your Alpha. Someone will be here shortly, but I...I had to take the chance to introduce myself."

Alton smiled suddenly. "Hi, Rene. I'm Alton. Would you like to go out to dinner?"

Sade rolled her eyes and muttered, "New Orleans." She was trying very hard not to panic. Varrick was flat on his back, unblinking eyes staring up at the sky. His glamour was fading right before her eyes. This was bad.

Very bad. After picking up Caleb at the airport, she'd called both Roman's cell and the Legation office. The Elvin secretary would say only that Roman had not returned.

She couldn't exactly call Crevan. *Le Vieil* didn't carry a cell and getting Varrick to use telepathy to notify the head gargoyle was currently out of the question, since he'd turned to stone. He was an ugly brute in his statue form. She also had no way of knowing if he was still technically alive.

"Mental note," she muttered. "Dig out those ancient tomes on Magicks one-oh-one."

Caleb appeared at her side. "Looks like I got here just in time."

"Yeah, things are going south in a hurry. I can't contact Roman. Any chance you have some other gargoyle on speed dial?"

Before he could answer, Sade's ears popped, followed by the curious *poof* sound and air displacement that occurred when a gargoyle teleported. A man in what Sade could only describe as "fighting leathers" knelt down on the other side of Varrick.

"What happened here?" he demanded.

Sade scowled. "Who the hell are you?"

The gargoyle scowled back. "I am Tabar Sheva, the new Second Sentinel."

"Then you should know how to contact Roman. Call him."

"Not until—"

Sade whipped out her badge and ID. "Do you know who I am?" Tabar's eyebrows climbed high on his forehead, but he nodded. Sade continued. "A sorcerer just knocked Varrick and a werewolf on their asses and kidnapped a woman who is under Roman's protection. Call him the fuck right now."

Tabar looked stricken for a moment, then his

expression blanked. "Roman cannot come here."

"What the motherfucking why the hell not can't he?"

"He has been called in front of—" Tabar bit off his words, then continued with, "The matter is within the purview of the Garragyion. I cannot explain further."

Sade skipped right over the use of the true and formal name of the gargoyle race and jumped straight into take-no-prisoners territory. "You're fuckin' telling me this is a need to know situation? Bull shit. You tell the gawddamned *Le Vieil* that Roman arrives in the next sixty seconds or there will be hell to pay."

The gargoyle, his hand and focus on Varrick's stony body, didn't bother to respond.

Pushing to her feet, Sade raised her face to the sky. Caleb choked back a growl as he cautioned, "Think before you act, Sade. The Old One isn't someone you want to mess with."

She snorted. "I don't plan on messing with him. I plan on pissing him right the hell off. I fucking *know* why Roman has been called on the carpet. And that's where he is." She turned her glower on Tabar. "You had your chance. Now it's my turn." Feet spread, she fisted her hands on her hips and yelled, "Crevan, you sorry sonavabitch! You get your gravelly old ass here right now. And bring Roman with you."

Tabar might have turned to stone for all that he wasn't moving, not even to breathe. Varrick rubbed his face with his hand and grimaced. "You shouldn't have pissed her off, Second. The *Enfant de L'homme* is not exactly known for her patience or her diplomacy."

Everyone still hanging around Jackson Square froze. To Sade, it felt like the air was sucked out of the space leaving a vacuum behind. Yeah, she'd really pissed the Old One off this time. Frankly, she didn't give a rat's ass. She was plenty sick and tired of the games the magicks played and she'd be damned if she let Roman take a fall.

"*Tödlich.*" The word fell into the silence created by the vacuum. Sade covered her laughter with a smirk. The word was at once a description, a type of being, and a curse. *Mortal.* She qualified on all three counts.

The Old One appeared in front of her. She supposed his hocus pocus was meant to make her nervous. She cocked one hip and tilted her head in his direction. "Crevan."

He ignored her. "Where is the witchling?"

Crevan was staring at Varrick and Tabar but it was Sade who answered. "Taken."

He was forced to look at her now. "By whom?"

"Three guesses and the first two don't count."

"The sorcerer?"

"Well fuck me running, you got it in one. Yeah, the bastard took her." She marched up to him and jabbed his chest with her index finger. When she stopped to think about it, that was going to hurt. "And he wouldn't have if you hadn't jerked Roman's chain. If he'd been here—where he was supposed to be, guarding her, this wouldn't have happened." She gestured with her other hand toward the blackened granite slab where the sorcerer and Verity had been standing. "This is on your head, Crevan. We had this covered until you fucked it up. You get Roman back here right now or I swear to God—"

Her ears popped again and when she turned her head, Roman—far worse for the wear—lay in a crumpled heap a few feet away.

Crevan's face morphed into its stone beast counterpart. "The death of every brother is now on your head, Roman Montagne. Find the Heart and destroy Crucible before she destroys us all."

CHAPTER EIGHTEEN
ONLY HUMAN

DESPITE THE TOURISTS pressing closer to see the spectacle, Sade didn't hesitate. She took two running steps and launched herself at Crevan. The whole notion of taking down the gargoyle leader was stupid for two reasons—she'd inconveniently forgotten that Crevan could teleport, and already had. The second was the arm that caught her around the waist, stopping her mid-flight. She struggled against the hard body she'd been hauled to and pinned by a second arm.

"Let me the hell go!" She kicked and squirmed against the vice holding her.

"I see nothing has changed, Agent Marquis."

Sade froze despite the fact that smooth, sexy voice in her ear ignited every cell in her body. Bloody fucking dragon. "What the hell are you doing here, Nikos?"

"The royal family wishes to celebrate Halloween here in New Orleans. As always, I have accompanied them."

She stopped struggling, but the damned lizard didn't put her down. They had a history, one she didn't want repeated with the Drakon of the Kholikikos Clan of dragons. As Drakon, Nikos was the head of security for the Clan. "Then why aren't you at the Monteleone babysitting them?"

"Because a little fairy told me that my favorite FBI agent was causing a scene in Jackson Square. I wanted to see for myself if it was true. I'm always one to enjoy it when you make a spectacle of yourself, Sade."

"Let me go, Nikos."

"Do I hear an unspoken 'or else' at the end of that sentence?"

"I'm in the mood to kick some dragon butt so yeah, I'll say it out loud. Or else."

He released her suddenly, but she was ready. They'd played this game before. She hit the walkway with bent knees, her body balanced so she didn't face plant. Sade whirled to face him, but he was already backing up, arms out in the dragon's version of *I come in peace, don't mind me, I won't bite.*

Nikos studied her, his amusement showing plainly in his expression. Sade hated that sneaky lift to the corner of his mouth, the crinkling at the corners of his eyes, and that one damn brow lifted just enough to show he was laughing inside.

"You do know it is unwise to enrage the gargoyles, yes?" he asked, his voice somber.

"Yeah, just so long as they remember they shouldn't piss me off either."

Yes, nothing ever changed with her, Nikos thought. And smiled. He would never admit how much he missed this woman—from her flashing emerald eyes that reminded him of his favorite jewel to the small beauty mark at the corner of her mouth that he longed to kiss, despite knowing she belonged to another.

Varrick had regained his glamour and was now sitting up, with assistance from Tabar. Sade made note of that as she turned and moved with an economy of motion to kneel beside Roman. The gargoyle was in human form, so the damage that had been done to him was far more visible. She glared at Varrick. "They fucking tortured him?"

"It's complicated," the gargoyle said in a low voice. He glanced over his shoulder at Tabar. "He did not break." It wasn't a question. Varrick knew Roman. He also knew what punishment Crevan had decreed.

Sade was fucking furious. Her hands shook as she tried to find one spot on Roman's bared torso that didn't show signs of abuse. She couldn't even recognize his face, knew it was Roman only because he *was* Roman and she would know him anywhere, in any guise.

"Tell me what to do, Roman? How do I help you?"

A tourist leaned into her view, a cell phone held out. Sade snarled and knocked the phone out of the man's hand. Surging to her feet, she brought her booted heel down on the phone with enough force to shatter it. The guy opened his mouth to protest then got a good look at Sade's face. He backpedaled out of her reach.

Two mounted New Orleans police officers arrived. Sade flashed her badge and announced. "I'm Senior Special Agent Sade Marquis, FBI. This is a crime scene. I want this area cleared." She got a chorus of "Yes, ma'ams." She turned her angry gaze on the crowd. "The next asshole I catch taking pictures, videoing, or posting this on line is going to jail. Do I make myself clear?"

Someone in the crowd began to protest. "You can't-"

"The fucking hell I can't." Sade's voice painted Jackson Square with frost. She stood sentry between Roman and the bystanders until they backed away, helped along by the mounted police, and several officers on foot who'd arrived to assist. Once there was enough distance between the small group of magicks and the onlookers, Sade crouched beside Roman once more.

"Roman?" She hated that her voice broke in the middle of saying his name. The gargoyle named Tabar crouched on his other side. "Get the fuck away from him!"

Tabar held his hands, palms out, in front of him. "I wish only to help, Agent Marquis."

"Fuck you. We don't need your gawddamned help."

Varrick was on his feet now, though still a bit

wobbly. Deacon Smith and his second, Lazare, had arrived. They had Alton well in hand. With the help of the elfin waiter, they were moving him away from the scene. Sade would check with Deacon later.

Caleb and Nikos stood side-by-side, uneasy allies for the moment. Sade looked to them because she wasn't trusting even Varrick at the moment. "We need to move Roman to the Legation."

"I'll teleport him," Varrick offered.

"Oh hell no," Sade spat. She gritted her teeth but managed to ask Nikos, "Will you take him?"

Nikos looked nonplussed for a moment. "You didn't ask if I could."

"You're a fucking dragon. I figure you're capable of transporting him, especially in his human form."

Approaching much as he would an angry cat, Nikos walked over. "Yes. I will transport him. Caleb and I can get him up and then I can carry him." He glanced at his pale gray suit then down at Roman's bloody body. He didn't quite hide the look of distaste in time.

"Fucking hell, Nikos. Send the gawddamned dry-cleaning bill to me."

Caleb shooed Sade out of the way, then bent to leverage—with Nikos's help—Roman into a position where the dragon could pick up the gargoyle. In the blink of an eye, and without the ear-popping change in pressure, he and Roman winked out of sight.

"Go to Roman," Caleb urged. "I can handle things here."

Her mouth pressed into a grim line, Sade nodded. Ignoring Varrick and Tabar, she turned on her heel and walked through the crowd with great deliberation. By the time she reached the front of the cathedral, she was all but jogging. As soon as the Legation's door was closed behind her, she sprinted up the stairs to the second floor, pounded down the hallway, and swung into Roman's bedroom.

An older woman Sade didn't recognize stood beside the door. She had the ubiquitous black bag carried by doctors for what seemed like centuries open on the bed. As Sade watched, the woman's index finger sprouted a razor-sharp claw and the woman divested Roman of his ragged trousers.

Sade gave Nikos the fish eye. He shook his head, crossing the room to her. In a hushed voice, he explained. "This is Dr. Pallas. She is one of the royal physicians. I called her to come."

Surprised, Sade rocked back and blinked rapidly. This was a side of Nikos she hadn't expected. Overbearing, yes. In charge, definitely. Sexy, oh hell yeah. But compassionate? Then she remembered his reactions the first time they'd met. Here in New Orleans. During a murder investigation.

"Where's Dr. Theo?"

It was now Nikos' turn for surprise. "You remember him?"

She lifted a shoulder in an off-hand shrug. "Vaguely." She leaned so she could see around him. "Thank you."

"You're welcome."

The sincere politeness shocked them both into a long moment of silence. Varrick appeared in the doorway, looking worse for the wear. "Magic won't heal him," he muttered.

"What?"

"You heard me, Sade. Creven stripped him of..."

"His what, Varrick?"

The doctor lifted her head to stare at them, her eyes glittering amber. "His mágikus?"

Varrick nodded, feeling numb. "He will have to heal as a human heals."

"What does that mean?" Sade demanded, stepping

closer to the bed.

Dr. Pallas looked grim. "Exactly what it says, girl. No get out of here, all of you. I have work to do."

Nikos and Varrick herded Sade toward the sitting room. There was no way to get past the two magicks. They were both huge, strong, and waiting for her to try. They settled onto the soft furniture. Sade paced.

Caleb eventually joined them, as did Deacon. The two werewolves raided the kitchen and returned with muffulatas and coffee. The men ate. Sade paced. Nikos eventually left, without saying a word. Sade took his departure as the opportunity to dash down the hallway to Roman's room. Varrick beat her.

"Fucking gargoyle magic teleportation," she groused.

"There is nothing you can do here, Sade," Varrick insisted. "You are only human."

"So the fuck what? I can stand guard. I can keep the motherfucking gargoyles away from him. I can—"

"Go to the hotel and get some rest," Caleb added. "I'll stay here. Deacon is here. And Varrick."

Sade snarled. Caleb shook his head at her. "Despite what you think, Varrick is on our side. On Roman's side. We need to find Verity, Sade. And you need to figure out how we are going to do that. You're the brains of this operation."

Only barely placated, but aware that she would plan better without the distractions and anger swirling around the Legation, she acquiesced.

"Okay. Fine. Whatever."

SADE SLOGGED down the hallway toward her hotel room. Nights like this, she really missed her old apartment. She'd done time at the FBI office here in

New Orleans back when she'd been a young agent. Her apartment, located above her favorite hangout—and which might account for Deja Vu *being* her favorite, was old school French Quarter. Shabby chic, with wooden floors, tall windows and that hint of history. She'd made the place into her first home.

Duty had called her elsewhere and when the Big Rip set the world on its ear, Sade ended up in Washington. Except she kept getting sent to New Orleans. Granted, *everyone* wanted to come to New Orleans. It was an amazing place, except she was coming to hate hotels. And dragons. What the hell was Nikos Constantine doing in New Orleans at this exact moment in time? She didn't believe for a minute his only reason for being in New Orleans was because the royal spoiled brats wanted to trick-or-treat on Bourbon Street. And finding her in Jackson Square? It was like he had some sort of internal tracking system where she was concerned.

They'd first met when she was in New Orleans investigating a series of murders, including the dragon nanny to the royal family. He'd expressed an interest in Sade—a *romantic* interest. And the damn lizard had continued to pursue her. She had her hands full with Sinjen St. John, the master vampire who'd claimed her heart during a case in Chicago. Sinjen and and Nikos in the same town was just...no.

And then tonight? After he'd taken off from the Legation and she'd been exiled? There she was walking down Bourbon Street minding her own business and who did she bump—literally—into? Nikolaus Constantine, Drakon of the Khokilokis Dragon Clan. She'd landed on her ass. He'd picked her up and insisted on buying her dinner. She'd finally ditched him by going to the ladies room and ducking out the back door of the restaurant. She had too much going on to deal with the libidinous dragon. Even if he had helped Roman. Nikos never did anything without ulterior motives.

She unlocked the door to her room. Her stomach grumbled as scents wafted from the plastic bag she carried. Settling at the work desk, she dug out the bleu cheese burger she'd picked up from Deja Vu and bit into it with a self-satisfied groan. She needed a plan. While she ate, Sade made notes. Wearing comfortable jeans and an FBI sweatshirt, she stared at the list she'd made.

1. Avoid the dragon
2. Find the girl
3. Avoid the freaking dragon
4. Get Caleb permanently assigned to this case
5. Avoid the bloodybuggeringfecking dragon
6. Find out where Ariel is to see if he can help find the girl
7. Avoid the muthergushingfirebreathing dragon
8. Other
    Things I found on the internet I need to ask about
        Sinjen re: gargoyles and Templars
        Ditto Roman and/or Varrick on gargoyle history
    How to avoid fucking dragons

Yeah, she'd get right on all that shit. Someone tapped on the door. She pushed out of the desk chair, her Beretta 9mm in her hand. Four strides later, she was looking out the peep hole. She stood there for a moment as emotions crashed through her. Relief. Surprise. Lust. Love. And then, as the tide rolled away leaving her limp, she found her personal demon—worry that Sinjen would stop loving her—hiding in the dark space under the stairs in her psyche.

"It's me, Sade. Open the door, love."

Sinjen's richly accented voice penetrated the door, soothing her almost as much as his touch would. She fumbled with the locks, jerked the door open, and fell into his arms.

"Well, no need to ask if you've missed me." He pushed into the room, kissing her.

Returning Sinjen's kisses with wild abandon, Sade kicked the door shut, but it banged into something solid. She froze, staring over Sinjen's shoulder at the other man standing in the doorway. So much for avoiding the fucking dragon.

"Did you miss me too, Sade?"

"No."

Sade sidestepped Sinjen and lunged. Nikos never saw her fist coming. Sinjen grabbed her around the waist but Sade kicked out and jerked against his hold—like she had a snowball's chance in a dragon's lair of getting away from the vampire. "Why is he here?" she demanded, a snarl in her voice.

"Ah, *khriso mou.* I have missed the lovely green fire of your eyes." Nikos spoke through the hand that was rubbing his nose. He turned to Sinjen, his expression cocky. "See, my friend, I told you she had missed me."

Sade glowered at the dragon. "Go to hell, Nikos."

"I am Greek. We don't believe in hell."

Sade threw up her hands. "What the fuck, Sinjen?"

The vampire stood very still, every muscle on his face frozen. If he smiled, she'd come for him next and while he enjoyed her fire probably more than the dragon did, he had other ideas for ways to extinguish it and none of them included the Greek watching them make love. "We bumped into each other at the Legate's office."

Glancing at her watch, Sade gave Sinjen a stink eye. "It's an hour after sundown. How are you even here?" She favored Nikos with a look that was both distrustful and disdainful. "And you've already checked in with Roman, or so you told me when you dragged me kicking and screaming to dinner."

"From which you disappeared in a most precipitous manner."

Sinjen was a master vampire. There was a story here but he kept his expression bland as Sade retorted, but she was addressing him.

"Bloody fucking dragon knocked me on my ass in the middle of Bourbon Street and then he literally dragged me off to a restaurant. I told him I had to pee. Not even a *dragon* can argue with that."

Cutting his eyes to the dragon, Sinjen didn't have to wait long.

"She ostensibly went to the loo and ducked out the back door. I must admit I was a bit disappointed. I was hoping she'd stay and argue." Nikos favored Sinjen with a knowing look. "And we all know how she likes to argue."

This time, Nikos saw the fist flying toward his chin.

CHAPTER NINETEEN
REUNION

_____

SINJEN GRABBED Sade's fist and examined the knuckles. They were already swelling and turning blue. He sighed. The human he'd claimed as his own was strong, willful, and completely fearless.

His gaze as sharp as daggers, Nikos focused on Sade. "Was that truly necessary? By my calculation, you owe me, Sade."

Only his arm wound around Sade's middle kept her from launching at the dragon. Sinjen bent to her ear. "Cease, Sade. We need to talk." He raised his head and focused on Nikos. "She does not owe you. You helped the Legate of New Orleans."

"At her request."

Sade threw up her hands, almost clocking Sinjen in the jaw. Had he been human, she likely would have put him on his arse. As it was, his reflexes saved him the embarrassment.

"Listen up you motherfucking lizard—"

Sinjen tightened his arm and Sade's breath whooshed out, effectively cutting off her tirade. "I said enough. Both of you need to put aside this petty competition—"

Angry words from both human and dragon drowned out the rest of his sentence. Sinjen rolled his eyes. "The two of you are acting like fae."

The bickering immediately stopped.

"That is so not fair," Sade muttered, but she relaxed against him. Sinjen dared take a deep breath as he waited for the dragon's response.

"Actually," Nikos said, rubbing his chin with thumb and forefinger in a thoughtful gesture, "we are."

"Fine. Whatever." Sade rolled her eyes at Sinjen as she wiggled loose from his hold before returning her attention to Nikos. "Care to explain what's going on?"

"As I explained in the square earlier, I'm here in my official capacity. The royal family comes to New Orleans every year for Halloween though the Old Gods only know why. Princess Elani, glamoured as a unicorn with a mane and tail colored like the rainbow, can prance around the royal palace just as easily as she can the Hotel Monteleone."

Sade choked back a laugh. "Wait. The kids actually glamour their Halloween costumes?"

Nikos hit her with a narrow-eyed glare. "As I was saying, I actually was headed to the Legate's office to register our party when the wave of black magic hit." Nikos rubbed the side of his neck, feeling a bit chagrined. "It was strong enough to stun me for a moment. By the time I arrived at the epicenter, you were launching yourself at *Le Vieil*." He didn't bother hiding the chiding tone in his voice.

Sade offered him a grim smile. "I might have caught him too, if you hadn't intervened."

"Then Caleb, Varrick, and I would have been mopping up pieces of you to deliver to your lover." Nikos gestured toward Sinjen, offering him the floor.

"*Le Vieil* popped in to say hello this evening." Sinjen took up the tale. "It appears that I'm not the only one who has a debt to repay. Except it's one of which I was unaware."

Sade's gaze darted between the two men. "Uh...huh." The corners of her mouth turned down and two sets of eyes focused on her beauty mark. She ignored their reaction, her brain already working on the puzzle. She began pacing.

Nikos moved to the space between the bed and the closet to get out of her way. Sinjen settled a hip on the desk, glancing down at the pad of paper lying there. He had to work to keep his expression carefully neutral—but for the self-satisfied smirk he winged toward the dragon. Sinjen was all in favor of the list Sade had made.

"I saw that smirk," Sade muttered as she brushed past Sinjen. She hit the exit door, pivoted and walked back to the windows overlooking the inner courtyard. She stopped and stared out at the patch of night sky just visible above the buildings crowding around.

"Black magic," she said. She glanced over her shoulder at Sinjen. "Like the Witch's?"

He shook his head. "No. From what I've been able to glean from the gargoyles, the dragon, and Caleb, it comes from a sorcerer."

Turning, she leaned against the windowsill. "I thought all the sorcerers were dead, and if they are, where did this one come from?"

"It's true the gargoyle sentinels hunted them down after the last war," Nikos said. "All practitioners were executed and their bloodlines cleansed."

Sade jerked and blinked. "Wait. Their bloodlines cleansed? What the fuck does that mean?"

"What you suspect it does," Sinjen replied softly. "Like the witch and wizard lines, magic runs in the blood. Also like the human magicks, blood does not always run true. That's why some humans have the barest touch of magic."

Dropping her head so that her chin rested against her chest, Sade closed her eyes. "How do we catch a sorcerer?"

"Very carefully," Sinjen said. "Especially one who can knock a werewolf, a gargoyle Sentinel and a dragon on their collective arses." He pushed off the desk. "You need to pack your things, Sade."

"Why?"

"Because you are checking out. We're moving into the Legation for the duration."

"Now you just wait—"

"No, Sade. Think about this. There is no protection in this hotel. For either of us."

She snapped her mouth shut and swallowed her angry rebuttal. Yeah...there were no metal shutters on the windows and unless Sade wanted to stick around all day, there was no guarantee that the maid or anyone else wouldn't just mosey on inside. Sinjen was mostly helpless during the day sleep.

"He's right, Sade," Nikos chimed in. "What safeguards could be activated would not keep out anyone—magick or mundane—with an ounce of talent. Until we pick up the sorcerer's trail—"

"We?" Sade's eyes flashed emerald bright, and both men noticed.

Nikos held up a hand. "We. As Sinjen pointed out, any sorcerer strong enough to incapacitate the ones he did this afternoon will require a combined force to take down."

"Don't look this particular gift horse in the mouth, Sade," Sinjen murmured under his breath. She growled in response but pushed off the windowsill and shooed them out of the way so she could pack.

"All my instincts are telling me to keep you guys out of this," she groused. "This is one ride-along I'm not sure you want to take."

NIKOS LEFT them at the door of the Legation. He intended to convince the royal family to return to their home in Greece if not the dragon realm itself. He, Xan, and Stavros would remain in New Orleans to assist with the hunt. Sade had agreed to the plan with reluctance.

Varrick met them on the second floor. He, apparently, had named himself Vice Legate and was running things. He showed them to an interior bedroom. Sunlight would not be a problem here and even Sade could feel the wards on the door. Of course, anyone stupid enough to attack the Legation would be facing the entire force of the Concilium Magicae. Not even a sorcerer could be that dumb. She hoped.

Just after midnight, Sinjen called a halt to the planning session Sade and Varrick had been engaged in. "I have not seen you in over a week, Sade."

Varrick took the hint and left with a muttered, "I need to check on Roman."

Sade eyed Sinjen. She was wary and dark circles below her eyes made her look bruised. "I don't like being away from you, Lady Sade," he said, his voice husky. "You look tired. I believe it is time for bed."

She waggled her eyebrows at him. "Something tells me if I go to bed with you, I won't be getting much sleep."

"You will afterward."

Sade was still laughing as he dumped her on the large bed in their assigned room. She bounced twice before he landed beside her, pinning her down with his hard, masculine body.

"Those clothes look uncomfortable. Allow me to help. Please." Sinjen trailed a fingertip along the plackets of her silky shirt, then dipping it beneath the material into the black lace bra cupping her breasts.

"Sure," Sade said on a breathless sigh as she arched toward him. "Help yourself."

He made short work of undressing her and when she reached to do the same for him, he captured her hands. Holding them pressed between his larger, stronger ones, Sinjen studied her face, blinking when the ghost of a memory danced between them. Even though she was lying soft and compliant beneath him, he saw the Sade who was present the first time they met. Brusque. Professional. Booted feet tapping on the concrete floor of his prison. He'd almost forgotten about the impact she'd had on him. At the time, he decided keeping an emotional distance between them would best suit his plans. even though his body demanded otherwise. The reality of her had been a bucket of ice water dumped over his head.

Later, when she'd finally given in, had finally accepted they were meant to be together, her sweet surrender had undone him. She'd had tears in her eyes when she touched him the first time, and he had taken her with such sweet tenderness that his own had been mist-filled. He didn't believe in fated mates like the shifters did, nor did he give the poets any more credence with their soul mate nonsense. At least not until he'd first laid eyes on Sade Marquis.

A week apart and he'd missed everything about her—the soft texture of her skin, the citrusy scent of her hair, the hungry little noises she made deep in her throat when he took her nipple into his mouth. He kissed his way down her body, spreading her as the heady scent of her arousal filled his nose. He looked up the long, lean length of her and smiled. Her dark hair was tumbled across the pillow, her eyes were closed, her body arching in anticipation. Then he lowered his head and the hot, rich taste of her filled his mouth. He gripped her hips, holding her close while kissing her most intimate place.

Sade demolished him—his desire burning him from the inside out. She was his everything. He looked at her and knew that as long as he had her, he would never want or need anything more. He refused to imagine life without her. The intense feelings he had for her was a mistake, but he didn't care. Hearing her breathless moan when he drove her over the edge, sinking into her welcoming depths, awaking to find her in his arms—any danger that presented was worth taking the chance. He smirked a little, knowing that element of danger was part of the allure. Still, he would lay waste to the world should something happen to her.

Sinjen concentrated on driving her wild and was rewarded by a keening moan and the arch of her hips as she surged off the bed. He held her in place by moving his body up hers. The little purring noise she was now making tickled his ear.

"I do believe you've missed me, Lady Sade."

She managed to control her breathing enough to mutter, "Yeah? Seems like the other way around to me."

He smiled. "We shall see," he murmured against her temple as he reached down and fitted his erection against her. When he surged inside her tight channel, she gasped and her nails raked across his bare back. Oh, yes. She *had* missed him. She wrapped her legs around his waist and he took the hint, rolling to the side. She adjusted her legs so that she was on her knees straddling him as he landed on his back.

"Hot damn." Sade growled a little as she rose up and then dropped back down on him. "This is a personal favorite." She rode him like a demon, hard and fast and when his fingers bit into her thighs, she stopped, holding the tip of his erection just inside.

Sinjen's sapphire eyes glittered as he stared up at her. "Hussy."

Laughing, Sade agreed. "Damn sure am and don't you forget it." She worked him slowly now, drawing out things, teasing and tormenting.

"Perfect," he murmured.

She smiled. "Yes," she agreed. "You are."

Before she could react, Sinjen turned the tables on her again. She was beneath him once more. His hips surged against her as he took over, setting a driving rhythm. He stared down at her, holding her gaze. He fisted one hand in her tumble of hair, gripping hard so she couldn't look away.

They were drowning in a storm of desire, lost in each other. His mouth found hers and he thought to feast on her but it was Sade who took over the kiss, Holding him, her greedy mouth fixed to his, sucking and tasting. She matched his thrusts with swiveling hips. Her inner muscles were as greedy as her mouth, gripping his cock each time he withdrew, clinging with tenacious need. More. He wanted—no, he *needed* more. He was desperate to have all of her.

"You do," she murmured into his mouth. "Always."

Sinjen wanted this feeling to last forever, the jolts of pure sensation rocking his core, the anticipation sizzling across his skin. It was always like this with Sade, had been from the first moment he saw her. "The night we met," he said.

"I remember."

"You terrified me. You still do." He hadn't meant to admit that.

"I know." A faint smile tinged with regret tugged at her lips—lips wet and swollen from his kiss. "That's a two-way street."

She cried out, her whole body jolting from the climax rocketing through her. He followed her, pumping his life into her. They lay sprawled together, tangled in sheets and covers, both breathless. Even after so many centuries of not needing to breathe, Sinjen found himself panting. Gaining a modicum of control, he watched her.

No longer quite so desperate to take her, he could finesse his desire. He cupped her face and his cock twitched to life. *Or maybe not,* he thought wryly. She blinked slowly and as her eyelids opened, he fell into the dazzling emerald fire lit within them. *He* did that to her. Only him.

Sade studied him, the knife-sharp lines and planes of his face, the shadow of the beard that always surprised her, and his eyes, the brilliant crystalline blue of sapphires. His black hair tumbled over his forehead and she reached over to brush it back. "Does it ever wear off?" she asked, her voice husky from their love-making.

"No." He knew exactly what she was asking. "It never does, nor will I ever tire of it. Of you."

She smiled then, a brief, hesitant quirk of one corner of her mouth followed by the period placed there by her beauty mark. Would she ever feel secure in his love? Sinjen planned on spending the rest of her life convincing her of it.

Something wicked glinted in her bottle-green eyes then she was pushing against him, urging him to his back. "I want to do things to you," she murmured, her gaze raking him from head to toe then returning to his groin.

He groaned but managed to say, "Do whatever you want to me."

She rolled on top, arching and curling against him. His lungs shouldn't burn and his heart should not be beating. He hadn't been alive since the time of the Crusades yet this woman brought him to life. His skin was so hot he felt like he was melting and that wasn't right either. Only Sade could do this to him. Only Sade *did* this to him. Sinjen was never *warm*. Not that he was cold or anything but vampires did not run at 98.2 degrees Fahrenheit like humans. When he was with Sade, when she touched him, her hands left trails of fire dancing across his skin. The feeling was glorious.

Her hands and lips explored his chest, his abdomen and then went lower. He sucked in air as his cock sprang fully to life. Her mouth was voracious as she took him inside. She owned him in that moment and he was her willing slave. Without conscious thought, he buried his hands in her thick, silken hair, tugging and pulling. He wasn't ready to let go. Not yet. Not until he was buried inside her sweet body once again.

Sinjen's strong hands lifted her head and then, between one breath and the next, Sade was flat on her back, and he was between her legs, his very nimble fingers stroking and teasing her until she was writhing.

"Inside me. Now!" she demanded.

He needed no further urging. He drove inside her. Any idea of taking her slow fled. He plunged into her time and again. He need for her was as sharp as broken glass. Her heartbeat raged beneath his hand as he cupped her breast. His vision blurred for a moment and he had to blink to clear it. He wanted to watch her come apart for him, because of him. Gritting his teeth as his own climax threatened, he watched her eyes darken, lose focus. He felt her shudders and then he buried his face in her hair, breathing her deep, knowing he would hold her inside him throughout eternity, as he emptied into her again.

Sade shudder again as aftershocks rocked her body. She felt Sinjen twitch deep inside her in response. "You okay?" she murmured.

His only reply was a very self-satisfied grunt. She laughed. He groaned, but he managed to get his arms under him and push up so she wasn't bearing his full weight.

"Gods, woman."

She gloated, and he laughed this time. Her hair spilled across her bare shoulders but he could see the throbbing pulse point in her neck. He could almost taste her.

Drenched in sweat, limp with the pleasure only Sinjen gave her, Sade calmed her body. His ragged breathing and Sinjen's intense focus on her neck satisfied her to no end. She reached up and tangled her fingers in his hair. "Yes," she murmured before closing her eyes.

Sinjen lowered himself to lay against her. He toyed with her hair, wrapping his fingers up in strands of it. When Sade lifted her chin and tilted it, he gave in to his basest instinct and fed at her neck.

Sade drifted as he fed, but then his hand slid between her thighs. He touched her, aroused her yet again, and when the hot wave of pleasure hit, she arched against him, flashing white hot with each pulse of her heartbeat.

A very long time later, she slid into sleep. Sinjen held her, his heart at peace, even as he worried. Sade was human. He was not. Would he be able to let her go when the time came?

CHAPTER TWENTY
OUT OF REACH

DESPITE THE STILTED CONVERSATION she'd previously held with Varrick, this was not a topic Sade wished to discuss with Roman. Roman was...if not a father figure exactly, he was a reasonable facsimile of a big brother. Still, the aura of sorrow clouding the air tugged at her conscience. She couldn't leave him hurting. Not like this. It was bad enough his physical wounds were slow to heal. The emotional scars were beyond her comprehension.

Roman had insisted on getting out of bed, of taking over his duties as Legate. He sat behind the wide desk, half-turned toward the window and the vista of historic buildings. She'd already reported no headway on tracking down Tremaine *or* Verity.

"We'll find her, Roman. I promise you."

She could only see his face in profile. "Perhaps it would be easier if you didn't."

"What the hell does that mean?"

"It's...complicated."

"No shit. Life is complicated." She threw up her hands to emphasis her point. "I'm not sure I understand the problem, Roman. You like her. She likes you. You're both old enough—" She choked back a laugh. Roman was a millenniums old gargoyle. "Well, you're both old enough. We'll bring her back, Roman, and then the two of you can work things out."

Roman scrubbed his hands through his shaggy hair, tried to marshal his thoughts. "My kind...we aren't...made for this."

Somewhere in the back of her mind, an old Eurythmics song played. Yeah, sweet dreams definitely weren't made of this, but what did Roman mean?

"Aren't made for what?"

He glanced around the room, expression troubled, his eyes shuttered. "For...*this*." He flicked his hand between them.

Sade's shoulders lifted in a half shrug, her elbows tight to her waist, but bent so her hands, palms up, were splayed wide, her expression torn between amused and exasperated. "This *what*, Roman? Carrying on a conversation?"

"Caring, Sade. There is a reason we are made as we are. We are guardians charged with upholding justice and meting it out when warranted. We were imbued with life by those with hearts of faith and righteousness. It was not until we gained the magic of glamour allowing us to move freely in the realm of Men that we learned of the..." The rest of his words were lost as he dropped his chin and muttered them into his chest.

Sade thought he'd said something about the sins of the flesh and whatever humor she'd found in this situation fled. She'd never seen Roman so bewildered. "Hey, it's not like you haven't...uhm...done it before, right?" She prayed she wasn't blushing.

"I'm no stranger to sex, Sade." Roman was oddly affronted by her implication, especially given his earlier reaction. Gargoyles weren't born of a loving act between a male and female. They were created whole cloth—or stone, technically speaking. Until they'd acquired glamour, they'd been asexual, their hearts truly made of stone.

"Then what's the big deal? Is your attraction so hard for you to believe?"

He stared out the window, the French Quarter unseen beyond. His voice came out ragged. "Some nights I can taste regret on my tongue, long after I have kissed her and she is asleep in my arms. Verity deserves a real man. One who can love her as she deserves, who can share life with her. A man who will give her hope and love."

Instead of death, Roman thought. At his hands. Judge, jury, executioner. The witchling's guilt or innocence his duty to decide. Regret remained a bitter taste on his tongue. And his heart, though carved from stone, shattered.

⁕

VERITY CHOKED down her fear as she tried to remember. What time was it? What *day* was it? Cobwebs clung to her memories, but she brushed them away. Roman. The attack in front of the cathedral. Roman. His bed.

She flushed as those memories washed over her and the image of them in bed made her squirm. Hearing voices, she held her breath. They moved off. She assessed the situation, thinking more clearly now. She was in a room. Shadows haunted the corners and she got the impression this was a large space. Focusing on her breathing, she slowed the rabbiting beat of her heart. Slow and steady, she reminded herself.

Her eyes adjusted to the gloom and she looked up. High windows, so grimy only a smidgeon of light penetrated, ringed the space. A warehouse? Perhaps. Or an abandoned church. Verity remembered a bit more— bits and pieces of conversation about a dark sorcerer. She slipped her hand into her pocket but there was nothing there. What was she looking for? Another flash of insight. The crystal ball she'd taken from that room in Roman's apartment. But it wouldn't fit in her pocket. And she hadn't taken her backpack when she slipped out for...lunch.

Everything came back in a crashing cascade—everything and...more. It was like she'd been living in a bubble and when she'd been transported to...wherever she was, the bubble had burst. She could feel the magic stirring inside her.

Would the crystal ball have saved her? If she'd taken it instead of the rose amethyst she'd slipped into her pocket? She didn't know but a hint of intuition intimated it was a good thing she'd left it behind. Verity was now positive she had to keep the crystal away from Tremaine. With that knowledge came a surge of strength.

She'd always been timid—not shy per se because she couldn't interact with the public the way she did had that been the case. No, she'd always felt...inadequate. Her magic was weak, shaky at best, though her intuition was strong, as was her ability to read people. But now? Her left hand curled into a fist, an ache radiating up her arm. She longed for the crystal ball, cognizant that it held real power—power she suspected only she could unleash.

With that soul-deep knowing, her crippling fear dissipated like morning sun burning off the river's fog. She felt invigorated but not cocky. No. She was still in danger but she could feel her magic stirring, unfolding, gathering inside her. She'd been asleep and now she was fully awake. And she remembered everything.

There you are, cher, Baba Rawnie whispered from the shadows. *I was wrong. The one you call Roman? You carry his heart of stone. Remember that. It will see you through the storm that is breaking.*

Somewhere, a door creaked, and the ghost of Baba Rawnie fled. That was okay. Verity understood now. She wasn't practiced but she had her instincts to guide her and the Old Gods had a way of making their wishes known. Her attention was drawn to one of the walls and she could just make out lines of light. The doorway. She shifted on the bare floor of that empty room, sitting lotus style, hands on her knees, chin up, ready to face whatever came through the door when it opened.

Footsteps echoed hollowly and then a key grated in the lock. The door swung open. Verity held her breath, then let it out slowly as Levant Tremaine stepped into the room.

"You have caused me a great deal of trouble."

Verity just continued to stare at him.

"Do you know who you are?"

She remained silent.

"Do not believe that obstinance will help you, girl."

She almost opened her mouth to protest. She wasn't a girl. Not anymore. She was a woman. Young still, especially where her power was concerned but she was not a girl. She gritted her teeth.

Tremaine was silent for several minutes. Then the door opened and two men wrestled a table through it. A third man followed, carrying a ladderback armchair. They situated the table not far from where she sat and the man set the chair on the side nearest the door. When Tremaine snapped his fingers, the first two men strode over and grabbed her. She squirmed, kicking and jerking, but she remained silent. She wasn't sure why but it seemed important. They deposited her in the chair and a moment later, she was trussed up, wrists tied to the arms of the chair.

Verity refused to show the fear welling up inside her. She had a part to play in whatever catastrophe was getting ready to hit the world. If Baba Rawnie hadn't hidden her talents, Verity would have felt the storm clouds gathering her whole life. She might not be any more prepared for what was to come, but at least she would have had some forewarning.

"I have a task for you," Tremaine said.

She looked up and shook herself mentally. She couldn't afford lapses in concentration like the one she'd just indulged in. The sorcerer now occupied a throne-like chair plumped with cushions and draped with rich fabrics. She half-way expected him to have donned a black satin robe emblazoned with stars, moons, suns, and various arcane symbols. He hadn't. He wore tailored black slacks with a knife-edge crease and a black dress shirt, open at the throat. He shifted on the chair and she realized the shirt was unbuttoned half-way. Was that supposed to be sexy?

After being with a gargoyle, this guy was just...pitiful. Still, she remembered bumping into him in the rain and the frisson of energy that ran through her during the encounter. She hadn't feared him then, even thought he was courteous in an old-world way that she sort of found attractive. Until he'd come back demanding she tell his fortune.

Tremaine pounded on the table, startling her. A wooden box now occupied the space in front of her. "Open it," he ordered.

She stared at him, fairly certain her expression implied her feelings—that he was Captain Obvious and had just been promoted to general. She made a show of trying to lift her arms, reminding him that her wrists were tied.

He turned, staring into the shadows. "Untie her once I am gone. One of you will remain to make sure she works the crystal."

She caught the low grumbles but none of the men articulated their opposition to his orders. He strode to the door, his heels tapping on the stone flooring like dance shoes. Once he'd departed, the three men materialized.

One slid a knife from the sheath on his belt and

sliced the ropes binding her. She sat silent and unmoving. The other two left the room. Knife man settled on the throne. He stared at her for a long period of time then he started cleaning under his nails with the tip of his knife. "You heard the man. Open the box."

Verity had no intention of doing so. She gripped the arms of the chair until her knuckles turned white.

"Suit yourself." The guy pushed out of the chair. He was tall enough that he only had to lean forward slightly to touch the box. He flipped the latch and opened it. The lid fell back on silver hinges. Inside, cushioned in a nest of black velvet, a chunk of quartz crystal with a bloodstone embedded the center seemed to glow in the anemic light. She had no desire to touch it. The thing didn't call to her, didn't make her blood sing like the one she'd found at Roman's.

The man dragged the throne closer and tumbled back into it. His booted feet landed on the table with a thump. "I've got all day but you don't. I guarantee that if you don't work your magic on that thing, Tremaine's gonna come back and make you wish you had."

Leaning back in her chair, Verity stared at him, ignoring the box and the crystal. She needed to think. Yes, she could touch her magic. Finally. But there was something missing. Some key she needed to turn to understand and control it. She wanted to curse Baba Rawnie. Her grandmother. Her mother. Her father. Her magic coiled a little tighter. Curious. She thought about Baba Rawnie. The magic stilled. Her grandmother. Nothing. Her mother. Nothing. She turned her thoughts to the man she knew nothing about, to the man whose seed had given her life. And to the leather belt with Celtic runes carved into the iron buckle that had a fire opal set in the center of it.

Her fingers tingled with the surge of power. Verity didn't know what to do with it, had no clue how to work magic. Baba Rawnie had done spells and while the old woman had taught only a few of them to Verity, she hadn't stopped Verity from watching and learning by osmosis. Except...that bright tendril of power inside her didn't power spells. She didn't know how she knew that, but the truth of it settled gently across her shoulders. She needed her father's belt, but it was safely tucked away, in her little house. She almost smiled again. Almost. Because she didn't know where she was and had the feeling she was a very long way from New Orleans. But once she got home, she would know what to do.

"Don't talk much, do you?" He scratched his crotch. "Never met a bitch didn't talk my damn head off. Maybe I'll keep you after Tremaine gets done with you."

CHAPTER TWENTY-ONE
CROOKS AND THIEVES

_____

ROMAN BLOCKED the doorway. With a shove, a hip bump, and a shimmy, Sade edged past him into the dismal little house. One room, it wasn't much more than a shack. There was a mattress on the floor, a battered dorm-sized refrigerator, a card table, a bean bag chair repaired with duct tape, and two stools. A plastic shower liner curtained off a sink, toilet, and a tiny shower stall. Broken plastic dishes, colorful clothes, and pages ripped from tattered paperbacks littered the floor.

She wasn't happy Roman had insisted on accompanying her and Caleb. He still looked battered and limped when he walked but he refused to stay behind. Sade was well aware that time was of the essence, but she worried about him, his grim-faced determination notwithstanding.

"Damn but those assholes did a number on this place." Roman grunted, his anger white-hot at Sade's back. She wisely ignored it. "What do you suppose they were looking for?"

"Good question," Caleb called from the front step. He didn't even attempt to get around the gargoyle. "Deacon's people are right. Death magic killed the human found here. Two other humans and a werewolf were along for the ride."

"Why go after a baby witch?" Sade mused. She turned a slow circle.

"Maybe she stole something from this guy," Caleb suggested. Roman rumbled and Caleb quickly added, "Or not."

Roman stared at Sade. "Verity is not a thief."

"Uh huh." Sade was unconvinced but Roman's decree carried the weight of magic. "Working in the dark here, pal. Any information you can give me might—" She broke off as all the hair on her body stood on end. She whirled to stare at Roman. The wash of power wasn't coming from him. She glanced to Caleb, who'd managed to squeeze inside. His eyes glowed with a red feral spark in their depths. He shook his head.

What was she missing? Sade studied the room again. "Caleb? Did we just trigger a spell or something?"

"Or something," he muttered. He moved, quartering the room. He pushed back the shower curtain hiding the makeshift bathroom and started tapping on the wooden shiplap wall.

"Stop." Roman's whispered command froze Caleb to the spot, one hand still raised to knock on the wall.

With a great deal of caution, Roman approached the werewolf. "Come away from there, Caleb."

Since the virtual ruff was standing up on Caleb's neck, he backed away without comment.

Roman stared at the wall wishing he had X-ray vision or something. Whatever was hidden held explosive power. It wasn't a spell. "A relic," he muttered. His face hardened. "Gargoyle."

Sade pressed closer in an attempt to see around him. "What are you saying, Roman?" She exchanged a glance with Caleb and mouthed, *Maybe Verity is a thief.*

Caleb shrugged, careful to stay out of Roman's line of sight.

"Get out." Roman's tone held no room for argument.

When it came to magic, Sade had learned to trust Caleb's instincts. Mostly. When he backpedaled away from Roman and headed for the door without a word of argument, she followed hard on his heels. She'd vacate the room but she would not leave Roman behind. She stopped in the doorway and watched. Dazzling light filled her vision and when she blinked away the afterglow, she discovered she was sitting on her butt about ten feet away. Caleb sat next to her, head down, hands clamped to his ears.

"What the fuck?" She rolled to her knees. Caleb's hand latched onto her arm.

"Don't," he said, forehead crinkled in pain. "As you would say, that's big bad fucking gargoyle shit. Roman can handle it."

Her butt hit the ground again. "How the fuck did our little gypsy fortune teller end up with some gawddamned to the big bad fucking gargoyle shit and why is it hidden in the wall of her house?"

"Good question," Roman gritted out the words from between clenched teeth. He held an old-fashioned metal cash box in one hand. "And one I intend to get the answer to as soon as we locate Verity."

ROMAN RETURNED straight to the Legation. He ignored Ceylin, carrying the cash box straight to his office. Setting it on the desk, he stared at it, once more wishing for X-ray vision. The thing was powerful. He retreated to the far corner of the room. The relic's power did not diminish. He moved the relic to the sideboard across the room from his desk, then slipped out the French doors onto the balcony. Nothing happened.

Entering his office, he sank into his chair, utterly weary. He'd always understood on some visceral level that humans were fragile. Now that he was experiencing their mortality firsthand, he understood a great deal more. One corner of his mouth quirked up in a wry smile he wasn't conscious of doing. This was not the lesson Crevan had wanted to teach him.

He stared at the box, could almost see the aura radiating from whatever lay inside. He now doubted that his presence had activated the relic. That meant something else triggered it. But what?

With great reluctance, he fetched the box and returned it to his desk. Merely holding it branded his fingertips. This was not his magic, though it belonged to his kind. A conundrum. And the mystery was only deepened by Verity's possession of the thing.

A sorcerer. A witchling. And a gargoyle object of power. What was wrong with this picture?

SADE SENT Caleb to the FBI offices to check in with Campos and scare the bejesus out of Reed. She figured she owed Campos that much. Caleb rubbed his hands together and used his best Saturday matinee villain's voice when he agreed. She had a very short list of addresses Campos put together and Sade planned to check them out. She'd left Sinjen under the influence of the day sleep with a note propped on the table next to his side of the bed. She fully intended to be home before dark.

Since driving in New Orleans drove her crazy, she planned her search. The first lead would take her to a cemetery within walking distance, so she left her government issue SUV parked around the corner from the Legation. Sade checked her watch. Déja Vu was on the way. She could grab lunch on the way.

Jax Martine waved to a stool at the end of the bar as she walked in the door. Her usual booth was full of noisy tourists. She hated leaving her back exposed but that stool was an acceptable substitute. She slid onto it at the same time Jax set two tall glasses of ice water in front of her.

"Breakfast or lunch, cher?"

"Breakfast."

He sailed through the door leading to the kitchen. Sade drained one glass. The humidity in New Orleans always made her thirsty. The door opened on a burst of chilly air. The weather was finally starting to feel like late October. Sade turned to check out the new arrivals. Locals. She went back to watching the rest of the place through the grungy mirror behind the bar. She reached for the second water glass and chuckled when she discovered two full ones. Yeah, Jax was not exactly human, but whatever magic ran in his blood was buried deep enough Sade couldn't figure it out.

A single guy walked in and took a seat on the opposite end of the bar. He ordered a beer and once it was delivered, the guy concentrated on drinking. Sade used the mirror to keep an eye on him, too, distracted only when her eggs, home fries, bacon, and biscuits arrived.

Wolfing down the food as she always did when eating alone, Sade kept track of everyone in the place. No one pinged her radar. She swallowed the last bite of buttered biscuit, tossed down a twenty-dollar bill, more than enough to cover her tab and a tip.

"Where ya off to, cher?" Jax called as he sailed by, arms loaded with full plates of food.

"I've got to see a voodoo queen about a sorcerer."

SADE HATED the dark. She hated waking up in it, disoriented and head aching, even more. Years of practice had her holding very still, breathing unchanged, eyes slitted as she surveyed her surroundings. Was she underground? That freaked her out just enough her breath caught. Chains rattled nearby. She wasn't alone. And if she was underground, she probably wasn't in New Orleans. The water table was too close to the surface—not to mention that the city was below sea level.

The clank of metal was followed by a hiss of pain. Not good. She ran a mental checklist of her body. She was dressed. Fully. And she wasn't tied up. That would be a fatal mistake for someone—or some *thing*.

A disembodied voice wafted through the darkness. "I know you're awake, bitch."

Huh. Either her fellow inmate knew who she was or he was a werewolf. Caleb, Romulus Jones, and Deacon Smith notwithstanding, most werewolves prowled on the crude side.

"Super," she replied. "Wanna tell me where we are?"

"Not really."

"You don't know either."

The answering growl confirmed both of her suppositions. Werewolf and clueless. She sat up and patted her body. Her cell phone wasn't in her jacket pocket. That would have been too easy. Then her fingers brushed across her shoulder harness. Her weapon was still there. What the fuck? Her kidnappers had to be total dipshits but she wouldn't look this particular horse in the teeth.

"I"m getting out."

"No, you aren't."

"The hell you say."

"Your humanity won't help. Not where we are."

Sade pulled her FBI standard issue Beretta 9mm. The one that should be loaded with the non-standard-issue bullets. "Your magic will?"

"Wolves don't have the magic needed for this, else I'd be gone already."

The werewolf shifted positions. A chain slithered

across the floor. Why the hell was he chained? For that matter, why the hell was she not? And why had whoever snatched her left her with her weapon? The last thing she remembered was getting cold-cocked outside Marie Laveau's crypt.

Except her head didn't hurt. And her mouth tasted like it was full of athletic socks. Drugged. The guy at the opposite end of the bar in Déja Vu. And friends. "Are you a Smith?"

"Huh?"

"Deacon Smith. Is he your Alpha?"

Another growl. "Fuck no."

Well, alrighty then. He was either a rogue or belonged to some other pack. Good to know. Sade was about to question him further when his voice sounded very close to her ear.

"I'm hungry."

She surreptitiously checked the Beretta's magazine. Empty. Oops. "And I want outta here." Her raised voice bounced back at her. "We don't always get what we want."

Metal grated and a shaft of light pooled on the floor. A disembodied voice behind the light said, "That can be arranged."

She didn't recognize the voice. "Who the hell are you and what do you want?"

"Where is the Heart of Stone?"

"The what?"

"Do not play games, Agent Marquis. Perhaps you'd rather wait until your cellmate becomes famished."

The wolf licked his chops. Yeah, a little too late for that. It'd help to know what was going on. Time to bluff. "I'll take you to it."

"Liar."

"Wait!"

"Yes, you will. Until your purpose has been served."

The light disappeared behind groaning metal.

"Any ideas?" she asked the werewolf.

"It's dinner time."

Well...fuck. "Besides eating me."

"Sounds like a plan to me."

"Don't make me hurt you, dude."

He laughed—until the magazine she'd clawed from her boot snicked into place. The special HE round blasted the wall behind him. Time to go. "Sorry I can't stay for dinner."

CHAPTER TWENTY-TWO
GOING ALL THE WAY

SADE WAS ALREADY through the hole she'd blown in the wall before she considered the consequences. A man rolled off a throne-like chair and came up snarling. He was halfway to her before her defenses kicked in. *Werewolf,* her brain decided. *Danger!* Her finger squeezed the trigger. The HE round tore a hole in his chest and kept going as the wolf went down. Sade processed the situation on the run. Throne. Wolf. Table. Wooden box. Verity tied to a chair.

She dove over the table, knocking Verity and the chair over just as the debris from the hole in the second wall rained down. Coughing from the dust, Sade snagged the knife hidden in her other boot. The hired muscle hadn't searched her beyond taking the magazine out of her weapon. Good thugs were hard to find these days.

In moments, she'd sliced through the ropes binding Verity. Sade hauled the other woman to her feet and pushed her forward. "Got the feeling we've worn out our welcome. Time to go."

Verity hesitated as they reached the breach in the wall. Sade stepped around her, peering through the murky air. An arm appeared through the haze and snagged Sade's arm.

"Sade, if you bloody well shoot me, I'll haunt you through all of eternity."

She peered through the smoke. "Ari? Is that you?"

"Aye, love. Out you come." Ariel Daoine, also known as the King's Seducer, hauled her through the hole.

178

Once Sade was safely on the other side, he reached through and snagged Verity. "You've made enough noise to wake a troll, Sade. Get a move on. Down this hall, right, right, left and if the door is locked, you can use your magic bullets again."

"Roger that." Sade took off at a jog, weapon in her hand.

Ari pushed Verity ahead of him, his head swiveling to watch for any pursuit. When Verity stumbled, he grabbed her arm to pull her along but the magic zapping through him almost drove him to his knees.

Sade heard his grunt of pain, slid to a stop and whirled. "What the hell?"

Breathing deep and pushing his own magic to recover, Ari shook his head. "Later. There's no time." There wasn't but he eyed Verity warily. "What are you, child?"

Verity was horrified, her eyes glued to his blistered hand, and kept saying, "I'm sorry, I'm sorry, I'm sorry" in a long litany.

"Don't got time," Sade barked. Tromping footsteps echoed behind them. She grabbed Verity's arm, felt a slight buzz but ignored it. She took off running, surprised when the little gypsy kept up with her. There was a tough woman lurking beneath the innocent waif. Good. Sade had the feeling Verity would need every ounce of strength she could beg, borrow, or steal.

A bullet slapped into the wood just above Sade's head a moment before she heard the concussion. She whiplashed Verity in front of her as they turned the last corner. "Go!" She waved Ari past her. Pistol out, she waited, then peeked around the corner. If she was going down, she'd take the bad guys with her. She trusted Ari to get the little witch back to Roman, Varrick, and Sinjen. They would do what needed to be done.

As the footsteps pounded closer, she counted off in

her head, then stepped around the corner, feet spread, Beretta raised, finger on the trigger. She never pulled it. The ceiling collapsed, almost burying the three men who'd been hot on her heels. Two pairs of leathery wings sent updrafts of dust spiraling through the space. The calvary had arrived.

Arms circled her waist and pulled her back around the corner. "There is something truly wrong with me that I find you with a weapon in your hand so arousing." The erection pressed into her butt provided the evidence to back up Sinjen's words.

Ari popped in, the air shimmering around him. "The bastard has escaped. I'll try to follow." Before he could disappear, Caleb arrived.

"Take me with you, Ariel."

Sade's jaw dropped as Ariel secured his long fingers around Caleb's wrist and the two of them winked out. "What the—?" She was so speechless she couldn't even cuss. Caleb and Ari had hated each other since...forever. When had they become friends? She felt like one of those people in the commercial where their heads exploded into purple smoke.

Roman and Varrick, still in their gargoyle forms, walked around the corner and the hallway got a tad claustrophobic. "All we need now is that damn dragon," Sade muttered.

"Someone mention my name?" Nikos asked.

⁂

VARRICK, Nikos, and Sinjen unearthed the three men trapped beneath the debris from the ceiling and the roof above it. Well, two men and a werewolf. Roman had gathered Verity into his arms, launched through the hole in the roof and disappeared. They were waiting on NOPD and Deacon Smith to arrive.

Sade stared holes into Varrick's back. He ignored her. Just like Nikos and Sinjen were ignoring each other. "Testosterone much?" she muttered.

"Speaking of," Sinjen said without taking his eyes off the prisoners. "How were you taken?"

"Good question. I had a lead that sent me to Marie Leveau's crypt. Somebody took me down from behind. I need to go by Déja Vu to check their security footage. I think the guy followed me from there. He's not one of these three." Her knitted brows crowned a deep frown of concentration. "Come to think of it, how *did* he get the drop on me? It's not like I'm magic blind or anything."

The three magicks exchanged telling looks but none of them deigned to enlighten her. She threw up her hands. "Fine. What am I missing?"

His expression settling into one she recognized, she grimaced at Sinjen. He saw the wince and fought not to smile. "I promise not to lecture you, but you are overlooking the tree for the forest."

"What does that even mean?" she groused.

"It means," Nikos said, "that we are dealing with a sorcerer. A sorcerer who is steeped in the black arts."

"I should have sensed a spell." Okay, she sounded a little petulant, but dammit, she *should* have. The vampire and fae marks she carried gave her a great deal of protection against magic, as well as the ability to sense it. She blinked. "Fuck. I didn't even know that guy in the room with Verity was a werewolf until it was almost too late." She deep-breathed through a flash of panic.

Sinjen, despite wanting to take her into his arms—a move Sade would detest and fight him over, placed only his hand on her shoulder. He didn't miss the fine tremblor beneath his palm. "There is much to learn about sorcery. It is a dark art that not many have experience with."

"You have heard of a null spell, yes?" Nikos asked. He continued when Sade looked puzzled. "A null spell is meant to hide magic. It is my understanding that the little witchling had one attached to her. It disguises the true nature of a magick, and is also used to disguise relics and artifacts." He gave a very nonchalant shrug. "It is quite useful to shield portals and shroud the Realms. The Veil, Sade, was the biggest null spell of them all."

After a long moment of consideration, she said the only thing that came to mind. "Huh." Then her brain processed the details she'd skipped over during the heat of battle. "Holy hell! Roman has his powers back. How the fuck did that happen?"

CHAPTER TWENTY-THREE
DIAMOND IN THE DUST

SADE STORMED UP the steps of the Legation, Sinjen hot of her heels. The place felt empty. If she'd stopped to think about it, she'd have been worried. Too bad she'd built up a head of steam. She charged straight to Roman's room, banged on the door and yelled, "Y'all better have fucking clothes on because I'm coming in."

When the door didn't open, she kicked it. The lock and hinges didn't budge. She knocked again, hard. "Dammit, Roman!"

She caught faint snickering and whirled to find Sinjen standing on the landing to the stairwell. "What?"

"They aren't here. And if you kick in that door, Roman will be most unhappy."

"If they aren't here, where are they?"

"In the Legate's office."

Blowing out a frustrated breath, Sade marched down the hallway and brushed past the vampire. "Why didn't you tell me?"

"You didn't ask." Sinjen knew the woman he adored well enough to have remained on the landing while she headed up the steps because at his words, she turned and would have nailed him with her fist.

She muttered all the way to the office. She was still full of adrenaline but she did knock and call, "Roman?" Sade heard rustling, then the click of the lock. The door opened and she was faced with one very pissed off gargoyle wearing jeans that hadn't been buttoned all the way up, which showcased hard abs and a shirtless chest. Resisting the urge to stick her fingers in her ears and sing *la la la*, she opened her mouth then snapped it shut. Roman still wore his wings, though he wasn't in his full gargoyle form.

"To answer your question, I don't know how, Sade. Nor do I know why." He stepped back from the door giving both her and Sinjen entrance. She took in the room with one look.

Verity sat in one of the high-backed guest chairs, her face tear-streaked. Varrick was in his customary position, one shoulder braced against the wall as if he was holding it up. She figured Ariel and Caleb were still hunting.

Before Sade could speak, Roman returned to the large chair behind his desk, though he leaned his arms on its back. Yeah, wings with a sixteen-foot spread, even folded up, weren't conducive to chair sitting.

Verity surged to her feet. "You don't understand, Roman. I have to go to my house."

"Why?"

"Because I do. There's something I have to get."

He reached under his desk and retrieved the metal box they'd found at Verity's little house. His fingers burned from the contact but he ignored the pain. He shoved the box toward her. "This?"

Verity gave the box a puzzled look. She stretched out a hand then jerked it back. "Is my belt still inside?"

Roman shrugged. Disregarding the blistering heat, he opened the lid. Verity gasped as the crystal ball she'd retrieved from Roman's room and hidden in her pocket throbbed with power. Roman was suddenly fully gargoyle.

Collapsing back into her chair, Verity began to shiver. Shaking her head in disbelief, she murmured, "I don't...how...? I don't understand."

"Uh, Verity?" Sade approached very carefully until she could peek into the box. She glimpsed a coil of leather, metal and something that might be a chunk of fire opal, but it was huge. When Roman shifted back into his human guise, she noticed the burns on hiss fingers. "Shit, Roman! What's wrong with your hands?"

"It's the power of the relic," Roman, his voice hard and cold, said without looking at Sade. "Where did you get it, Verity?"

Verity stammered out sounds then stopped. Something bad was happening. Something awful had already happened to Roman. He hadn't taken off because he had business, leaving without even saying goodbye to her. No, something had occurred while he was gone. His face looked battered and angry fires burned in his eyes.

"I f-f-found it." She pulled her legs up, thighs to chest, her arms circling them. "The n-n-night Baba Rawnie died."

"Tell me."

She couldn't keep silent, no matter how badly she wanted. Roman was implacable. Verity closed her eyes. "It was the dark of the moon, on Samhain's Eve. Men came to the cabin. Baba Rawnie told me to stay out of sight. She stood on the front porch, arguing with the men. Then they dragged her out into the yard. They had guns and dogs and..." She gulped. "Fire."

"They killed her?" Sade asked, keeping her voice even.

"Yes. And they set the house on fire. I hid behind the stove and the Fridgedaire. The fire burned so hot." She glanced at Roman. "I told you about the wooden box in the stove. I didn't tell you about the metal one. There was a loose board and when I pried it up, thinking to slip out through the crawl space, I found it."

She shuddered, her eyes going unfocused. Verity continued after several steadying breaths. "That old ice box was as tight as a coffin but I crawled into it."

"With the box?" Roman interrupted.

"Yes. I curled up in there, figuring I would die from suffocation. Smoke got in but the smoke? It's much better than the fire, you know?" She looked around at her audience. When they all nodded, she continued. "When the floor burned up, the stove and the ice box fell through. That door popped open, spilled me out, and when I quit rollin' I was almost in the bayou. Nobody saw me. I hid the woods and in the morning, I found Baba Rawnie's *gris gris* box in the stove. It had her cards, the stones, and her crystal ball."

"What happened then?" Sade again.

"I started walkin'. Hitchhiked a time or two. Stopped walking when I got to New Orleans."

"And the belt?" Roman reminded, his voice a harsh rumble.

"I stole one of those fancy pocket knives." She glanced up. "The one with all the tools, you know?" Roman nodded. "I used the little curly spiral thing to pry the lock. When I opened it, there was the leather belt and wrapped in cotton wool I found the buckle. The letter—" She paused to reach into the box. After withdrawing the paper, she handed it to Roman. "You can read for yourself."

He unfolded the brittle paper and studied the fading ink. Sade watched him closely. When he looked at Verity again, his eyes were haunted and his shoulders slumped in defeat.

The paper fluttered to the desk from his nerveless fingers. "You are exhausted, little witch. Come with me." Roman rounded the desk, bent and lifted Verity into his arms. Without a word, he carried her out of the room.

As soon as they were out of sight, Sade reached across the desk. Varrick grabbed her wrist. She hadn't even seen him move.

"Leave it," Varrick ordered. "It is not for you."

186

"The hell you say!"

"Sade." Sinjen said only her name, his voice low and compelling. She turned her head to look at him. "Leave it."

"But—"

Varrick shook her arm. "Look at the box, Sade. *Really* look at it."

She did. Her eyes watered and her lungs complained about the heat she was breathing in. She backed away. "What the fuck?"

"This is about the Garregyion, Sade. It is not for humans. Not even one such as you." Varrick stepped away from the desk. "Just...leave it. This is for Roman to deal with." He swiped the back of a hand over his mouth. "I need a drink."

"That makes a bunch of us," Caleb drawled as he stepped through the door. His suit was filthy, the dark five o-clock shadow scruff along his jaw competed with the tired, dark shadows beneath eyes still showing feral red glints.

Ariel followed the werewolf into the office and stopped long enough at the sideboard to splash brandy into a crystal snifter before he dropped onto the couch drawn up in front the fireplace. "We chased the bloody bastard through every realm but one."

"Let me guess," Sade said dryly.

"Yeah, for some reason, he was smart enough to stay out of the gargoyle realm."

Sade glanced at Varrick who was drinking Kentucky bourbon straight from the bottle he'd found tucked inside the sideboard. Her gaze was drawn to the paper but before she could reach for it again, Sinjen was there, handing her a cold beer. She noticed Caleb also had one. She accepted the bottle, lifted it in a toast and took a long swallow.

She settled on the arm of the nearest guest chair

and listened while Varrick debriefed Ariel and Caleb. She was still having trouble wrapping her head around their apparent camaraderie. "No fucking sense," she muttered.

Sinjen leaned on the back of the chair and raised a quizzical brow. "Oh?"

"They've nipped at each other's heels for fucking years. Caleb was my guard dog, Ariel was like the high school bad boy in the leather jacket trying to get in my pants. It didn't stop when I grew up. Yip. Yip. Growl. Dig. Snipe. And now they're like Valley Girl BFFs. I just don't get it."

"You're female."

She raised her chin and scowled. "Since when did you become so misogynistic?"

He chuckled and the sound of it made her breath catch. Sinjen enjoyed doing that to her. "Men and women are not the same, love. A fact for which I am eternally grateful." He snagged a tendril of her hair with his fingers and played with it. "I suspect a lot of that had to do with their affection for you. They were in competition."

"And now they aren't?"

"And now they aren't."

"Huh." She wasn't quite sure how she felt about that but before she could question Sinjen further, Nikos walked in. She rolled her eyes. "And speaking of."

Roman chose that moment to return.

The butler followed him in, pushing a cart filled with cold cuts, cheese, various types of bread, and condiments. There was eating and talking. Talking and drinking. More eating. A lot more drinking. And then Sade noticed that Roman was standing at the French window behind his desk staring out into the night. She sidled up to him.

"You ready to talk to me, Romo?"

"We've just spent the last hour talking, Lady Sade."

"Not about the important stuff."

She could almost hear rocks grating as he turned his head to look at her. "Making plans to catch the sorcerer isn't important?"

"A little. But you—" She patted his chest. "You, my friend, are far more important. I'm worried about you. Talk to me."

"What is there to say, Sade? There is duty and honor. And then there are personal feelings. Which should come first?"

"You care about Verity."

He didn't attempt to deny it. "Yes."

"You can choose who to serve, who to protect. You can choose light or dark, good or evil. But, dude? Trust me in this. You can't choose who to love." Sade's gaze slid past him to focus on the handsome vampire standing across the room talking to Varrick, Caleb and Ariel. Her voice softened as she continued, "Who you love isn't a choice."

Roman understood that but his heart remained shattered. "Destiny is not that kind, Lady Sade."

Sade laughed. "You're telling me? Destiny is a bitch, Roman. I know that first hand." She sobered, and softened her expression. "Tell me about your little witch."

"She was there...just...there. She was a diamond. In the dust at my feet, staring up at me with those eyes of endless sorrow, and I knew. God help me, Sade. I knew. How do I slay my heart, my soul?"

Sade rocked back on her heels and carefully pulled her poker face into place. She had the best one in the entire Bureau. "You need to talk to me, Romo." She hoped the childhood appellation would have the intended effect.

Roman scrubbed at his face with the heels of his

hands. "I can't." He shook and it was like a small earthquake going off. His next words sounded like they'd been jackhammered from the depths of an abandoned mine. "To do so is to break faith."

"Gawd—" Sade snapped her jaw shut before he could chide her. It suddenly occurred to her that whatever was going on went to the very core of the Gargoyle race. They were guardians. Protectors. Created as wardens for cathedrals and buildings—and humanity itself. Gargoyles were the sentries, the first line of defense standing against all the big bads the dark could throw at magicks and mundanes alike. They'd been...her brain stuttered to a stop. Were gargoyles created whole cloth by some magic spell known only to *Le Vieil*? She'd never seen a female gargoyle, hadn't gotten an answer when she asked. Were they kept in some...what had Roman called it...a rookery like nesting hens? Roman's natural form resembled carved granite. Is that how they were made? Some artist carved them from stone and the magic brought them to life?

And she was back to the questions she'd stopped herself from asking Varrick the night she'd seen Roman in bed with a human woman. Which freaked her right the hell out because yeah, she figured gargoyles did it. And all the magicks had a thing for doing it with humans but...this was *Roman*.

"You are thinking too hard, Lady Sade."

"Probably, but it occurs to me that I know nothing about you, about your kind. Well, I know a little. I know about the Old One and the Sentinels. I know that your kind has some sort of base in or near Paris. But..." She breathed deeply a few times. "Where do you come from?"

"We are not born, Sade, not in the sense humans are, or even many of the magical races. Elves and Fae create life just as humans do. As do werewolves and trolls. You know how ghouls come about and vampires. We have our secrets, Lady Sade, and we keep that faith close."

"If I'm to help you, Roman, to help all of your kind, I need to know."

"Yes."

Before he could speak again, the sound of leathery wings beat against the still, night air beyond the window and something heavy landed on the balcony. Crevan, *Le Vieil*, walked in through the window.

"You would break our code, Roman? Again?" The Old One sounded tired yet also oddly pedantic, like a professor bored by the miscreants in his class. "And you, *mortal child*, why should we entrust you with our secrets?"

Sade met his gaze with her own steadfast stare. "Because I care, *Le Vieil*. Because I understand duty and loyalty. Because Roman is my family. Because I know...*here*—" She pounded a loose fist against her heart. "I know in my heart that evil is coming. Old evil. Evil the gargoyles have faced before and I'm afraid the evil prevailed that other time and that if it does so again in this day, in this age, everything that's gone before will be for naught."

Crevan sneered at her. "Pretty words for a human whose light will be snuffed out in the blink of my eye."

"Yeah?" She leaned toward him, her feet shoulder-width apart, knees flexed and arms loose at her sides. She was ready for a fight, even it meant taking on one of the oldest creatures in all the Realms. "Magicks have been trying to kill me my entire life and yet here I stand."

What a picture she makes, Roman thought. Tall and lanky, that wild brunette hair falling in messy waves across her shoulders. Her stubborn chin with a full mouth men dreamed of kissing and that beauty mark adding punctuation to her expression. She was beautiful enough and fierce enough to have been a Valkyrie, though none of the shield maidens had survived, but it was her eyes that stopped the world. Brilliant as emeralds, the color of green bottle glass in the sun. They saw *everything*.

"Would you sacrifice the Crucible of Eve, *Enfant de L'homme?* To save humanity?"

Sade recognized the subtle shift in the tone of Crevan's voice. He'd often called her that, it's translation something along the lines of "child of man," meaning anyone human in the formal language of the Gargoyles, but when he'd said it just then, it had power behind it, like he'd bestowed it as a title and the words should be capitalized. Now she had to figure out two things—who the bloody freaking fuck was this Crucible of Eve everyone was so freaked out about and just what did he mean by "sacrifice?"

CHAPTER TWENTY-FOUR
NO MORE CHANCES

The entire room vibrated with tension. Sinjen was already halfway to Sade when Crevan raised his hand, palm out, to stop him. "You don't control me, Old One," he said, his tone deadly. Gargoyles weren't immune to death and he *had* been alive when the last war was fought.

"I will not harm the human," Crevan said. "I have spent my entire existence protecting them. As much as this one vexes me, she is safe."

Sade opened her mouth to retort but Roman's quelling look silenced her. Her jaw shut with an audible snap. Both gargoyles stared at her until Sinjen wrapped an arm around her waist and forcibly pulled her across the room. He deposited her on the couch between Caleb and Ariel. Caleb offered her a bite of his sandwich—rare roast beef, horseradish sauce, and Provolone cheese on a brioche bun. She bit and chewed but before she could take it away from him, Sinjen leaned over her shoulder and handed her an identical sandwich. It wasn't until she inhaled it that she realized none of the gargoyles remained in the room.

* * *

ST. LOUIS CATHEDRAL had long been closed for the night. The three gargoyles stood in the second-floor gallery overlooking the high altar. Crevan and Roman faced off against each other. Varrick, wisely, stood apart. His arms hung loose at his sides, but that did not mean he wasn't prepared to leap into action should the need arise. Ghostly echoes filtered in through the stained-glass windows—the patter of a ghost tour guide down in the alley below, telling the story of how Père Antoine, a priest buried beneath the cathedral, still haunted both the church and the alley.

Varrick briefly wondered what the tourists would think if they discovered three gargoyles inside. St. Louis had never needed their kind, as New Orleans had been a sanctuary and neutral from the beginning. Only the stupid would break that keystone precept.

"Who is she?" Roman demanded of Crevan.

"She is the Crucible of Eve, Roman. And it is time for you to discharge your duty. You vowed to me, standing before the high altar of the Basilica d'Le Creche, amid the broken shards of our brothers, that you would guard the Heart of Stone and hunt down the Crucible."

His voice an inhuman growl, Roman asked again, "Who is she, Crevan?"

"You know who she is. What she is. A danger to us all." Crevan spread his arms and wings wide. "To all of humanity. Your duty, Roman, is to destroy her before she destroys everything we have pledged our lives to uphold. To protect. There are no more chances."

"Why does she have the Gargoyle's Fist? Why is there a letter saying it came from her *father*?"

Crevan's voice was as sharp as polished obsidian when he answered. "Because each of us carries the seed of our own destruction within. Because each of us can sow that seed and reap the harvest of carnage that is prophesied to follow." A moment later, Crevan was gone, but a lingering echo of his voice remained. "Because I failed in my duty to the brotherhood."

Moments later, both Roman and Varrick teleported away. Neither saw nor heard the little mouse crouched beneath a pew down below. When she realized they were gone, Verity crawled out and dashed the tears from her eyes. She would have to scurry back to the Legation before her absence was noted. The crystal ball in her pocket throbbed against her hip. *I will help you*, it seemed to say.

ROMAN STRODE in from the balcony. The people still gathered in his office all looked up. The only one who started to comment was Sade but Sinjen's hand on her shoulder, Ariel's on her arm, and Caleb's on her knee kept her silent. The large bite of food in her mouth also helped, Roman thought wryly.

The box, its metal scratched and dented, remained open on his desk, as did the old letter. He had his suspicions, especially now after the cryptic words he'd exchanged with Crevan. Varrick remained at his back, just inside the open window, and Roman wondered if the gargoyle was there to protect his flank or to deliver the *coup de grâce*. The spot between his shoulder blades itched. That was not a good sign.

Sade had swallowed and set her plate aside. Never one to shy away from the crux of things, she said, "Will you tell us what the fuck is going on?" Her eyes shifted to the box on the desk. "And what the hell that thing is?"

Varrick cleared his throat but Roman silenced him with a slash of his hand, cutting the air between them. "I cannot give you the details of our creation, Sade. Still, war is coming and despite the cliché, to be forewarned is to be forearmed."

Roman, his voice dry and curt, outlined the history of the Old War, recited the story of a sorcerer who stole the Heart of Stone which imbibed the gargoyles not only with life but with free will. He told of the creation of the

Crucible of Eve—a human woman imbued with black magic who could control the Heart and the Garregyion warriors who had pledged their immortal lives to protect humanity—though he didn't speak to how she was created. He spoke to the duty a chosen gargoyle accepted when word came that the Crucible of Eve had been reincarnated—a duty to slay the Crucible, often at great sacrifice.

"I have been the guardian of the Heart of Stone for centuries," Roman said quietly. "And it is my onus to carry out the vow."

"Oh fucking to the hell fuckityfuck shit and piss *no*," Sade snarled. "Verity? The little street rat fortune-telling witchling? *She's* a danger to us all?"

Roman nodded gravely while Ariel, Sinjen, and even Caleb chimed in with the various versions they were familiar with. All the tales were the same. The Crucible of Eve would bring great danger and destruction not only to the gargoyles but to all the magicks.

After they'd all finished, Sade brushed them off. "Not going there. Not yet. Tell me about that thing in the box."

Varrick stepped forward and spoke before Roman could. "The buckle on the belt is made of rune-inscribed iron and holds the Gargoyle's Fist. It is a weapon."

"Of course it is," Sade muttered. "It has a fucking name." Louder, she said, "Tell me what it does."

Lifting one shoulder in a shrug that appeared nonchalant, he offered a grim explanation. "It kills gargoyles. And sorcerers. It's been missing for—"

"Twenty-six years," Roman said.

"What does the letter say, Roman?" When his shook his head in the negative, Sade pushed. "It's important."

Once again, it was Varrick who responded by reading the letter where it lay on Roman's desk.

"My sweet baby girl, you are the truth of me, and of

your father. I know now what I did. What he did. What we did. I have to leave for your own good. Your Paridala Zara will keep you safe. She has to. I stole this from your father. It is your legacy—the one bequeathed by him, no matter how unknowing he is. Before you were born, my precious child, I went to Baba Rawnie. She foretold of a great battle, of a greater love, of a prophecy only you could fulfill. It's up to you, heart of my heart. Baba Rawnie assures me that you will know the time, the place, and what to do. I love you. Your Mama."

Out in the hallway, the little mouse who'd been sitting with her back against the wall had heard enough. Verity pushed to her feet and came inside. "It's me," she announced. "I'm the Crucible of Eve."

"No," Roman denied, starting toward her. She held up her hand and the belt, in a shower of sparks, flew into it.

"Whoa, lighting!" Sade quipped, but no one laughed.

"I'm a danger," Verity said, proud her voice didn't shatter like her insides had. "To everyone."

"No!" The windows vibrated from that one snapped word. Roman's fury swelled until no one in the room breathed—no one but the little witch.

"That's what everyone says," Verity insisted. Fearless now, she approached the gargoyle. She expected his chest to feel as cold as granite when she placed her palm against it. She found instead a beating heart and warmth seeping into her skin. When had she grown so cold?

"You cannot do this, little one. I refuse to allow it." He gazed down at her, drinking in her face, her wild tangle of hair. He would drown in the silver-blue of her eyes if she didn't blink.

"This is my destiny, Roman. You know this..." She patted the spot over his heart. "Here."

His hand covered hers, dwarfing it. "No." His denial came on a sighing breath. Roman cupped her cheek, bent to kiss her. To hell with duty, with honor. Verity was his to cherish and protect.

Verity leaned against him then, absorbing his warmth. She would give him this night. And a day. A day spent together doing the things lovers did when in New Orleans. She understood that despite his centuries of living, this fragile thing growing in their hearts was as new to him as it was to her. She would take this time to make memories for both of them. Memories sweet enough to last eternity because that's all they would ever have—memories.

Sinjen cleared his throat and then the room emptied, leaving her alone with Roman. "Love me," she whispered.

"I do," Roman said, though she hadn't asked a question.

Feeling a little shy now, though her skin zinged like someone was running a 4th of July sparkler across it, Verity smiled. "No, silly. *Make* love to me."

She hadn't even finished speaking when he swept her into his arms and carried her from the room. He all but flew down the stairs and while soft voices were audible as they passed the sitting room, Roman didn't slow down. Inside his room, he lay her on the bed like she was a priceless piece of porcelain.

He undressed Verity with utmost tenderness—her shoes, her skirt, her blouse. She wore nothing underneath. He stripped his own clothes with a flick of magic. He settled on top of her, watching her. The trust in her eyes was a living thing—fragile, a gossamer thread of spider web easily broken by a careless word. He would not speak, then. He would do only as she asked. He would make love to her.

The shadows in Roman's bedroom offered a kind of

intimacy. A tugboat's lonely horn whispered through the window. Once upon a time, that loneliness might have touched Verity but not tonight. She raised her head to find Roman's mouth, to build a sparkling bridge made of magic and moonlight, of love and desire. Roman. Her. Just the two of them. Tonight and tomorrow would be their eternity.

She wrapped arms and legs around him, kissing him harder, showing him that they were meant to be. Like this. Like liquid silver. Like love. Skin to skin. Mouth to mouth. Heart to heart.

She tasted wonderful, rich, ripe, full of magic and promise. Their hearts beat in time and Roman knew there would never be another like her. There was no simple explanation for the why of them. He knew only that they were. No matter what tomorrow brought, they had tonight.

He stroked his palms over her body, feeling the tease of magic that left her skin prickled in their wake. He meant to arouse and to pleasure, to soothe and to entice. She breathed his name, a demand and a plea. Roman slipped his hand between them and his fingers found her hot and slick and ready. With eager anticipation, he slid inside her, a slow glide into her depths until her inner muscles surrounded him with caressing heat.

He made love to her, as he had to no other woman. He offered her his heart, his pride. He gave up his secrets to her, and she did the same. Wild kisses followed by tender ones. He pumped into her hard and she arched to meet each thrust, and then they stilled, hearts pounding, only to do it again. And again. Both knowing, in the depths of their souls, this was their last chance to love.

When they came, they came together, their breathless sighs so lost in the sound of silence that no one heard.

CHAPTER TWENTY-FIVE
HURTS LIKE HELL

ROMAN WATCHED the shifting patterns of light dance on the Mississippi. Behind him, noise from the French Quarter blared. Mardi Gras was still months away but the party on Bourbon Street went on year-round and this time of the year was prime. He longed to be far away, to take Verity with him, but duty kept him here. Besides the hunt for the sorcerer, he couldn't shirk his duty as Legate. Too many Magicks were in town to celebrate Samhain and Halloween. And too many drunk humans.

"Their reckoning will come."

He glanced at the tall gargoyle standing beside him. "Have you now become a mind reader, Varrick? I thought you had a date."

"I did. *Did* being the operative word. Doc was called in to cover the Halloween insanity." Varrick and the human medical examiner, Dr. Toni Allison, had met during a previous incident, when a rogue fae was murdering magicks in New Orleans. That the human ME and Varrick had an on-going, if erratic, relationship was not a state secret.

"Ah." Roman was distracted. After their night of love-making, Verity had asked him to spend the day with her. They'd done silly things. Human things. They'd had breakfast at Brennan's Restaurant. They'd strolled through Jackson Square admiring all the arts and crafts. They'd had cafe au lait and beignets at the Cafe Du Monde. They'd ridden the St. Charles Street street car. They'd held hands and kissed and laughed like they had all the time in the world. And all the while, Roman knew he would eventually have to kill her.

"Where's the little witchling?"

"In my quarters. Sleeping."

"And you aren't with her because?" The other man stretched out his feet, slouching down against the metal-slated back of the bench. Varrick cut his eyes to Roman then returned his gaze to the river. "If you're doing that whole *I'm the Legate* thing, why aren't you on Bourbon Street? I figured you and the witchling would either be in the midst of the party—" He stopped at Roman's snort and laughed a little before continuing. "Or you'd be out there policing the damn fae."

"This isn't Venice during Carnival," Roman replied dryly.

"Praise be for that!" Varrick's voice was fervent. "Been there, done that, had to wear the freaking costume. What is it about the fae and dressing up? And those masks?" He gave a mock shudder. "Mardi Gras in New Orleans is fun at least. Halloween is better though."

They sat in companionable silence as the joyful, if muted, noises of the continuous party that was New Orleans wafted from behind them.

"You haven't answered my question, Roman."

"Which question was that?"

"Why are you sitting here instead of spending time with your little witchling?"

Why indeed? He was old—millenniums' old. The shiny had worn off long ago. Like Varrick, he'd been there, done that. Still, as Legate, he had duties to perform. That his orders from Crevan weighed heavy on his mind was no excuse.

"Where did you say Verity was?"

Roman closed his eyes, head drooping. A man created from stone should not ache like this. "She's sleeping."

"Are you sure?"

Something in Varrick's tone alerted Roman. He sat up and looked around. Further down the riverwalk, he caught furtive movement—a swirl of material creating a phantom dance. Timid steps pattered against the pavement, echoing softly. He caught the flash of blue fire at the apparition's waist when she turned to look, not that he needed the surge of power from the Gargoyle's Fist to know the ghost's identity.

Without a second thought, Roman pulled more glamour around him and strode after the shadow. His warrior's stride caught up to her almost immediately. Even in the dark, caught as she was between two streetlights, Roman could see the whites showing in her eyes. She was terrified but her stiff body and clenched fists held anger too. And determination. Her head swiveled from side to side as if she was sniffing the air, like a wolf. When her head stilled, her gaze came to rest on the spot where Roman stood. She stared as if she could see him behind the invisibility glamour in which he was cloaked.

She blinked and her face softened. One hand reached out before she caught herself and forced her arm to drop to her side. "Please understand," she said. "I have to do this. I have no choice. It's in my blood." She backed up three steps, her eyes glinting with unshed tears. "I'm sorry," she murmured, then she turned and fled.

In that moment, at those words, Roman's heart cracked and he knew without any doubt. She *was* the one he'd been seeking, the one he would have to sacrifice. What was the price of one frail human's life in balance to the lives of hundreds—of thousands of his brothers? What mattered the cost to his heart in lieu of that debt?

Varrick's hand landed on his shoulder. He'd known all along but understand that Roman had to come to his own conclusion, his own decision. With that done, he could take this burden from his friend and mentor. "I'll do it."

"No. She's mine." And she was. His. Always. He would deliver her fate into no hands but his own.

"I am sorry," Varrick said, his voice echoing the sound of far-off thunder.

Roman looked to the south, beyond the lights of Algiers Point, toward the Gulf of Mexico. A storm brewed out there, the clouds amassing on the horizon full of lightning flashes.

Varrick watched the building storm as well, then said, "And all our yesterdays have lighted fools the way to dusty death. Out, out, brief candle! Life's but a walking shadow, a poor player that struts and frets his hour upon the stage and then is heard no more: it is a tale told by an idiot, full of sound and fury, signifying nothing."

"I didn't realize you were so well-versed in Shakespeare's plays."

"Only a few, one being MacBeth." Varrick offered Roman a rueful grin. "Who also had trouble with witches." He leaned slightly to see past the other gargoyle. "It appears your little witch plans to leave you in the dust."

Roman dropped his glamour and spread his wings. "She'll not get far."

⁘ ●

VERITY RAN. Not that she was very fast. And the farther she got from Artillery Park—from the specter that was real, though she had only sensed him—the more she realized she was doing the right thing. Maybe

204

she'd been wrong and that disturbance she'd felt hadn't been Roman. Didn't matter. She had to get away, had to get to the End of the World. Her head throbbed in time with her labored breathing. She wasn't a runner. Never had been. But she ran now for all she was worth.

You're doing the right thing. Right thing. Right thing. The voice chanted in her head. *End of the World. End of the World. I'll meet you at the End of the World.* She recognized the compelling sound of it and smiled grimly. Yes, she would meet her tormentor at the spit of land the locals called the End of the World, but given what she'd learned in the past twenty-four hours? The sorcerer was not ready for her.

The stitch in her side made it hard to breathe. She'd reached the point where the riverfront park dead-ended at the Governor Nicholls Street Wharf. She dodged the fence around the wharf and slowed to a fast walk along the railroad tracks. Gravel crunched beneath her feet and the lighting was spotty. She slowed more, worried about twisting an ankle. No one pursued her so maybe she'd been wrong. Maybe she hadn't sensed Roman back there along the river.

Holding her side, she kept up her determined march. The leather belt she'd cinched around her waist rubbed against her bare skin. The iron and fire opal buckle was her secret ace in the hole and she needed every advantage. The sorcerer was strong and could control his magic. She was...a witchling. Barely. But she had a plan.

Thunder rumbled in the distance. She wondered if the storm was natural or something conjured up by the sorcerer to hide the evil spells he was getting ready to invoke. She had to stay alive long enough to learn what he planned. She had to figure out how to defeat him. And she had to hope that if Roman *didn't* come for her that her death would be clean and quick.

The pain lessened a bit and she could breathe easier. Verity picked up her pace. She felt wild and free as the wind capered around her, teasing her with a myriad of scents. The tang of the far-off Gulf was a brief counterpoint to the heavy moss and mud of the Mississippi River. A whiff of cayenne and shrimp boil spices sprinkled the air. But there was something else. Something sharp like licorice, and thick and oily like the sludge that sometimes lined the shore. She could almost taste the evil riding the winds of the storm.

The sorcerer. He was waiting for her. She had to do this. Had to keep Roman and Varrick and Alton and Mama Two and all the rest safe. She was the only one. She knew that in the deepest part of everything that made her *her*. Running again, she kept to the shadows of the train cars parked on the siding, darting along the wharfs and then a jogging trail through another park until she at last came to the fence blocking off the barren finger that stuck out into the river at the mouth of a canal, as if pointing the way toward the Mississippi Delta.

There was a fire at the End of the World, the wind teasing it until it tossed up embers. The hulking shadow just beyond surprised her, though it shouldn't have. She'd known, when she sensed him, that Roman would try to stop her. He probably followed her, flying above her like a bat, soundless in the silence just before the storm.

Verity stopped, keeping the fire between them. She had to tell him, but how could she without breaking? Would she have the right words—the ones to make him understand? She ached all the way down into her soul. She loved him so much, but no matter what she said, no matter what she did, she would lose him when this was done. And it hurt like hell.

"You know." Her voice was flat, no accusation.

"I suspected. Do you have the Heart?"

Her fist clenched around the smooth crystal ball tucked into the pocket of her skirt. "I didn't steal it." She hadn't. She'd found it when it called her. He had to understand that but she doubted he would, doubted he would accept her explanation.

"I know." Roman kept his voice gentle. He could give her that. Because he did know. He'd been in possession of the Heart of Stone for centuries, safeguarding, bringing it to light with each new flock of fledglings. By the One God and by all the other gods old and new, he love her. The pain in his heart flared, as hot as the fires of hell.

She breathed again, for a moment anyway. He told the truth. He knew. Gods but she loved him and it hurt. "I fell in love with you." She offered a smile half apologetic, half heartfelt. "You were like a dream, one I used to have but couldn't remember when I woke up." She fished the Heart of Stone out of her pocket. "This is the key, but you know that too."

He nodded, and tried to speak but his jaw was clamped so tightly he couldn't move it—like the Tin Man in the *Wizard of Oz*, only Verity was the oil can he needed to give him the heart he'd long denied having.

"I'm the lock. The...what did that other gargoyle call me? The Crucible? Yeah..." She nodded. "The Crucible of Eve. I can't escape this, Roman. Neither of us can. It's Destiny." The storm broke around them and the bonfire flared, shooting flames and embers swirling into the sky, blocking each of them from the sight of the other. "You can't stop me."

CHAPTER TWENTY-SIX
ASH AND WATER

THE FURY of the storm raged around them. Despite that, Roman stilled, forcing his hands to remain at his sides, palms flat against his thighs. Verity was a wild thing, hair and eyes looking fey in the thrashing wind and uncertain moonlight. He didn't know what this was, was almost afraid to even consider the consequences. He was sure, though, that he had never seen what he thought he was seeing in her this moment. Her skin had always carried the faint sheen of magic but now? Now she blazed as brightly as the fire flaring between them.

Verity cocked her head as if hearing something. He listened too, caught the baying of far-off hounds, the sound of horns, the shouts of men and thundering hooves. No matter how unearthly Verity looked at this moment, he knew to his very soul that she was not fae, nor was she prey for the Wild Hunt.

"She is mine, Oberon!" He threw back his head and challenged the very air. He thought he heard the Fae King's laughter riding the wind and though the sounds of the hunt faded, he didn't relax. Lowering his head, he sought out the slip of a girl who'd stolen his heart. Verity no longer stood in the firelight. She'd moved, standing now on the small jetty of rocks poking into the Mississippi.

"This can never be," Verity whispered. "*We* can never be." The wind caught her words and brought them to his heart. "I will lose you. No matter how hard I try to hold on, you and me...we just aren't meant to be. I am the Crucible of Eve."

A shudder rocked her and Roman feared she'd fall into the angry water lapping at her feet. With stealthy moves, he sidled closer. She didn't seem to notice. When he was close enough, he reached for her, but she leaned away, her perch far more precarious now.

"Is it true?" she asked. "What they say about witches? That we can't drown?" Not that it mattered. There would be no river where she was going. She could hear the sorcerer calling her. She didn't have much time.

Roman's lungs turned to the stone that was his natural form and he couldn't breathe. "No," he answered but the wind blew the word away.

"The damage is done, Roman. I can't fix it. I can't make it go away. You are good and light and...I'm not. The darkness in my heart, in my head..." She spread her arms wide, as if welcoming the lashing rain. "I am the foulest of the foul, Roman."

"Not true, Verity! You are goodness. You are truth."

She lifted her shoulders in a small shrug. "Maybe. I don't know. But I *am* the Crucible of Eve, Roman." She reached into her pocket, her fingers curling around the cold glass of the crystal ball. It heated at her touch. Pulling it out, she opened her hand to show Roman. "I am the Crucible, Roman, and I have the Heart of Stone."

Unsurprised, he waited, silent. Wild balls of light appeared and danced around her. The fire opal at her waist glowed bright as the magic built within her.

"It called me, you know. And came to my hand. I didn't steal it."

"I know."

Her hand closed over the Heart but it glimmered between her fingers. "I know what to do, Roman."

Before he could move, she was gone. He hadn't seen her move. Hadn't seen her body tumble into the river. But she was gone, the shining-bright wild light that had been Verity was snuffed out as surely as a candle in a gale.

He screamed, the wind tearing his voice from his throat and flinging it into the tempest.

"Gone," the wind told him.

"Forget," the water insisted.

Roman sank to his knees, head bowed. The storm kissed his forehead then danced away as if it never was, and the sound of silence wrapped around him.

THEY ARRIVED at dawn, Sade leading the way. She knelt in the mud beside Roman, uncaring of any damage to her tailored slacks. Gesturing behind her back, she silently ordered Caleb, Sinjen, and Ariel to quarter the area. A shadow of broad wings drifted over them as Varrick and Nikos flew cover above them.

Caleb caught her attention. He stood next to the river, a few feet from where she knelt next to Roman. She winced at the implication—that Verity had fallen, or was pushed, into the river. Or worse.

"What happened?"

Roman didn't move.

"Did you kill her?"

Roman surged to his feet, the motion spilling Sade onto her butt. "By the One God, Sade. Do you truly believe that of me?"

"Well." Sade made a big show of looking around. "Last any of us knew, you'd gone after Verity. And Crevan sorta ordered you to kill her."

He stared down at her. "I have never shirked my duty, *Enfant de L'homme.*"

Sade grimaced. "Not you too. You damn gargoyles totally freak me out when you get all gravel-voiced and intone those words like they start with capital letters and contain the weight of the world."

She pushed off the ground. Glancing at the mud on her hands, she rubbed her palms against her slacks. "Tell me what happened?"

Roman bristled. "Are you asking in your official capacity, Agent Marquis? Because I will remind you that I am the Legate of New Orleans and—"

"Damn it, Roman. Pull the stick out of your butt. I'm asking as your gawddamned friend. Okay? I want to help. If she went in the river, we need to start a search."

"No need," Caleb said. "She didn't go into the river." Roman and Sade both stared at him like he'd lost his mind. "Portal spell."

Roman was stunned. It hadn't occurred to him. Verity didn't have that kind of magic... Then he remembered how she'd glowed last night. She had the power but he would swear she didn't have the experience. Had she so completely fooled him?

"Not hers," Caleb continued.

Latching onto that, Roman stared at Caleb. "Are you sure?"

Caleb rolled his eyes while tapping the side of his nose with one finger. "Best nose in the business, boss. You know that. Verity has some kind of crazy magic going on but she's untrained. No way could she work the spell, much less conjure it." He breathed deeply and crinkled his nose. "Black magic. Definitely not Verity."

Roman froze. Had he heard Caleb correctly? Sade saved him the trouble of asking.

"How do you know?"

Caleb shot Sade a narrow-eyed look that said, "D'uh" as plainly as speaking it aloud. "There's nothing dark about our little witch. Like I said, there's some kinda crazy mix of magic in her but nothing even hinting at the black arts. No death magic. Nothing dark that I can sense."

All but sagging in relief, Roman glanced at the group surrounding him. "Can she be tracked?" His gaze rested on Caleb.

"I don't know. We'd have to do what Ariel and I tried yesterday."

The fae groaned. "My head is still reeling from that."

"Can you get a fix on who did conjure the portal?" Roman wasn't about to give up.

"Maybe. The magic is way off. Pretty sure we're dealing with the sorcerer."

"We are."

Caleb exchanged a look with Ariel. "To borrow Sade's favorite phrase, well fuck."

CHAPTER TWENTY-SEVEN
POSTCARD FROM THE EDGE

_____

VERITY'S HEAD still spun and she wondered how stupid she could get. Just because the Heart had fallen into her hand—almost literally—and she wore what she'd learned was the Gargoyle's Fist, she had no experience with magic. And this man—was he a man? She rubbed her temples and tried to focus her thoughts, and plug the holes in her memory. Tremaine. Levant Tremaine. She focused on him, on the *feel* of him.

She tried to feel his magic. But it was...wrong. Off. Nasty. Her nostrils flared, filled with the stench of it. Like turgid swamp—dead fish and fetid mud. Like things dead and dying. She shivered. She was in so much trouble now. But she'd learned something in the past few days. She was not a little mouse—not unless she needed to be small and silent. No. She did have power. She could be strong. And she would be. She would protect Roman. She would keep the sorcerer from starting a new war.

She would *not* fulfill the prophecy.

Footsteps echoed outside the door. Panic bloomed inside her but she fought it down, inhaling deeply. A memory of walking to Vacherie after Hurricane Katrina slid into her mind, along with Baba Rawnie's voice.

Do you see, cher? See dat big oak dere, d'one lying broken and splintered? Now look over dere. See d'willow tree? People, dey tink d'oak is the strong one, but a big wind come and dis is what happens. Fire wood. But the little willow? She dances and bends with the wind and when d'big wind is over, she be jus' fine.

Folks like us, cher, we gotta be d'willows, yeah?

Yeah, Baba Rawnie, Verity agreed. She would be a willow and she would survive—come big wind, bad magic, or hell itself.

VERITY had no idea of how long she'd been confined in this room. Hours? Days? Time passing felt like one of those black and white vortex optical illusions, a weird convolution that contracted and expanded. When she'd first arrived, Tremaine and been all "good cop." When she didn't cooperate, things got dicey. When she admitted she couldn't work magic, he got downright pissy. Angry, he'd lashed out at her with his magic and he'd stormed out, leaving her a quivering puddle of misery.

Thing was, she *had* worked a bit of magic. She could feel the belt cinched around her skin but even when the guards had searched her, they hadn't noticed it. And the Heart? It resided in the pocket of her skirt. She could feel it when she slipped her hand inside, but if she patted her skirt from the outside? Nothing. It occurred to her that maybe the artifacts were protecting themselves rather than the other way around.

The door slammed open. Verity jerked out of the drowsy state into which she'd fallen. Tremaine barged into the room, his eyes pools of black. Was that lightning dancing in their depths? She shuddered as a wave of oily malice rolled over her.

"I am finished with your childish games. Do you know who I am?"

She found her stubborn streak and raised her chin, unblinking as she met the storm in his eyes. "You told me your name is Levant Tremaine. Names have power. Therefore, I think you lied. So no. I don't know who you are."

Face suffused with red, he stalked toward her. Palms slapped against the scarred wooden table then he leaned forward, cutting the distance between them in half. "I am the Rising Rock, the scion of the gargoyle realm. I am the son of Cybele Tremaine." He paused for dramatic effect, expecting a reaction from Verity. When none came, he scowled.

"You're too stupid to even be scared." He straightened and with a wave of one hand, a cushioned chair appeared. He sank into its comfort with studied grace. "Let us hope that you aren't too stupid to learn what you should have been taught from the beginning." He held up an index finger. "Lesson one. I am Levant Tremaine, son of Cybele Tremaine, one of the strongest witches to ever live. I am the son of Azeria Karandzav, the First Sentinel of the Garregyion."

Verity blinked but managed to keep all other reactions off her face. This Azeria person was *not* the First Sentinel. That was Roman. Or had been, she corrected. Because of her, he'd lost his position.

"And as the only son of Azeria Karandzav, the Stone Fox, then I am entitled to wield the Gargoyle's Fist. You stole it. I want it back."

She blinked again. Tremaine sounded like a five-year-old pouting because someone took his favorite toy. The leather around her waist pinched. She held her breath, waiting. No knowledge came to her. "Not yet." She mouthed the words, remaining silent.

Tremaine raised another finger. "Lesson two. Who are you?"

Verity blinked at him. "You know my name."

He sneered. "Poor little witchling, isn't that what your gargoyle seducer calls you? Verity La Croix. The Cross's Truth. See, little witchling, not only is there power in knowing a name, the naming itself creates power. Except you have so very little. Your mother was a fool."

Stiffening at the aspersion he cast on her mother, Verity managed to once again control all other reactions.

"Your whore of a mother..." He smirked at her. "Let's see, Celestine Cross. She didn't live up to her name either. Nor did she have the talent to work the necessary magic. No, the power all came from our father."

Unable to stop the gasp, Verity could only stare at... She began to hyperventilate. Her half-brother? Was that even possible? They looked nothing alike. His eyes were dark at night, his hair black. She was blonde, blue-eyed. The belt pinched her again and the buckle heated. Control. She needed to get it back. She held her breath. Exhaled slowly. Opened eyes she hadn't realized she'd closed.

"Dad liked me best." As soon as the words were out, she wanted to call them back. Too late.

Tremaine's face drained of color then two red splotches appeared on his cheeks. The lightning returned to his eyes. Verity's hair stirred as electricity kissed her scalp. Hair lifting in the currents of magic swirling in the room, she fought to remain still. Calm. In control. She could not reach into her pocket. She could not touch the iron and fire opal at her waist. And then a thought occurred to her. Tremaine was not as powerful as he thought he was. Had he been, he would have sensed both the Heart of Stone *and* the Gargoyle's Fist. For the first time she had hope. Unfortunately, she smirked with the knowledge.

Two things happened simultaneously—a spell of some sort, one that stained the air black, and Tremaine's fist came flying at her.

VERITY AWOKE to darkness. She reached out with her senses—the physical ones anyway. Cold stone beneath her cheek. The SOB had knocked her out of the chair when he'd hit her. Her cheek—the one pressed to the floor—ached, but she suspected the chill emanating from the stone had helped. She listened but detected no other presence. Sitting up slowly, she held her head and fought a surge of nausea.

After a few minutes, she felt steady enough to stand—at least long enough to get off the floor and onto the chair, which she had to set upright. Her stomach grumbled around the queasiness. Had long had it been since she ate? Or drank for that matter. Her throat felt like sandpaper wrapped around the imaginary cotton stuffed in her mouth. She licked her lips, feeling how dry and cracked they were. She could live longer without food than she could without water. She needed a plan so she could negotiate when Tremaine came back.

Levant Tremaine. Her brother. *Half*-brother. Or so he claimed. She now understood, at least, why he'd taken her. It was all about the Heart of Stone and the Gargoyle's Fist. He thought she could work the Heart, use it to transform stone into breathing beings. Gargoyles, but unlike Roman and Varrick, the ones Tremaine wanted to create would have no free will. But he didn't understand. It was the Heart that *imbued* free will.

She needed to get into Tremaine's head. If she could discover why he believed himself to be this scion of all gargoyles. She'd play along. Give him a little. Accept these so-called magic lessons. Knowledge was a good thing. The more she learned to control the artifacts, the more she could fight. Hurt, hungry, and thirsty, she pulled her knees up to her chest, laid her uninjured cheek against them, and dozed off.

· ·/¡·• •

TREMAINE eventually returned. He'd put off confronting the fucking witch. He watched through the window in the door. She'd awakened at some point. Crawled off the floor. He studied her aura. It was lackluster and tattered around the edges. He grabbed his anger in an iron fist and crushed it. His mother's voice buzzed in his head.

She is the key. You cannot kill her until she has delivered your army. Until she has sacrificed he whose blood runs in you both.

"Yes, mother," he agreed without hiding the bitterness in his voice. "I know, mother."

Do not disappoint me, Levant.

He stood ramrod straight, waiting. When he could no longer feel her presence, he eased the door open and approached the table. Breath rattled in the witchling's lungs. His *sister,* he sneered. She was weak, like all females. Even his mother was weak. She thought he was still under her control. Little did she know. He'd never been under her thumb, not from the first breath in his lungs.

Returning to the hall, he called to one of the guards. "Bring water and food. Our *guest* is in need of reviving."

The werewolf nodded and padded off. Soon, he would replace all these inferior magicks with those of his own creation. The cavern below them was filled with statues carved from every stone. His *sister* would bring them to life and he would control them. He'd read about the Old War. He'd studied the tactics, discovered the fatal flaws that caused the renegades to fail. He would not fail. He had the Crucible of Eve. He didn't fight the sardonic grin spreading across his face. He'd tip his hat—if he'd been wearing one—to his mother. She'd played that game well, tricking his sire into creating the being guaranteed to ravage the Garregyion race.

Pah, he thought. Gargoyles were not meant to be slaves to humanity, to uphold stupid laws laid down by other, weaker magicks. Gargoyles, under his command of course, would conquer them all. He leaned against the door jamb and watched the little witch. So weak. So stupid. He would crush her and turn her to his will, and then he would rule the Realms.

・・゛い゜・　　●

"YOU NEED TO FOCUS."

Each word sliced Verity, the sound as sharp as any razor. Her skin pulled back from the cuts, blood beading up before spilling like mourner's tears. Four wounds on her left arm—the arm closest to her heart. Four rivers of blood. Birth. Life. Death. Infinity. But what was the fifth word?

Verity lifted her gaze to meet Tremaine's. Her lungs collapsed beneath the hatred in his eyes. Why was he doing this? Why was he hurting her? He'd promised to help her. To teach her. Her head pounded.

"Tell me the last word, witch, and the pain will stop."

No. He was wrong. The pain would never stop. It would follow her into the death she now knew he promised just as surely as the blazing heat of his hatred seared her skin. She wanted to close her eyes—shutter her soul from his seeking—but she couldn't. She was too weak. He was too strong. Nothing would save her. Nothing but the last word. But she couldn't reveal it. The Heart of Stone. The Gargoyle's Fist. Both remained inert, silent against her pleas for strength.

219

She had to remember. Something. What? Blood pumped through her body. She was the Crucible of Eve. Her blood was the answer, a slow fountain of death dripping from her wounds. What little strength she had waned as her soul fluttered free, hovering near the ceiling, looking down, judging. Her body failed. Her heart failed. But her soul was free. Free to live again. Love again.

Her head lolled on the body of a rag doll without stuffing as he shook her. "The last word!"

So very long ago when her soul had first taken flight on the wings of a baby's cry, the wind had whispered in her ear. Her soul knew. *Love.* "Roman." They were the same.

The outer door shattered. Roman crashed through, locks, hinges, and wood pulverized beneath his onslaught. The sorcerer flashed out, escaping his wrath, but the death rattle of the figure tied to the chair stopped Roman from following.

Verity.

CHAPTER TWENTY-EIGHT
RELEASE ME

_____

ROMAN WAS TOO LATE. All thoughts but those centered on Verity fled. He cut the ropes binding her and gathered her into his arms. Varrick had followed him but now stood just inside the door.

"The magic," Roman gritted out. "Cleanse it."

Varrick nodded. He would sear the magic from the room. Hell, he would burn this place to the ground if that's what was needed. "Take her. Heal her. We will have need of her in the times to come." He didn't know the why of his prognostication but he felt it in the very roots of his soul.

A moment later, Varrick was alone in the room. His nostrils flared and the stench of blood magic made him breathe through his mouth. He built a ball of fire in his hands—he was one of the few gargoyles who carried that particular talent. Magic teased his senses. The portal. He cast around, looking for the sorcerer's escape route. Finding it, Varrick tossed the ball of fire over his shoulder and stepped through the crack that hadn't quite closed.

. ./¦• •

THE FIRE BURNED hot and fast, voracious in its appetite. It scoured the room. *Find and destroy,* its master had commanded. *Magic.* When there was none left in the air, in the runes drawn upon the floor and walls and ceiling, the fire found the table. There was much magic embedded in this wood. It hissed and spit and danced. The wood caught, flashed into flame. The fire continued to hunt. It found the chair. It tasted the sweet, savage blood that had soaked into wood and fabric. And fire wavered. It had tasted this blood before.

When it found the thick puddle of blood pooling around a drain in the cold floor, the fire was bloated, sated from other magics. It contemplated the viscous fluid, curious. There was life in this blood. Magic and life and prophecy. Fire had devoured the death magic as its master had ordered. Its duty was done. It would rest, it decided, would hunt another day, another time. It flared and then snuffed out.

In the cavern below, carved figures stood in rows of perfect symmetry. The first drop fell from a stalactite onto the head of one. It shook its head and by the time the drops had coalesced into a steady stream, there was enough of the blood for all.

Their collective hearts began to beat. Thoughts formed. And then came the compulsion. As if they shared one brain, all heads turned to the east. That way lay...what? Heaven? Hell? Deliverance? Or dominance? Redemption or corruption? They had to find out. One by one, they tested their wings, tested their powers, and then they were gone.

·· ·ʃᵛˢ•   ●

VERITY AWOKE in Roman's arms. Her brain foggy, she wondered if she'd had a nightmare. She remembered being cold—so very cold. But now she was warm. And she'd been in pain. So much pain.

"Verity?"

She smiled at the hesitancy in Roman's voice. Her gargoyle was never hesitant. He was brave and true, rock hard, steadfast. Hers. And then, as if this was the dream, it all came back. She sat straight up gasping for air, unable to draw oxygen into her lungs, the air thick and liquid like water, like she was drowning.

"Breathe, Verity!" The order freed her lungs. Precious oxygen rushed in and she got lightheaded. Muscled arms banded around her and she discovered she was now sitting across Roman's brawny thighs, her head tucked beneath his chin, as he sat on the edge of the bed.

"Breathing now," she murmured and felt his sigh of relief beneath her cheek. She pushed against his hold and he loosened his arms enough she could look up at him. She searched his face, understood that her jumbled memories were not a nightmare but the truth, especially when she glimpsed the bandages on her left arm. "And safe, thanks to you. You came for me."

"Always, little witch." He bent his head to capture her mouth with his. The kiss was sweet, almost hesitant and so unlike her gargoyle.

"I'm okay, Roman."

"Your heart stopped beating, Verity. I held your lifeless body in my arms."

She cupped his face in her palms and kissed him. "But I am the Crucible of Eve. I give life, Roman. And I had both the Heart and the Fist. I just needed you so I could come back."

Roman rested his forehead against hers. "I've never been afraid. Not until you, Verity. Your very presence terrifies me."

Her face crinkled into a look of confusion. "I'm not scary."

"No, little witchling, but losing you? Forever? I could not go on living."

Fists pounding on the door drowned out the comfort she was about to give him. "Roman!" Varrick's voice eclipsed the pounding of his fists. "We have to go. Le Creche. There's been an attack."

Verity was already pulling on clothes. "I'm going with you."

There was no denying her.

TOO LATE. They'd come too late to make a difference, to save the fledglings, to save the guards who stood unwavering before overwhelming odds.

"Hundreds," the fledgling said, his broken body frozen in human guise. Roman held him in a gentle embrace. "Maybe thousands. Gargoyles fighting gargoyles." His voice cracked as a shudder racked his body, then his heart beat no more.

Roman stared up at Crevan and Varrick, at the gathered escadron of Sentinels. They'd been tracking the sorcerer, with only a handful of guardians left to guard the very heart of the Garregyion. They'd all come too late. With gentle care, he set aside the fledgling's body and pushed to his feet.

"How?" he asked of those who should know.

Crevan stared at Verity, who stood at Roman's back. "The Crucible of Eve." *Le Vieil's* voice echoed in the apse. "This is her doing. You should have killed her, Roman. You should have done your duty. You have no honor left."

Verity's fingers curled on his arm, her nails digging into his skin even through his leather jacket. "No," she whispered.

"You betrayed the brotherhood, Roman Montagne. You shirked your duty, and as a result you have rained death and destruction down upon the heads of your brothers."

A low, growling hum started and swelled. "Traitor. Traitor. Traitor."

Varrick stepped between the Sentinels and Roman.

"Not true." He met Crevan's angry glare without flinching. "This is my doing. When Roman and I rescued the witchling, she was dying. Roman tasked me to cleansing her cell of magic. I set loose a flame then followed the sorcerer through the portal."

"If he had sacrificed the witch, Varrick, her blood would not have been spilled." Crevan pulled his authority around him, a thick cloak of magic and age. "Rectify your mistake. The rest of us will hunt. Kill the Crucible, Roman."

Roman fell on his knees amid the rubble. The air seemed to compress as the Sentinels teleported one by one. When only Varrick remained, he turned to his mentor. "I am sorry, Roman."

And then he was gone.

Roman, his faith as shattered as the altar he knelt before, raised his ravaged visage to the massive hole in the basilica's roof. Clouds, like dirty lace, drifted across a moon so full it chased the stars into the shadows. "Forgive me!"

His guttural cry echoed off broken walls. Verity could bear his despair no longer. Stepping to him, she cradled his now-bowed head to her breast. She'd never seen the gargoyle so defeated. This magical being was the epitome of strength and now sorrow swamped him.

"I am damned."

His voice broke her heart. "No," she whispered.

"Heaven is lost to me." His words were muffled against her. "Heaven is lost to my brothers."

"No."

The quiet word startled both of them. Roman surged up, leathery wings unfolded, sword in hand as he stood between her and a spectral figure, cloaked in gloom, that stepped out from one of the small chapels lining the apse. The chimera floated closer, a feminine face flickering in and out of focus. "Choices are the hinges on the door of destiny, Roman Montagne. What you choose in this moment will determined the fates of many." She turned to Verity. "Verity La Croix, you are not cursed, despite what you believe, what the Old One believes. You must have faith. Both of you." She nodded toward Roman. "Trust in life. Trust in love." The entity pointed a finger at Verity. "She is the key, Gargoyle. Turn it."

Then the spirit was gone.

Roman pivoted, gathered Verity into his arms and launched toward the hole in the roof. "I will *not* sacrifice you!"

Verity cupped his face. "You have to. This is your challenge. Have faith in—"

"No!"

"Then it's up to me. I have faith. In us. In you. I am the Crucible of Eve, Roman. I am the Heart of Stone. Now let me be the Gargoyle's Fist. I know what to do." She kissed him. "I will love you forever. If nothing else, have faith in that." Verity prayed it would be enough. She didn't want to die. And that was a very real possibility. "It's time to release me."

CHAPTER TWENTY-NINE
BATTLE CRY

DESTINIES are a dime a dozen especially when Fate was acting the bitch. Roman once again knelt in sorrow amid the ruins of the Basilica d'L'Creche. So many of his brethren gone, the renegades leaving naught but destruction in their wake. He glanced at the woman standing nearby. He shouldn't have been surprised to see her but he was.

"How did you get here?"

Sade offered a cheeky grin. "A gargoyle, a dragon, and a fae walked into a bar."

"Ah."

"And I forgot the vampire, werewolf, and me. You didn't think we'd stay behind, did you?"

"This doesn't concern the dragons, fae, vampires, werewolves, or humans." Roman said without much conviction. This child of man was far too stubborn—and loyal—for her own good.

"You're wrong. A sorcerer is bad news for everyone and if he takes over the gargoyles? Dude, that means war in all the Realms because you know damn good and well that a megalomaniac like this Tremaine asshole is not gonna just sit around with his thumb up his butt." She glanced around the ruins of the basilica. "This is gonna suck."

"You are mortal."

"Yeah, d'uh."

"I'll take you home."

"Fuck that. I'm staying. Bullets won't do shit now." Sade offered a very Gallic shrug of her shoulders. "I'm loaded with high explosive rounds."

"Their magic is strong."

"Yes." Sade tilted her head, brow crinkling. "Wait. Where's Verity?" She suddenly had a very bad feeling. "I thought she left with you."

Roman remained silent. How could he explain? He wanted both of the human women he loved safe. Except neither of them were quite human. Not anymore. Sade, with her vampire marks and touch of fae magic, would bleed like any mortal. And die just as easily. Verity was...more. Human with witch magic in her blood but she'd been sired by a gargoyle—a possibility that left him reeling. Untrained as she was, Verity still managed to be powerful. And just as stubborn as Sade.

"Verity is..." He closed his eyes, chin dropping to his chest as he rubbed the back of his neck. "Verity has her own agenda," he finally said.

"Oh fuck." Sade was stunned. "Please tell me she didn't go over to the dark side."

"No."

She didn't approach him but her understanding of that one word draped over his bowed shoulders like a warm cloak. He pushed to his feet, feeling the weight of his age for the first time in centuries. "This was once a place of peace, of beauty."

Sade now stepped to his side, laid a hand on his arm. "You were born here."

He offered his own Gallic shrug. "It was home. Once."

Her gaze met his, sure, strong, steady. Pride swelled for the woman the child he'd once rescued from the faerie court had become. Twilight cloaked them in blue silk while the full hunter's moon squatted on the horizon like a Chinese lantern. How had things come to this? Gargoyle against gargoyle? If his granite chest contained a heart, it would have been ground to dust by now. Together, they stepped outside to be met by fae, dragon, werewolf, and vampire—a motley crew of crusaders.

"Let's go kick some rogue gargoyle butt!"

Typical Sade. "Yes," Roman said. "Let's."

⁕ ⁕

THE SKY filled with winged gargoyles, one group led by Crevan, the opposing force fronted by Jago Leron, the former Second Counselor.

"Motherfucker," Sade snarled when she recognized the traitor.

More gargoyles waited down below in stoic ranks. Between the two armies stood a henge of standing stones, as the sacred circle had from time eternal. Roman recognized some he'd considered friends in the renegade army. He found no sign of the sorcerer, nor did he sight Verity. His chest tightened at the thought of losing her, then he almost laughed. It was most likely neither of them would survive this battle. Still, he would know should anything happen to her. She lived inside him, in his heart and soul. Yes, he would feel the instant her life ended. But that was not going to happen. Not today. Not ever, if it was within his power to prevent it.

Nikos, flanked by Stavros, one of his watch dragons, walked up to Roman. "We can be most effective in the air."

"Yes," Roman agreed.

"I would like to flank the flying squadrons but I do not wish to have those we've come to assist turn on us."

Varrick appeared, and was met with weapons both magical and mundane. He held out empty hands. "I'm guessing you're the calvary. Do you have a battle plan? I'll pass it along to Crevan."

Sade stood beside Roman, Sinjen at her back.

229

Seemed daylight in the Gargoyle Realm had little effect on vampires. She'd have to remember that. Caleb stood on her left, Deacon Smith at his back. Nikos remained to the right of Roman, Ariel next to him. A glittering array of mounted fae warriors waited not far away.

No witches or wizards had accepted the invitation to join in the fight—on either side. They'd decided to remain neutral, which was probably a good idea. Sorcerers were a little too close to the witchy family tree for comfort.

Roman explained the strategy his group had planned. Varrick nodded. "There is a reason you are the First Sentinel, Roman."

"I am that no longer, Varrick. I would have seen you in my place. Tell *Le Vieil* that we will help but our aim is to end the sorcerer." Roman paused, staring up at the Old One. "And to save the Crucible."

"Understood, old friend," Varrick said, clapping Roman on the shoulder. He grinned at Nikos. "No sniping dragons from the sky." His gaze turned to Ariel and Caleb. "Nor cold iron against the fae, silver against the wolves. The brotherhood thanks you."

"Jeez," Sade muttered. "What are humans, chopped liver?"

"If you don't stay out of the line of fire, *Enfant de L'homme*, that is precisely what you will become."

A man popped in behind Nikos and everyone tensed. "Report Xan," Nikos ordered. People visibly relaxed and Sade recognized the newly-arrived dragon from that murder case in New Orleans when she'd first met Nikos.

"The countdown has begun."

Sade looked up at Roman. "That's our cue,"

VERITY PACED the room, counting off the steps in her head. She had to play this game while balanced on a knife's edge. Only Roman suspected her plan. She would not tip her hand to Levant Tremaine. *Rising Rock,* my ass, she thought.

The door opened and two gargoyles entered. She stopped moving and studied them. They weren't as tall as Roman or Varrick. In their gargoyle form, their skin was gray and covered with a fine coating of dust. Their expressions were empty of emotion and she wondered if there was any intelligence behind their dull eyes. This was so not good. She approached one.

"Hello."

It stared at her, unblinking. She reached out to touch it and the gargoyle didn't move. A synapse in her brain fired. Roman and Varrick, even the terrifying *Le Vieil* were very definitely male. These two were...not. There was no sense of life, of gender, of anything. Foggy memories coalesced. The drain in the floor beneath the table. Tremaine losing his temper and screaming at her. *"You have to know this! It's in your blood, bitch."* And then he began to cut her.

Her *blood.* Of course! Tremaine had it backwards. She was the Crucible of Eve. Her blood could animate stone, but it took the Heart of Stone to bring them truly to life. The sorcerer must have come back after Roman rescued her and taken her blood to create his army after all.

Startled, Verity realized there was warmth beneath her palm. She was still touching the gargoyle and his tough epidermis was heating. With sudden insight, she fished the Heart from her pocket and pressed it against the gargoyles chest. A second ticked by. More. Nothing happened. She was about to hide the Heart away when the gargoyle's eyes flashed and he crumpled to his knees groaning. The second gargoyle didn't move, didn't notice the commotion.

Verity stuffed the Heart back into her pocket and went to her knees. The gargoyle's eyes held intelligence now, and confusion. She wanted to bang her head against the wall. There was probably some long and involved ceremony when a new gargoyle was made and she'd just willy-nilly used magic she had no control over and no real knowledge of to imbue this creature with...what?

"A soul," the gargoyle murmured, as if in answer to her internal questions. His face held wonder now as he gazed at her. He grabbed her hand and he was too strong. She couldn't jerk away. He placed it over his heart and she felt it beating.

"Will you bestow my name?"

She almost stopped breathing. Names were important. Names...defined magic. She riffled through her brain searching for the right one. "Herluin," she said suddenly. "Herluin Bec."

The gargoyle nodded solemnly. "It is a noble name..." He trailed off, brows now mobile enough to furrow. "I do not know how to address you."

She smiled. "I'm Verity. Verity La Croix."

"Yes," he agreed, still solemn. Then he noticed the second gargoyle and shuddered. "Half life," he murmured, as footsteps echoed outside the door.

Verity panicked. She should have waited. Tremaine would know she'd done something. Herluin placed his hand on her shoulder.

"Silence. The magic comes and I understand. Fear not. I will not betray you."

In a blink, he appeared an exact match to the bookend on the other side of the entrance. By the time the door opened, Verity stood on the other side of the room, fighting for control as Tremaine walked in.

"Seen the errors of your ways, bitch?"

She gave him a disdainful look. "Lets call a spade a spade, shall we? You're nothing but a bastard." She plastered on the biggest bitch face she could muster on. "Takes one to know one." Strutting toward him, she let her power flare slightly. "Though I should thank you, brother dear."

Tremaine took a unconscious step backwards. When he realized the retreat for what it was, he stopped. "I thought I'd killed you."

Verity smirked. "Witches are hard to kill." Something in his expression triggered another memory. His mother. Realization hit her like a bucket of cold water. She scrabbled to hold her control in place. "But I see you've already discovered that fact. How many times have you tried to kill your mother?"

His expression twisted into a snarl and his hands clenched at his sides. "Never."

"Liar, liar, pants on fire. Doesn't matter. You can't kill me either." She was about to put the rest of her plan in motion when the room exploded.

⁕

ROMAN, standing in the center of the sacred stone henge, demolished another gargoyle. He'd lost count of the number he'd taken down. These weren't fighters. They weren't even fledglings. They reminded him of Emperor Qin Shi Huang's Terracotta Army. With every one he cut down, his heart bled a little more. He paused to check the battle.

Varrick was in the air now, wingman to Crevan. He would protect their leader. By default, Roman assumed command of the land-based troops. On the left flank, the troop of fae warriors harried renegade gargoyles—those who had followed Jago. They were holding their own. On the right, Deacon and Caleb, with a handful of werewolves, had cornered the few rogue wolves working for the sorcerer. The rogues didn't put up much of a fight. The three dragons attacked the center from the rear. The huge silver dragon was easy to identify. Roman had watched Nikos fight before. The bronze and ebony dragons were slightly smaller but no less adept at aerial warfare.

"Roman!" Sade's shout had him turning, but a fraction too late. He went down from the blow to his head. A second later, his attacker was blown to smithereens and Sade was sliding on her knees beside him. "Gawdammitgawdammit." Her curses were almost a crooning lullaby. "How bad are you hurt? I couldn't get a clean shot, not until you went down."

Blurry vision and ringing in his ears left him disoriented. With considerable care, he reached up and touched his head. It hurt, but was intact. Cautious, he tested his neck, tilting his head one way then another. That, too, worked. Fingers. Arms. Wings. He closed his eyes, willing his head to clear. When he opened them, he was fine.

Sinjen stood over them, a belt-fed 12-gauge shotgun in his hands. He glanced down. "Everyone still breathing?"

"Yeah," Sade assured him. "I think it's time to go find Levant Tremaine, the little pissant. He has totally pissed me off."

Extending a hand, Sinjen hoisted Sade to her feet and while she stood guard, he assisted Roman. "There have been no reports of him on the battlefield, Sade. Just where do you expect to find him?"

"Well the gawddamned bomb didn't work or we wouldn't be fighting so we need to get inside his...whatever the fuck that place is." She waved a hand in the vague direction of an edifice carved out of the side of a granite cliff.

"Stronghold," Sinjen supplied.

"Yeah, whatever. We need to find the asshole." She glanced to Sinjen. "How the fuck do we kill a sorcerer?"

VERITY HAD READ a quote somewhere that said, "Grace starves anger." Good thing she was the most ungraceful person she knew. At the moment, she was running full out on rage. Seconds before the ceiling collapsed on top of them, Tremaine cast a spell and disappeared. She didn't have time to follow him through the portal and was in imminent danger of being crushed when Herluin snatched her off the floor, her ears popped, and when she opened her eyes, she was standing on the top of a mountain.

Stunned, her brain wasn't ready to process what she was seeing. Gargoyles wheeled in the sky like flocks of giant seagulls. And were those dragons? Flaming dragons? Below, in the valley, two armies clashed. This was a nightmare, surely. She desperately wanted this to be a dream, or a movie because the battle below her was even more epic than anything in the Lord of the Rings movies.

"Lady Verity?"

With reluctance, she turned away from the fighting to focus on the gargoyle. "Thank you, Herluin. You saved my life."

"You wish to track the sorcerer?"

She reared back, chin tucked in surprise. "Yes. We have to stop him and I'm the only one who can."

"Then we will go to him." He offered his hand and she grasped it.

The world went topsy-turvy and she counted her heartbeats. One. Two. Three. She opened her eyes. Levant Tremaine, his back to her, stood about six feet away on a wide ledge. The fire opal of the Gargoyle's Fist flared and the runes cared in the iron buckle pulsed with power. There'd be no hiding it now. Tremaine was aiming some sort of weapon at one of the gargoyles flying overhead. *Le Vieil.* The Old One. Like falling dominoes, truth came to her. Azeria Karandzav. The Stone Fox. Crevan Stonehenge. Crevan was an Old Irish name for fox.

Without thinking, Verity lunged for Tremaine, yelling "Watch out, Father," at the same time. She hit the sorcerer in his low back with her shoulder and the force of her blow tumbled them over the side of the ledge. Thank all the gods that it wasn't a straight drop. They rolled, arms and legs tangled, both scrabbling to stop their tumble while also fighting for control of the other.

When they teetered to a stop on a lower ledge, Verity was on top, straddling Tremaine. "I am so done with you," she shouted, hitting him with her fist.

He fought back, only with magic. The first wave blasted her against the rock wall behind them. Going strictly on instinct, Verity unbuckled the belt and wrapped the leather around her right hand, until the knot and fire opal rested across her knuckles. She then clutched the Heart of Stone in her left.

Tremaine stalked toward her, his face twisted with hatred. "I will kill you now, witch." He raised his hands and Verity braced herself. She was running strictly on intuition and prayed it would be enough to protect her.

A dark shadow dropped from the sky. Verity waved her arms to distract Tremaine, hoping she wasn't wrong to trust the ancient gargoyle who touched down behind the sorcerer.

Crevan watched the tableau for a time. He recognized both the Heart of Stone and the Gargoyle's Fist. That the Crucible of Eve could wield both was a revelation. He didn't move when the sorcerer spoke.

"You think to finish me, *sister*?" He spat on the ground. "My blood runs with the magic of Cybele and the pitiful gargoyle she seduced. Give me the Fist and the Heart and I might let you live."

Rocked to his very soul, Crevan fought to understand. Cybele. The name conjured up the image of a beautiful woman with black hair and blacker eyes. She was a powerful witch? Was it possible the sorcerer was *his* son? The idea staggered him. The first tenet of the brotherhood was plain. *Do not lay with a witch.* And this was the reason. A witch powerful enough could create a child with a gargoyle. In the Old War, sons had murdered their fathers and fathers had slain their sons. Then the rest of the sorcerer's words penetrated. Sister.

"Yeah...no," Verity said. "I think I'll hang on to them. It's not that I don't trust you...well. Yeah, it is. And you're only my half-brother."

Regret filled Crevan. When he'd gone to the sweet Celestine, he'd known the destiny he was about to force on her, and her child. Verity looked like her mother. His fingers curled at the memory of the golden silk that was Celestine's hair shimmering across his hands. "Daughter," he whispered, his heart twisting at what he must do next. Verity had to die.

"Hi, Dad," she called, smiling brightly.

Tremaine whirled. His eyes bugged when he recognized the gargoyle standing there. "You!" he gasped. Then he smiled as ice rimed the black of his eyes. Wasn't that just like dear old mum? She'd begetted him by seducing the Old One himself. *Le Vieil* of the Gargoyle Sentinels. Payback might be hell, but in this case, it would be a hell of a lot of fun. He forgot about everything but taking down the most powerful gargoyle in existence. Raising his hands, he prepared a spell.

Verity reacted on instinct. She was positive she was

the only one who could take down the sorcerer. Like him, she carried two kinds of magic, but unlike him, she was the Crucible of Eve. She darted toward him and leaped on his back. Once again, the impetus of her lunge pushed them both over the ledge. She thought she heard Crevan shout something but the wind rushing past her ears left no room for sound. This time, there was no slope or ledge to break their plunge. This time, they were free-falling through space and Verity had no clue how to conjure up a parachute.

She clamped her legs around Tremaine's waist and her left arm snaked under his shoulder and side so she could press the Heart of Stone against his chest, directly over his heart. Her left hand, knuckles still covered by the Fist, pressed against the back of his neck. The ground hurtled up at them but she held on. She had no clue why.

Frantic, Tremaine flailed his arms and legs but he couldn't dislodge the witch. He threw back his head and clocked her in the face. Her grip loosened and he fought to get free. She immediately clamped around him again.

Verity's eyes stung with tears from her nose connecting with the back of Tremaine's head. That hurt like hell. She could feel blood trickling from one nostril and then she knew. Blood magic. Blood sacrifice. Blood to blood. She'd been right in her conclusion that she was the only one who could slay the sorcerer.

Blood dropped on the Fist and it flared. She ducked her head and rubbed her nose against the bare skin on the side of Tremaine's neck, leaving a red smear. The Heart throbbed in her hand. Light flared, leaving her blind and stunned. It took a few seconds for her to realize that she was plummeting to earth all by herself. Tremaine was nowhere to be seen. She could only hope that he was truly gone because if he was still alive, her sacrifice was going to suck. And hurt.

She closed her eyes, waiting to hit the rocks below.

"VERITY!" Roman yelled her name, watching in helpless dread as she fell from the cliff face. He'd seen Crevan land on the ledge moments before Verity and Tremaine plunged over the edge. Filled with horror, he couldn't take his eyes off the scene. Jago landed on the ledge and Roman watched the two gargoyles fight. Crevan could defend himself. Verity couldn't.

Roman was lifting off when he was blinded by a supernova. The blast of sound that followed deafened him. His wings straining against the wave of energy, he flew through the silence, searching for Verity. A speck of black spiraling through the sky caught his eye. Verity.

He caught her around the waist and the added strain jerked on his wings. One folded, broken by the combination of the energy blast and the force of Verity's fall. He couldn't stop their descent. Cradling her to his chest, he found peace knowing they would die together. "I love you," he told the woman who held his heart.

THE SURGE of energy crashed into the earth, flattening everything in its path. Stones toppled. Bodies folded. A gargoyle fought to his feet, unfurled broken wings, and knew he was about to watch the man he considered his father die. A dragon, blown from the sky, shifted to human form, the blast temporarily robbing him of magic. Those still alive could only watch in helpless horror as Roman and Verity fell.

Then a second figure appeared, rocketing from above, wings folded tight. Varrick shaded his eyes. It wasn't Crevan. It wasn't a gargoyle he recognized.

Beside him, Sade raised her weapon. He clasped the barrel of the gun and forced it down.

"No. They are dead anyway. If he means to save them, he is their only hope."

The figure passed Roman, with Verity in his arms, dropping below them before twisting and gradually flaring his wings. He came up from underneath, supporting the side of Roman's shattered wing. Their flight slowed, grew more controlled. They landed roughly, but in one piece.

Verity grabbed Roman's face and kissed him. Hard. "I love you too!" she proclaimed. Then she reached for the gargoyle who had saved them. "And you're my hero, Herluin." She kissed him as well. Then the smile faded from her face. "Levant Tremaine, sorcerer and my half-brother, is dead."

"Thank fuck," Sade said fervently while swaying from exhaustion. "Does this mean life goes back to being normal?"

"I suspect," Roman said, "that there is no such thing as normal."

"But did we win?"

Roman pulled Verity into his arms and kissed her before answering. "Yes. We won." And his words echoed in the sound of silence.

EPILOGUE
IN THE END...

ROMAN GAZED at the carnage. The standing stones of the sacred circle lay scattered like a child's building blocks after a tantrum. Fallen gargoyles resembled crushed statuary. In a millennium of life, the Sentinel thought never to live so long as to watch his brethren fight each other again. Though he'd told Sade that they had indeed won, there was no victory here.

"Could we have avoided this?" He asked no one in particular.

Crevan appeared at Roman's shoulder. The oldest gargoyle of them all spoke, his voice grating. "No. Not even the death of the Crucible could have prevented this. Indeed, had she died, this catastrophe would have happened sooner, the devastation complete." The Old One swiveled his head to sweep the valley. His gaze narrowed on a small island of people not far away. "You have true friends."

Roman watched the vampire help the fae to his feet. The two of them pulled up both the werewolf and the dragon. Two human women—women who were far more than they seemed—braced each other up, their exhaustion obvious. "Yes," he said. "Will you claim her?"

Silence stretched between them. "She is...unique," Crevan eventually said. "The daughter of prophecy. Cherish her, Roman. As she is the first, so are you. We will all learn to navigate this new order of things, but it will be you who must lead us."

Considering Crevan's words, Roman watched the

women. The raven-haired woman was his daughter by choice. The other, her hair a shining gold torch against the gray skies? Before her, before Verity, there had been no life in his soul. She awakened him from the dull existence to which all immortals were doomed. She brought light and laughter into his world. She, like her name, had shown him the truth. She turned, smiled, and he understood the gift he had received. Verity was his—to hold, protect and to love. Forever.

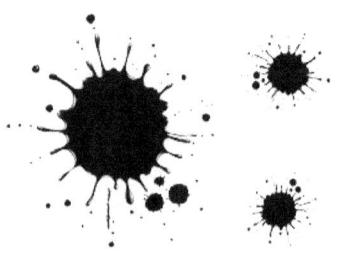

Keep reading to learn more about Silver's books and check out the playlist of songs for this book.

Music is a large part of my creative process and this is especially true with The Penumbra Papers books. If you are curious about my playlist, here is the soundtrack by chapter, artist and song title. All rights to these songs belong to the composers, lyricists, artists, and/or recording companies. I've listed them here for informational purposes only.

Playlist

Intro & Prologue – Gregorian, "Sound of Silence"

Chapter 1 - Destiny: Lenny Kravitz, "Destiny"

Chapter 2 - Sticks and Stones: Arlissa, "Sticks and Stones"

Chapter 3 - A Little Help from My Friends: The Beatles,
"A Little Help From My Friends"

Chapter 4 - The Storm is Coming: Milck, "The World is Unraveling:

Chapter 5 - A Time To Hunt: All That Remains, "The Thunder Rolls"

Chapter 6 - Watchers In The Rye: The Butterfly Effect, "The Window and The Watcher"

Chapter 7 - Broken Dreams: Seether, "Broken"

Chapter 8 - No Sanctuary: Angus Powell, "Monsters"

Chapter 9 - Sound and Fury: Skillet, "Fire and Fury"

Chapter 10 - Past vs. Present: Harry Styles, "Sign of

ABOUT THE AUTHOR

Silver likes walking on the wild side and coffee. Okay. She loves coffee. LOTS of coffee. Warning: Her Muse, Iffy, runs with scissors and can be quite dangerous. An award-winning author, she's been a military officer's wife, mother, and has worked in the legal field, fire service, and law enforcement. Now retired from the "real world," she lives in Oklahoma and spends her days at the computer with two Newfoundland dogs, the cat who rules them all, and myriad characters all clamoring for attention. She writes urban fantasy, dark paranormal romantic thrillers, and sexy contemporary romance.

If you're ready to walk on the wild side or want to find out more about Silver and her books, you can connect with her on social media.

WEBSITE: www.silverjames.com
FACEBOOK: AuthorSilverJames
TWITTER: @SilverJames_

Be sure to sign up for Silver's newsletter (instructions on her website) to get first looks at upcoming projects, fan-only contests, and other sooper sekrit stuffs.

Thank you for reading this book!

Dear Reader:

I hope you enjoyed your visit with Sade and the gang. Sade is a character of my heart. She first came to live in my imagination over a decade ago. I finally decided to get serious about this writing gig and one of the first things I did was sign up for National Novel Writing Month. Sade and Sinjen's story, THE SEASON OF THE WTICH, was started that year and after much revision, came to life a few years ago. I knew the rest of her "Scooby Gang" needed their own Happily Ever Afters, even though the Penumbra Papers is Urban Fantasy. It was finally Roman's turn.

Reviews and word of mouth help other readers find books to read. I appreciate every review. Please consider leaving one at the site where you bought this book and/or Goodreads. Don't forget to look for my other books. If this is your first Penumbra Papers book, please check out the rest of the series and my other series, too. Keep reading for the list of all my titles.

~Silver

TITLES BY SILVER JAMES

Penumbra Papers:
That Ol' Black Magic
Season of the Witch
The Devil's Cut
The Sound of Silence

Moonstruck Genesis:
Moonstruck: Secrets
(Contains the novellas Blood Moon and Bad Moon plus
additional chapters and cut scenes)
Moonstruck: Lies
(Contains the novellas Hunter's Moon and Wolf Moon plus
additional chapters and cut scenes)

Moonstruck:
*Blood Moon – Book 1
*Bad Moon – Book 2
*Hunter's Moon – Book 3
*Wolf Moon – Book 4
*Bride's Moon – Book 5
*Rogue Moon – Book 6
*Christmas Moon – A Moonstruck Novella (#7)
*Blue Moon – Book 8
*Moon Shot – Book 9
(A Moonstruck/Hard Target Crossover Novel)
*Special Forces: Operation Alpha: Rescue Moon
(A Moonstruck companion novella set in Susan Stoker's
Special Forces: Operation Alpha Kindle World)
*Special Forces: Operation Alpha: SEAL Moon
(A Moonstruck companion novella set in Susan Stoker's
Special Forces: Operation Alpha Kindle World)
*Special Forces: Operation Alpha: Assassin's Moon
(A Moonstruck companion novella set in Susan Stoker's

Special Forces: Operation Alpha Kindle World)
*Dallas Fire & Rescue: Blood & Fire
(A Moonstruck companion novella set in
Paige Tyler's Dallas Fire & Rescue Kindle World)
*Dallas Fire & Rescue: Crash & Burn
(A Moonstruck companion novella set in
Paige Tyler's Dallas Fire & Rescue Kindle World

Also set in the Moonstruck World:
Hard Target
Double Cross – Book 1
*Double Trouble
(A Hard Target companion novella set in
Roxanne St. Claire's Barefoot Bay Kindle World)

Nightriders MC
Night Shift – Book 1
*Remember the Night – #1.5
Night Moves – Book 2
*Remember the Night
*Night Fire – Book 3

From Harlequin Desire
Red Dirt Royalty
Cowgirls Don't Cry RDR#1
The Cowgirl's Little Secret RDR#2
The Boss and His Cowgirl RDR#3
Convenient Cowgirl Bride RDR#4
Redeemed by the Cowgirl RDR#5
Claiming the Cowgirl's Baby RDR#6
The Cowboy's Christmas Proposal RDR#7

From Wild Rose Press:
Faerie Fate
Faerie Fire
Faerie Fool
*Faerie Reign
(Digital 3-book boxed set at a special price)
*Faerie Faith (Twelve Brides of Christmas)

Class of '85 Reunion Series:
*Fairy Tales Can Come True
*Promises, Promises

Dearly Beloved Series:
*Best Laid Plans

Novella:
*Café Midnight
(Paranormal Noir Mystery)

*Available in digital format only

www.ingramcontent.com/pod-product-compliance
Lightning Source LLC
Chambersburg PA
CBHW070910180626
46817CB00003B/997